And a Time to Dance

BLUE FEATHER BOOKS, LTD.

*As always... to my Little Phyllis Valentine. I love you.
And in memory of my father, Morris Conrad Paynter... I love
you and miss you, Dad.*

And a Time to Dance

A BLUE FEATHER BOOK

by

Chris Paynter

This is a work of fiction. All characters, locales and events are either products of the author's imagination or are used fictitiously.

AND A TIME TO DANCE

Cover design by Ann Phillips

A Blue Feather Book
Published by Blue Feather Books, Ltd.

www.bluefeatherbooks.com

ISBN: 978-1-935627-64-7

First edition: June, 2013

Printed in the United States of America and in the United Kingdom.

Acknowledgements

From the very beginning, I've felt blessed to be a part of Blue Feather Books. My publisher, Emily Reed, is a cheerleader, a nurturer, and a good friend to all of the authors at Blue Feather. She was especially kind to me over this past year of pain and sorrow. She sent me e-mails, simply to ask if I was okay and to let us know that we were in her thoughts and prayers. "Thank you" seems inadequate, but... thank you, Em, for your thoughtfulness, your compassion, and your friendship.

To my esteemed editor, Nann Dunne, thank you for your expertise and for making me look better with each pass of my books. I learn something every time we work together, and I'll never tire of it. Please keep teaching me. You have such a vast knowledge, and I want to continue to be a sponge and soak it all in.

Jane Vollbrecht, thank you for all you've taught me about writing. I still hear your voice in my head as I create a new book... and in a good way. More than anything, thank you for your friendship, which I treasure with all of my heart.

Thank you, Mom, for your love and support throughout the years. I love you. And to my brother, Dave: I hope you know how proud I am of you. We grew closer as we got older, and for that, I'm grateful because you're one cool dude. I love you, too.

My father passed away in April of this year after a sixteen-month battle with lung cancer. My dad was my best friend and confidante. He taught me so much—a love of history, of baseball and sports, and with all the hours we shared talking about anything and everything, a love of storytelling. He gently asked me before he died, "How's your writing coming along, Sis?" because he knew I was struggling with it. His soft-spoken question nudged me into finishing this book. I did so about two weeks before he passed. So, thank you, Dad... for everything.

And to my wife, Phyllis... you also battled cancer this last year. You did so with dignity and with grace, never complaining. In fact, as you suffered through chemo and radiation, plus battled a serious infection, you worried about me and how I was doing. But that is who you are—the kindest human being I've ever met and known in my life. You are my hero, and you always will be. Thank you for your love, which sustains me in the best of times and in the depths of despair. I love you, sweetheart.

Last, I would be remiss in not thanking all of my friends, including my Facebook friends, for your e-mails and for your posts on Facebook. Your positive thoughts, energy, and prayers kept us going. You have no idea how many times when I was feeling down, an e-mail or post from you on Facebook would lift my spirits, if only for one moment out of a difficult day. So from Phyllis and me, thank you and God bless you.

The journey to finishing this book was a long one. I started writing the story right after I submitted *Survived by Her Longtime Companion* to Emily for her first reading. Everything came to a screeching halt in January 2012 when my father was diagnosed with Stage IV lung cancer, followed closely by Phyllis's uterine cancer diagnosis in February. My mom also suffered through a serious illness in July 2012. I couldn't focus on anything, let alone my writing. But like my father, Phyllis gently prodded me to begin again. *And a Time to Dance* will always be special to me for so many reasons, but particularly because I wrote it and finished it during the most difficult time in my life.

To every thing there is a season, and a time to every purpose under the heaven:

A time to weep, and a time to laugh;
A time to mourn, and a time to dance;

—Ecclesiastes   3:1,   3:4

Chapter 1

"Where did *she* come from?" Corey Banner said.

Her best friend, Penny Maloney, turned to where Corey was looking. "I think her name's Judy Wagner." She threw a softball to Corey as they warmed up before their game—their typical Thursday night outing in Lansing, Michigan.

"I've never seen her before." Corey tossed the softball back to Penny but watched Judy out of the corner of her eye. Streaks of gray peeked through Judy's dark hair. Corey couldn't help it. She'd always been a sucker for gray hair. Focused so much on the newcomer, Corey flubbed Penny's next throw. The ball struck her in the left shoulder.

"Still learning to catch, Corey?" Penny teased. She glanced over at Judy again. "Mel works with her at the plant, I think. And from what Mel told me"—Penny lowered her voice to a conspiratorial tone—"she's a ringer."

Corey watched Judy wind up and fire the softball into Fran's glove. Judy sure looked like an all-star pitcher who would catch their opponents off guard. Fran, their shortstop, took her glove off and shook her hand out. She was laughing, but Corey didn't think she was pretending too much. It sounded like Judy's fastball had left a red mark on Fran's palm.

"Want to meet her?" Penny said.

"Yeah, I do."

"Hey, Banner, where were you last week?" Fran asked as they approached.

"Had a lousy cold."

"Right. Sure it wasn't because we were playing Tammy's team?"

Corey colored at the remark. Yes, her ex played for last week's opposition, but Corey had long since adjusted to seeing her, either at a game or around Lansing. They had a halfhearted truce—well, halfhearted from Tammy's perspective. Corey had gotten over her

1

the day she'd discovered Tammy was cheating on her. Once was all it took.

"Quit being a dick, Fran." Penny gave her a shove. "Corey had a cold. I even brought her my famous chicken soup while she was sick in bed."

Judy stood a few feet away throwing the ball up in the air and catching it behind her back.

"Judy Wagner, right?" Penny said.

Judy stepped forward. "That's right." She stuck her hand out.

"I'm Penny Maloney." She hooked her thumb at Corey. "This is Corey Banner, our left fielder."

Corey offered her hand and met Judy's gaze. "Hi."

Judy held her hand lightly but didn't let go. "Hi."

They stood staring at each other for a long moment.

Penny shifted in place. "Uh, Judy, you might want to quit looking so good. You're supposed to be our secret weapon. You've kind of attracted the attention of the Cardinals."

"The Cardinals?"

Penny motioned to the women on the opposing team who were talking among themselves, obviously taking a sudden interest in watching Judy warm up.

Judy grinned. "I'll try to play it cool then."

"So, Corey, want to loosen up some more?" Penny said.

She didn't respond.

"Yo, Cor." Penny nudged her. "Come on. I don't know about you, but my arm's not warmed up yet." Penny tugged on her sleeve. "Nice meeting you, Judy. Can't wait to see what you can do on the field."

"Nice meeting you, too, Penny." But Judy never took her eyes off of Corey.

After they got a few feet away, Penny whispered, "Jesus, Banner. I've never seen you act like this."

"Act like what?" Corey said with some irritation.

"Like you wish you were all alone with her. And anywhere but on a softball field."

"Shut up, Penny."

"You were staring."

"No, I wasn't. Besides, I don't think she's interested."

Penny snorted. "Think again." She raised her chin in Judy's direction.

Corey chanced a quick look behind her and found Judy still watching. Judy smiled, and Corey couldn't help but smile back.

* * *

Penny set two full buckets of iced beer in the middle of the table. "You're buying the next round, Banner."

The team had assembled at Charlie's Place, the local lesbian bar, after solidly beating the Cardinals, 8-1. Corey had a good game with two singles and a two-run double, and she made some key defensive stops in left field. But the big hero was Judy with a bases-clearing triple and a two-run homer that soared above the centerfield fence by several feet. She also struck out ten batters. As they slapped hands with the Cardinals after the game, the glares the opposing players shot Judy's way were almost comical.

Now, though, Corey was even happier, sitting next to Judy at the table. She'd sat down first, and a surge of excitement pulsed through her when Judy hurried to sit next to her. Corey had ignored Penny's pointed look.

Corey twisted the lid off a Budweiser and took a sip. "No problem, I'll buy the next round. I can't stay too long, though. Got to get up at five with my dad. We're working on Mr. Shelby's place, remember?"

"What kind of work do you do?" Judy asked.

"Construction. My dad owns the company, but he trusts me to oversee a lot of the projects. Penny said you work at the plant in town?"

Judy nodded. They talked about their jobs and had to move even closer as the women around them got louder. Their legs touched under the table, but neither withdrew from the contact. If anything, Judy pressed against her more. The blaring music changed to a milder, slower tune, Bette Midler's "The Rose."

Judy tilted her head up at the speakers. "I love this song."

"It's the owner's favorite," Corey said. "She plays it at least once every night."

Judy gave her a shy smile. "Will you dance with me?"

Corey flushed. "I'm not much of a dancer, Judy. I don't—"

Judy stood and held out her hand. "Come on. We can't go wrong with this one." She led her onto the dance floor.

When Judy took her in her arms, Corey noticed right away how effortlessly they fit together, the feel of Judy's body against hers— the absolute rightness of it. She didn't even think about the dancing. Her heart thumped hard, and she swore she felt the echoing answer from Judy's. She knew then this was the beginning of something special, something life-altering.

As the song ended, Judy stepped back and cradled Corey's face in her hands. She lightly brushed her lips against Corey's. Their eyes met, and she didn't miss Judy's obvious desire.

"Wow," Corey mouthed.

"Wow is right."

Corey hated that she had to leave, but five came pretty damn early in the morning.

"I need to get going," Corey said, her voice laced with regret.

"Let me walk you to your car."

After they left the bar and stood beside Corey's car, Judy grabbed her hand. "Can I call you?"

"I hope so."

They exchanged cell numbers. Judy kissed Corey again, this time a little longer and with a lingering hint of what was to come. She opened the driver's door.

"I'll call you this week, Corey."

Corey was reluctant to start the car and drive away, as if this whole night were a dream and as soon as she woke up in the morning, the memory would vanish in the mist.

Judy touched her shoulder in a move of soft assurance. "I promise."

Corey relaxed. "I can't wait to hear from you."

As she pulled away, she watched Judy in her rearview mirror. Judy raised her hand, and Corey waved back. She lowered her car window and leaned her elbow on the door. Oncoming headlights reflected off the street's dividing lines, keeping rhythm with her thoughts about the night… and the promise of the days ahead.

Chapter 2

"Six years and you still can't keep up with me, huh?" Judy teased. She and Corey were hiking on their camping trip to the Upper Peninsula of Michigan. As always, Judy's competitive nature made her set a blistering pace.

"Jesus Christ, Jude, does it have to be a race with you? It's supposed to be a leisurely hike, not part of an Ironman Triathlon."

"Bitch, bitch, bitch." Judy disappeared around the bend in the trail, and her muffled laughter drifted back to Corey.

Corey welcomed the reprieve and sat down on a nearby tree stump. She untied her Timberlands and rubbed the soles of her feet through her thick socks. She didn't even worry that Judy might be a half-mile ahead of her by now. She put her boots back on and gazed up at the brilliant blue sky that peeked through the thick pines. After she had enough of a second wind, she got up to find Judy.

She went around the trail bend, but Judy was nowhere in sight. Hell, maybe she *did* get a half-mile ahead. Corey was beginning to feel the first pangs of worry when Judy jumped out between two trees and tackled her. Thankfully, the spongy, moss-covered undergrowth softened their landing.

Judy straddled Corey and held her hands above her head. "Never let down your guard when you're in the wild."

"Damn it, Judy, you scared the shit out of me!"

"Not only can you not keep up with me after six years, you still don't anticipate my moves."

"Yeah, I do," Corey mumbled. She was a little sore from being thrown onto her back and more than a little irritated about it.

"You do? What's my next move then?" Judy leaned over and pressed her breasts against Corey's.

"You'll kiss me." Corey's bad mood was diminishing fast as her body reacted to the hard muscle of Judy's thigh pushed between her legs.

"Maybe I was wrong then." Judy nibbled on Corey's lower lip.

Corey opened her mouth to allow Judy's tongue inside, and they battled for dominance. Corey moaned as Judy thrust her knee in rhythm with the thrusting of her tongue.

Judy nipped at Corey's neck and licked her way up to Corey's ear. "How about we get back to our campsite and have a roll in our sleeping bags?"

"Funny, that's what I thought your next move would be."

Judy kissed her again and stood up, pulling Corey to her feet. "I'm glad you know me so well."

The burning embers of their campfire were almost hypnotic to Corey's tired eyes. She leaned back against Judy's chest. Judy tightened her hold around Corey's waist.

"This is nice," Judy said softly, as if afraid of disturbing the night sounds that surrounded them.

Corey sighed in contentment. "It is."

"You know what would make it even better?"

"Going back into the tent and picking up where we left off from this afternoon?"

"Tempting, but no." Judy let go of her waist and gave her a playful shove.

Corey toppled over onto the ground and landed on her shoulder. "Hey!"

Judy stood up and offered her hand. "Come on. I know that didn't hurt."

Corey frowned at her, debating whether to give in to her request.

Judy wiggled her fingers. "You know you want to find out what I'm up to."

Corey grabbed her hand, and Judy lifted her up. She slid her arm around Corey's waist, pulled her close, and stepped forward with her.

"What are you doing?" Corey asked.

"Dancing." Judy hummed a tune that Corey didn't quite catch, but then Judy started singing the first line of "The Rose." "Remember when we first danced to this?"

Corey closed her eyes, and in her mind, they were on the dance floor at Charlie's Place. "Yes." Her voice shook with emotion. She rested her cheek against Judy's, lost in the feel of their bodies swaying in perfect rhythm.

"And you told me you couldn't dance…"

* * *

Dust particles floated in the swath of sunshine edging its way into the tent. Tiny flecks shifted in the light as if they were pulsing in time to the sound of a silent symphony. The synchronized movement reminded Corey of the dance she'd shared with Judy the night before.

Judy shifted beside her. She yawned and squinted at Corey.

"Good Lord, don't you sleep?"

Corey dropped from the elbow she'd been leaning on and cuddled up next to Judy. "I just woke up. I love it when we're in the UP. Everything seems so magical."

Judy pressed against her under their joined sleeping bags. "I'm not sure 'magical' is what I'd call it this morning. It's frigging freezing." She shuddered as if to emphasize her point.

Corey quickly swung a leg over Judy's body. She bent over and placed a gentle kiss on the lips she loved. Ones she'd never grow tired of kissing. She ran her fingers through Judy's short gray hair.

"Have I ever told you how sexy you are? All these years, and you're still damn sexy. And your hair? God, I could run my fingers through it all day."

Judy kissed her again, this one a little more passionate. "You find me sexy, huh?" Her eyes twinkled in the morning light.

"Mm hmm." Corey edged her fingers under Judy's sweatshirt to brush against her breasts.

Judy hissed. "Jesus! Cold, cold, cold!"

"Sorry." Corey gave her a crooked grin.

Judy chuckled. "No, you're not." She fell to the side and cradled Corey in her arms.

Corey rested her cheek against Judy's left breast and listened to her heartbeat. She couldn't remember the amount of times she'd lain like this. She marveled at the solid thumping that gave her such comfort and clutched Judy's waist a little tighter.

"Hey, you all right?" Judy said as she kissed Corey's forehead.

"I was thinking how lucky I am we met at that softball game six years ago."

"Me, too." Judy leaned her cheek against Corey's hair. "This was a much-needed getaway. Especially after all the overtime I've been working at the plant. Do you know how much I've missed you?"

"I think so."

"You think so? You do know how much I love you, don't you?"

Corey didn't answer fast enough.

"Let me show you," Judy said.

Corey sighed with pleasure as Judy settled over her. With each caress and each touch of Judy's lips to her body, she fell even further in love with her. Something she had never thought possible... but it happened every time.

*　*　*

"I can't get over how refreshed I feel after one of our outings to the UP." Judy signaled to pass a slow-moving semi. She reached over to take Corey's hand. "I hope you feel the same."

"You should never doubt it. Anytime alone with you is precious, whether it's here or on a walk in the city." She leaned against the headrest and sighed while she watched the passing trees that hugged the highway. "It'll probably be awhile before we can do this again, huh?" She awaited Judy's reaction and didn't miss the pained expression that flitted across her face.

"I'm not sure. Jim said to be prepared to work my butt off when I returned from this week's break."

Corey closed her eyes briefly and withheld another deep sigh. Judy worked too damn hard. She had since the day they met and most likely before that, too. Corey put in long hours with her dad's construction company, but he rarely asked her to work into the night on any project.

"Hey, it'll be all right, Cor." Judy brushed her fingertips over the top of Corey's hand. "We'll make it up here again before the weather turns too cold. I promise."

Corey didn't respond.

Chapter 3

Corey thought she heard the doorbell. Again.

She pushed the shower curtain aside and cocked her head to listen, hoping she was wrong. Nope. There was the annoying sound. She chose to ignore it and tugged the curtain back into place. It was after nine on Halloween night, well past the cutoff for trick-or-treating. Besides, it was raining.

Corey had performed her sentry duty at the door as she'd shoveled out candy from a bowl she and Judy had filled.

Judy ruffled her hair before she left for the auto plant in town to begin her swing shift. "Quit scowling. You'll scare the kids off."

"I'll quit scowling if you get yourself back home so I can rip off those clothes and finish what we started this afternoon."

Judy kissed her long and hard. "There's plenty more where that came from. I'm scheduled until midnight, but I might surprise you."

Corey held out hope Judy really would surprise her. Since their camping trip in late August, Judy's overtime had increased even more. She sometimes worked sixty hours a week. It was about time for a serious talk, especially when Judy said she was doing it for them—to buy that cabin in the Rockies they'd always dreamed about.

Pounding on the door supplanted the ringing of the bell.

"Damn kids."

Corey twisted the faucet to shut off the water and quickly toweled down. A rumble of thunder rattled the windows and reverberated under her feet. She threw on her boxer shorts and T-shirt, donned her terrycloth robe, and cinched it tight around her waist before going to the door. She peeked through the peephole. Her stomach fell to her feet at the sight of two Michigan state troopers.

Corey tried to muster a smile. With a shaking hand, she opened the door.

"Corey Banner?"

9

She nodded.

"You're listed as next of kin to Judy Wagner?"

She nodded again and gripped the doorknob even tighter. "She's my partner." Numbness infused her body, and her knees felt like they'd give out at any minute.

"I'm State Trooper Hendrickson." The porch light caught the reflection of the water droplets dripping down his plastic-encased hat. "This is Trooper Morris. May we come inside?" he asked, his expression one of pain and regret.

She staggered backwards. "No. Please don't tell me something's happened to Judy. Please."

They entered the foyer, and Hendrickson shut the door. When he faced her again, Corey knew.

"No," she wailed. "Please, God, no." She started to sink to her knees, but Hendrickson caught her. She grabbed hold of his rain-slickened jacket and fisted it in her hands.

"Ms. Banner, your partner was involved in an accident about two hours ago on 496. We think her vehicle might have hydroplaned. I'm sorry to inform you she died from her injuries en route to the hospital. We found your contact information in her billfold."

Corey's racking sobs quickly morphed into hyperventilation.

Hendrickson led her to the couch and helped her sit down. "Lean over and try to slow your breathing," he said softly. He rubbed her back as she clutched her sides.

Several seconds passed while Corey tried to get her breathing under control.

"This can't… be happening." Corey fought for air. "She was… at the plant. She shouldn't have been…" She remembered Judy's parting words. *Oh, no. She left work early for me.*

She tried to focus on Hendrickson's weathered face as his lips moved, but she didn't hear him. It was if she were peering through a tunnel. An image of Judy crumpled behind the steering wheel, splashes of blood everywhere, battered Corey's mind.

The tunnel grew smaller and smaller, and she slowly slipped away.

"Ms. Banner? Ms. Banner?"

She welcomed the suffocating darkness that consumed her like a black hole.

* * *

A thick fog cloaked the days that followed. Corey put one foot in front of the other to make it through each twenty-four hours that bled into the next twenty-four hours and another painful memory. Her parents, Daniel and Vera, were there for her, as were her sister, Betty, and her friend Penny. But her life also felt like it ended that Halloween night. What made it even more painful was their wedding anniversary was tomorrow, November fourth. They'd been married in Provincetown the year after they'd met.

Corey stood over Judy's grave in the buffeting, driving snow and wind after the funeral service, wishing and praying for God to open up the earth in front of her and let it swallow her whole. She sobbed, but the tears froze on her face.

"How could you do this to me, baby?" she cried. "Damn you!" She fell to her knees and pounded the fresh mound of dirt, already covered in a layer of snow. She lay over the grave and pushed her head into her arms. "We were supposed to live our lives together. How can I go on? Tell me… please. Because I'm lost."

A hand tugged into the crook of her arm and an arm circled her waist.

"Come on, Corey." Betty and Penny gently lifted her to her feet. "You'll catch pneumonia." They started leading Corey to Betty's car.

"I don't care. I don't fucking care if I die."

Penny gasped.

They stopped and Betty spun Corey around to face her. She gripped her shoulders tightly.

"Well, I do. Mom and Dad do. My kids do. Penny does. We all love you. We'll help you get through this. Just don't shut us out."

Corey collapsed into Betty's arms and gave in to her grief once more. Betty gently rubbed her back in a soothing motion while Penny, tears rolling down her cheeks, patted Corey's arm.

Betty murmured in her ear, "That's it, hon. Don't hold it in."

Chapter 4

Two years later…

Corey bolted upright in bed, her hair and tank top drenched in sweat. The bed shifted slightly, and a hand touched her shoulder.

"Corey? Anything wrong?"

In the dim light, her girlfriend Sandy's brow furrowed with concern.

"I'm fine." Corey got out of bed and left for the bathroom to splash water on her face. When she returned, Sandy sat propped up against the headboard with her arms folded across her chest. Corey stopped at the foot of the bed, not wanting to hear what came next. It always came next.

"Are you ever going to let me in?"

Corey took in Sandy's beauty and agonized again why she hadn't moved on from that Halloween night two years before. Here was a vibrant, gorgeous, loving woman in her bed. But it wasn't enough. They'd been together going on five months. It wouldn't have mattered if it were five years.

"I don't know what you mean," Corey said.

"Yes, you do. Can't you at least try to talk about her?"

"She was killed driving home from work." Corey tried to shut out the voice in her head that screamed, "To get home earlier to you."

"But what about *her?* How you met. Her favorite foods. Her favorite movies. What you did for fun."

Corey sat down on the edge of the bed next to Sandy. She picked at the comforter, not wanting to meet Sandy's pleading eyes.

"We met at a softball game. She loved sushi and old 1940s' black-and-white movies. For fun, we went on long hikes. We had season tickets to the Tigers games. We liked to camp…" She bit her lip as she swallowed her tears.

Sandy grasped her hand. "Go on."

12

"I can't, Sandy," she choked out. "Please don't ask me to."

Sandy swung her legs to the side of the bed. She didn't say anything while they sat shoulder-to-shoulder. She eventually stood up, went to the window, and drew the curtain aside. The streetlight illuminated the room enough for Corey to see her glistening eyes.

"This isn't working, Corey," she said softly. "I love you. But I'm selfish. I need all of you. Not the bits and pieces you've rationed out to me in our time together." She faced Corey, her cheeks streaked with tears. "I've tried talking to you about Judy when you wake up drenched in sweat after another nightmare. You've shut me down every time. We can't make this work without both of us participating in the relationship, but you have to trust me enough to let me in."

Sandy was right. All along, Corey thought it would come to this. She'd dated a couple of women since Judy's death. Sandy had almost broken down her defenses. But Corey's walls were high. No matter how much Sandy had chipped away piece by piece at the mortar, the stones held strong. And it wasn't fair to Sandy to live with half a woman. She could argue with Sandy it would get better, to give her more time. But Corey knew that wasn't true.

She walked to her and brushed her fingers through Sandy's hair. "You're right. I'm sorry this is all I can give you. You deserve so much more."

Sandy cupped Corey's cheek and kissed her. In her heart, Corey knew it was a kiss goodbye.

* * *

"Erin Elizabeth Flannery, aren't you awake yet?"

Erin moaned and squinted at the clock. God, she wished she didn't have to get up at four every morning. *Every fucking morning.* But a mountain lodge didn't run by itself.

"I'm up," she mumbled into her pillow. As she was starting to drift back to sleep, Aunt Tess's voice called to her again.

"Don't make me come up there! It won't be pretty."

"I'm up!" Erin rolled out of bed, staggered to her feet, and padded over the hardwood floor to the bathroom. On autopilot, she flipped the shower on and shed her nightshirt. She leaned against the cool, tiled wall as she waited for the water to warm. She almost dozed off again but jerked awake when her chin lolled onto her chest. She stepped into the shower spray.

After washing and rinsing her hair with water as hot as she

could stand it, she gradually twisted the faucet to straight cold. She resisted the urge to shift it back to warm water. This was the best way for her to wake up every morning.

She dried off and dressed in faded jeans and a denim shirt. She twisted her shoulder-length blonde hair into a ponytail and stared at her reflection in the mirror. At twenty-eight, she often thought her light blue eyes were her best feature. But other women had singled out her high cheekbones and one deep dimple that creased her right cheek when she smiled.

A photographer had stayed at the lodge a few nights. She and Erin spent an energetic night together at the photographer's cabin. The next morning, the woman took a business card from her purse and left it on the bedside table. "Call me," the fiery redhead told her. "I'd love to take some shots of you."

The redhead had been one of Erin's many summer affairs. She never dallied in anything too serious, although there had been Anna. They'd spent the entire summer together, unlike the other women who'd come and gone in a night or two. Anna arrived to work at the dude ranch located a couple of miles away from the lodge. But by September, she was ready to move on. Erin still wondered what Anna was doing in her native Chicago. Anna told her she wanted to experience the "Wild West" before settling into her high-powered job at a brokerage firm. Erin wasn't sure how wild a Colorado mountain lodge or the dude ranch was when populated by people with cell phones and pagers constantly going off.

She tromped down the stairs to the kitchen where Tess was fixing her usual heart-attack-here-I-come breakfast. Erin snatched a piece of bacon from the plate and munched on it while pouring a cup of coffee.

"How's my favorite aunt this morning?" she said.

Tess grunted. "Considering I'm your only living aunt, that's not much of a compliment. But I'll take it."

In her sixties now, Tess wore her thick, gray hair piled up tight in a bun. Maintaining a lodge with twenty cabins helped keep her figure trim.

"Have you called your mother recently?" Tess asked as Erin set the table in the dining room.

"No." Erin awaited the rebuke.

"Erin, my sister can be an ass, but she's still your mother and likes hearing from you."

Erin walked into the kitchen and leaned against the counter as she watched Tess dole out the scrambled eggs.

"Mom wants me to settle down. She thinks I'll still grow out of being gay and 'meet that special guy.'" Erin framed the words in air quotes. "We both know it'll never happen."

"But you have to admit, she's been pretty accepting."

"I guess so."

Tess brushed past her to put the eggs on the table. Erin grabbed a mitt and lifted the biscuits out of the oven. She stacked them on a plate before helping Tess bring out the juice and coffee.

"You'll call her?"

Erin sighed and sat down at the table. "Yes, I'll call her tonight."

Tess poured out two glasses of juice. "Don't act like it's such a burden."

"You know her first question will be if I'm dating anyone, and if I'm not, 'well, there's this son of a friend of mine...'" Erin stabbed at her eggs.

Tess laughed. "Kate's never been the sharpest crayon in the box."

"You can say that again."

"Let me ask you. *Are* you dating anyone right now?"

Erin raised her head in surprise. "No. Why?" Tess had never shown any interest in her love life before.

"Because, like my sister, I want to see you happy. And I don't think you're happy bedding every good-lookin' young thing who stays at the lodge."

Erin dropped her fork to the plate with a loud clatter. "Aunt Tess!"

Tess reached for Erin's hand. "I'm not sure why you do what you do, but I sense you're not happy. Tell me I'm wrong."

Erin stared down at her plate. "I'm happy enough."

Tess squeezed her hand. "Look at me and repeat those words."

She raised her head but wouldn't meet Tess's eyes. "I'm doing okay."

"That's not what I'm talking about, and you know it. Please look at me."

Erin finally met her gaze.

"You're a beautiful woman, Erin. You deserve someone who'll appreciate you for who you are, not how you perform in bed."

Erin's mouth dropped open. "Oh. My. God. I cannot believe you just said that."

"You know it's true."

Yes, Tess was right, but it didn't make it any easier to hear.

Erin flitted from woman to woman, enjoying the sex and the fact the woman would be gone in the morning—or at least in a few days. Except for Anna. Even then, she thought Anna wouldn't have remained interested if she'd stayed permanently. It had been too easy for Anna to say goodbye on her last day.

Tears threatened to spill over. She stood up abruptly and took her plate with her unfinished eggs and bacon to the kitchen sink. She pondered Tess's words as she shoveled her uneaten food down the garbage disposal.

Tess entered the kitchen and leaned her hip against the counter. "I didn't mean to upset you, but I thought it high time I quit tiptoeing around the subject and say what I thought. Why haven't you been able to settle down?"

Erin flipped on the water and garbage disposal while seeking a reprieve from answering the question. But she couldn't grind up nonexistent food forever. She switched the disposal off.

"Do you remember Bonnie?" Erin asked.

"Your roommate from the university?"

"She was more than a roommate. We were lovers all through school and for two years after we graduated."

"Didn't she move to New York?"

Erin laughed but without humor. "Yeah, with an artist from Steamboat Springs she met at an exhibit at the university. I didn't find out about it until Bonnie was packing up her stuff from our apartment." She thought back to that horrible day...

"Hey, Bonnie. I'm home a little early. Did you want to go out for dinner?" Erin set down her laptop case and purse on the coffee table. She heard noises coming from down the hall and trotted toward them. "Where are you?" She skidded to a halt at the doorway to the bedroom. "What are you doing?"

Bonnie was removing clothes from the closet and haphazardly throwing them into several cardboard boxes on the floor. Erin couldn't quite comprehend what she was seeing.

"I'm packing my clothes."

"But... but why are you putting them in those boxes?"

Bonnie grabbed the masking tape that lay nearby and taped up a box with quick precision. She straightened and thrust her hands on her hips. She stared at Erin with an expression that very much reminded Erin of her own mother.

"Look, I didn't want it to end this way..."

"What do you mean? End what way?" Erin felt like someone

had dumped a cold bucket of water over her head. She tried not to shake as frigid fear gripped her insides.

"You and me. It's not working."

"Wait. Are you... are you leaving me?" Erin hated that her voice quivered.

"Erin, you have to feel the distance between us. We've not been close for months."

Erin thought about it. Maybe it was true, but Bonnie had been so busy with her job. "That's because you've been at the office so late almost every night..." Then it hit her. "Oh, my God. You're seeing someone, aren't you?"

Bonnie held her hands out in front of her as if to ward off Erin's accusation. "I didn't want you to have to find out this way."

"What the hell? You were hoping to leave before I got home, weren't you? Were you even going to leave me a fucking note?" Bile rose up in Erin's throat, but she swallowed it down.

Bonnie couldn't maintain eye contact.

"You weren't, were you? I can't believe this. Who is she?"

Bonnie picked up a box and hurried past Erin on the way to the front door. Erin wasn't about to run after her and discuss this in front of their neighbors. She waited for Bonnie to return. As she waited, she looked around the apartment. All of Bonnie's personal items were missing. Including a photo of the two of them.

When Bonnie came back inside, Erin stabbed her finger where the picture frame used to hang. "Why would you even want that?"

"I wanted something to remember us by. We were happy then."

Weak-kneed, Erin collapsed in a nearby chair. She didn't even look up as Bonnie carried each remaining box out to her car. Finally, there was nothing left.

Without raising her head, Erin said, "You should at least have the guts to tell me who she is."

"Does it matter?"

Erin stared at Bonnie who stood in front of her, her expression closed off and cold. "Yes. It does. Who is she?"

Bonnie focused at a spot on the wall over Erin's head. "Megan Reynolds."

"The artist?"

"Yeah. We met her at the school exhibit when her paintings showed there, remember?"

"I know where we met her." Erin rose to her feet so fast that Bonnie jumped back. "And all those late hours you've been working? You were with her?"

Bonnie didn't say anything, but the look on her face was answer enough.

"She can't even fucking paint."

Anger flashed in Bonnie's eyes. "Apparently someone thinks she can. A prestigious gallery in New York has accepted her work for a permanent exhibit. We're moving there. In fact, I'm picking her up in fifteen minutes."

At that moment, the finality of their relationship landed squarely on top of Erin. The weight of it pressed down so heavily against her shoulders, she wondered how she was still standing.

Again, Bonnie looked at her as if she were a child. "Listen, it's not like it's the end of the world. You'll get through this. You're strong." She started for the door, but as she put her hand on the doorknob, she turned around. "Goodbye, Erin. You'll find someone again. Someone who'll love you the way you deserve to be loved."

She shut the door behind her. The sound traveled through the living room and struck Erin like an arrow straight through her heart.

As tears slid down her face, Erin thought about Bonnie's parting words. She was wrong. Because when Bonnie walked out that door, she took every last modicum of trust with her...

Tess's voice brought Erin back to the present. "Then you returned to the lodge to work." Her expression softened. "That explains your quiet demeanor for several months after you moved back to Grand Lake."

"She broke my heart," Erin said around the lump in her throat.

Tess cupped her face. "But, honey, it doesn't mean you give up on love."

"I thought she was the one, Aunt Tess. I gave her everything I had. I gave her my heart."

Tess wiped away a stray tear with her thumb. "The funny thing about our hearts is a piece might go away with someone we once loved. But you need to see it as now there's more room for your true love to move in and fill that emptiness."

Erin tried to lower her head, but Tess held firm. "Don't you give up, baby girl. You hear me? You have a whole lot of living to do. And there's a woman out there waiting to meet you and love you the way you should be loved."

Erin remembered Bonnie had said the same thing as she was leaving. "I don't know..."

"I do." Tess kissed her forehead. "Why don't you go look in on the number four and six cabins? Those lodgers checked out late last night and left their keys in the drop box."

Erin hugged Tess tightly. "Thank you."

"You only need to thank me if you heed my advice."

Chapter 5

A month had passed since Sandy had moved out.

Corey was restless, but not because of the empty house. It felt like ants had taken up residence under her skin. She was unable to sit still. She thought she'd burn off the nervous energy in her construction work, but she still felt wired. She could get together with friends to attempt to shake off the unease, but since the night Judy died, socializing became almost nonexistent.

Corey joined her friends on poker night every other Friday, and she went to an occasional movie. She met Sandy at one of the poker nights. Penny had arranged the introduction. Thinking back, she saw how things had moved much too quickly. They'd only dated a month when Sandy began leaving her things at the house. Before Corey knew it, she'd moved in.

But the uneasiness consuming her now was wearing on her to the point of distraction. She opened the refrigerator and pulled out a bottle of water. She flopped down on the couch and picked up the nearest magazine on the coffee table. It was a three-month-old issue of *Outdoor USA*. She opened to an article about the Rocky Mountains. The photos of majestic peaks and stunning scenery jumped out at her as she flipped the pages.

She stopped on a photo spread on Grand Lake, Colorado, a town located at the western entrance to Rocky Mountain National Park. One photo of a lodge overlooking Grand Lake took her breath away. The clouds dipped in over the lake, and a rainbow rose from the water to a thunderhead above.

"My God." She remembered how she and Judy had talked about taking a vacation to Colorado and the cabin they wanted to build. Corey had even sketched plans as if to make the dream more real. But they never had the money or something inevitably postponed the trip. A sob rose in her throat. She threw the magazine onto the floor and curled up in a ball, not even trying to stop the tears.

"I miss you so much." She allowed the pain to pour out of her like her therapist had told her to do. But, oh, how it hurt. Like someone had taken a jagged blade and sawed her heart in two. A piece of it was missing that left a constant ache deep in her very core. And within the ache lay a strong sense of guilt that she was partially responsible for Judy's death. Guilt her therapist unsuccessfully tried to talk her through.

Corey cried herself to sleep and dreamt of her last camping trip with Judy. Judy's smile was all she could see, and her laughter fell on her ears like a rushing waterfall. She jerked awake. The laughter seemed to linger in the room.

"Judy?"

Darkness and silence answered. Corey switched on the lamp beside the couch. She stood up and accidentally stepped on the magazine, still open to the photo of the mountain lodge. A sudden thought came to mind. It seemed crazy. It seemed irrational.

But it felt right.

* * *

"Mom, it's not such a ridiculous idea."

"If that's the case, why aren't you asking your father's opinion?"

Corey's mother, Vera, all five-foot-one of her, was pacing around the kitchen. Corey sat at the dining room table trying to enjoy her mother's chocolate chip cookies while also incurring her wrath.

She waved one of the cookies in the air. "These are excellent, by the way."

"And don't try to change the subject. Daniel! Come in here and talk some sense into your headstrong daughter."

Her dad entered the kitchen and grabbed a glass from the cabinet. "Is she talking about joining the Peace Corps again?" He winked at Corey as he poured milk.

Corey favored her father in build and hair color. She was three inches shorter than his six-foot height. Her dad had turned sixty two months before, but his dark hair was almost free of gray.

"No, she's not joining the Peace Corps. That would make more sense than moving more than halfway across the country to live in Colorado."

Daniel looked surprised. "Is that what you want to do?"

"I can't stay in Lansing any longer." Corey tried to swallow the lump in her throat. "Judy's memory is everywhere. She's on the trail when I go for walks. She's at the grocery store when I can't decide what head of lettuce is fresh. She's..."

Daniel and Vera sat down on either side of her and held her hands she'd unconsciously balled into tight fists.

"I know how rough you've had it these past two years," her dad said. "Your mother and I both know. You lost a lot of your spirit the night Judy died in the accident. And you haven't gotten it back yet."

Corey shifted away from them and cradled her head in her hands as she silently cried. *Will I ever stop crying?* Her mother slipped an arm around her shoulders.

"Is this really what you want to do, honey? Where will you live? You don't even know anyone in Colorado."

Corey wiped her tears away with her sleeve. "There's a lodge in Grand Lake. I think I'll stay there until I find something more permanent. I've barely touched the money from Judy's life insurance policy. That should keep me on my feet until I'm settled. And I have my savings from working construction. Maybe I can find a job where I can use the skills Dad taught me."

"I'll miss your work," her dad said. "You're the best on my crew. More than anything, I'll miss my little girl. But if this will make you happy"—he glanced at her mother—"then we'll support you. Won't we, Vera?"

Her mother had tears in her eyes, but she nodded slightly.

"Mom, please don't cry. It's not like I'll lose touch with you. I'll keep in touch with Betty and the kids, too." She thought about her sister's deadbeat husband, Hank. Him, she wouldn't miss.

"All right, honey. I agree with your father. We only want to see you happy."

"I don't know if I'll ever be happy again. But I at least want to breathe air I've never breathed before."

* * *

Erin shoved the last of the dirty bed linens into the laundry bag and dragged it out of cabin six. She was making up the bed with fresh sheets when her cell phone went off. She didn't recognize the number.

"Hello?"

"Hey, there, Erin. How goes it in the wild, wild west?"

"Anna. I didn't think I'd hear from you again. How's the Windy City?"

"It's Chicago. What can I say? Listen, I've set aside a week's vacation in July. I was thinking of coming out there. Do you have openings for July twelfth through the nineteenth? I'll fly back to Chicago on that Sunday."

"Oh. Um, I'm not at the desk right now. I'm in one of the cabins. Can I call you in about an hour?"

"In one of the cabins, huh? Tell me, is one of them cabin four? I have some fond memories of our time spent there."

Erin felt the heat rise to her cheeks. "I'm finishing up at cabin six and heading over to four when I'm done."

"Mmm… wish I were there with you. We'd muss up some sheets together." Anna's husky voice had dropped even lower, which sent shivers down Erin's spine.

"Let me finish up what I'm doing, Anna, and I'll give you a call in a bit. I can reach you at this number?"

"Yes. This is my cell."

Erin almost said something about Anna not giving out her number before. "Talk to you soon."

Erin finished cleaning cabin six and had a difficult time concentrating on cleaning cabin four, especially when she recalled the extracurricular activities she and Anna had shared here. On the bed. On the floor. On the couch. Against the wall. In the shower.

She dragged the two laundry bags to the main lodge. An elderly couple passed her on the trail. Mr. and Mrs. Johanson? Erin took a chance.

"Good morning, Mr. and Mrs. Johanson. You're up early today."

Mr. Johanson flicked his wrist and glanced at his watch. "It's eight-thirty. I'd hardly call it early."

"I must have lost track of time. I hope you both enjoy your day," she said as she moved past them.

Eight-thirty? It never took her three hours to clean two cabins. The phone call flustered her more than she realized. Erin pulled the laundry bags to the back door, which led into the laundry room. She took out her set of keys to unlock the door and lugged the bulging bags to the washer. After she dumped in the first load, she returned to the front desk where Tess was talking to one of the lodgers.

"Erin, I told Mr. Torres you could take him to the ranch and introduce him to Bill. Mr. Torres would like to go trail riding."

"I'll be with you in just a sec. I need to check the computer for a potential lodger."

Erin hustled to the PC and opened the reservation calendar for

July. There were a couple of cabins still available. Erin smiled when she noted one of them was the number four. She typed in Anna's name. She'd call her later to get her credit card information.

"Come on, Mr. Torres. I'll take you over in the Rover."

They walked outside and down the steps of the long porch.

"We're right over here." Erin motioned toward a beat-up, pale yellow, 1973 Land Rover. It didn't look like much on the outside but was dependable for mountain driving.

They chatted on the way. About a mile down the road, she pulled into the gravel parking lot of the ranch. She steered him toward the office.

"Mr. Torres would like to do some trail riding," Erin said to Joel at the counter. "Is Bill around?"

"Out in the back corral, Flannery."

Erin resisted the urge to tell Joel, a nineteen-year-old brat, once again to address her by her first name. As they trudged toward the corral, a woman rode toward them on a tall chestnut horse. She touched the brim of her cowboy hat and grinned down at Erin.

"Ma'am," the woman said with a slow drawl. She held her gaze for a few seconds and then touched her hat again at Mr. Torres. "Sir."

Erin almost stumbled as she turned around to watch the woman's butt sway in the saddle. She realized Mr. Torres had asked her a question.

"Excuse me? I missed what you were saying, Mr. Torres."

"I've not ridden that much," he said with a sheepish expression.

"Not a problem at all. Bill will take you on the easier trail. It stays pretty even but still gives you some fantastic views."

A gray-haired man with a goatee waved at Erin as they neared the corral.

"Why if it isn't Miss Erin. You haven't been around in a while, young lady."

"Been staying busy at the lodge, Bill. Mr. Torres here would like to take one of your easier trails today. Can you get him saddled up?"

Bill held out his hand to Mr. Torres.

"This is Bill Cooper. He should get you all set."

The two men clasped hands and launched into a discussion as to what kind of horse would be best suited for Mr. Torres's experience level.

Erin left them to return to the Rover. The woman who'd ridden past on her horse was leaving the barn.

"We meet again," the woman said with a smile. "I'm Lee." She offered her hand to Erin.

"Erin." Erin welcomed the warmth of the touch. Lee, who'd tilted the cowboy hat back on her head, was even more attractive off her horse.

"I don't suppose you'd know a good place in town to get a bite to eat for dinner?" Lee asked.

"Gerry's Diner in town is nice. Reasonable, too."

"I don't suppose you'd like to join me?" Lee's smile widened.

Erin didn't hesitate to accept the offer. "I need to get my work done at the lodge, but I could meet you there around seven."

"You're at the Rainbow Lodge?"

"I'm part owner with my aunt."

"And you still have to work?" Lee teased.

"We're not exactly rolling in employees. My aunt wanted to hire someone for repair work but hasn't found anyone reliable yet, so I'm it. We do have some part-timers, but she wants someone who'll work full time to help maintain the property."

"I know where the lodge is. I can swing by and give you a lift if you like since you know where we're going."

"See you at seven."

* * *

Erin extricated her arm from under Lee. She leaned on her elbow and studied Lee's nude body as she slept. Picking up her watch from the bedside table, she hit the dial to illuminate the face: 2:45. She debated about waking Lee but decided to let her sleep. They were in cabin four. *What is it about this cabin?*

Erin tried to be quiet as she rose and began dressing. Lee shifted in the bed and greeted her with a lazy grin.

"Don't tell me you're the type who screws and runs."

Erin sat down on the side of the bed and tugged on her boots. "I need to get back to the lodge. You're welcome to stay here until daylight. The cabin hasn't been rented and won't be until Monday."

Lee moved behind Erin. "Sure I can't persuade you to stay a little longer?" she asked as she nibbled on Erin's earlobe.

Erin craned her neck to kiss her. She meant it to be a gentle kiss, but Lee quickly made it something more when she thrust her tongue into Erin's mouth.

Erin withdrew from the embrace and stood up. "In about an

hour, my aunt's going to wonder where I am." She thought about the conversation from yesterday morning. *Well, maybe not.*

Lee fell back onto the bed. "Ah, a conscientious worker. Figured as much."

Erin ignored the remark. She walked to the door and put her hand on the doorknob. "I enjoyed our night together."

"Me, too. See you around?"

"I'll be here." Erin left the cabin and plodded down the trail to the lodge. She veered onto another trail leading to the lake. She was risking injury by venturing there in the dark, but a full moon helped illuminate the path. Having reached her destination—a large boulder at the edge of the water—she climbed onto the rock and tucked her knees against her chest. She tried to draw peace from the moon reflecting off the still water.

Instead of peace, a penetrating loneliness gripped her very being. So much so, she clutched at the pain in her chest. The water lapped against the shore, slapping a sad rhythm that matched the beating of her heart. Aunt Tess was right. But it didn't mean Erin's behavior would change anytime soon.

Her aunt's words only accentuated the fact Erin was alone, despite leaving the bed of a beautiful woman only minutes before. A woman who wanted her to stay. But Erin did what she did best. She ran as fast as she could to the false comfort of her loneliness.

Chapter 6

"So, dude, when are you leaving in the morning?" Penny peered at Corey over the lip of her beer.

"Probably around seven. If I can get my ass up any earlier, I will."

Corey took a sip of her Budweiser. When she'd called Penny to tell her of her plans to move to Grand Lake, Penny first had reacted negatively. Well, "freaked out" would be a better way of putting it. She thought Corey was overreacting to the break-up with Sandy and needed to give herself some time, not move thousands of miles away. After Penny settled down, she'd agreed to meet for a couple of beers at Charlie's Place.

Penny frowned and picked at the label of her bottle.

Here comes the lecture. Corey was hoping they'd avoid a serious talk. She'd had a hard enough time with her parents.

"You know, at first, I didn't get it. Like I told you, I thought you needed to chill, and you'd be fine. Sandy was okay, but she was a little clingy."

"She wasn't clingy." Corey stared down at the well-worn table. "She deserved more. You and I know that, Pen. I'm a mess." She raised her head and met her friend's eyes. "I need to leave town and start over. And I want to do it in a place that Judy and I had always planned on going."

Penny reached across the table and touched her hand. "Hey, I understand now. I had to think it over and see it from your point of view. You're talking to your best friend, remember? I know how hard Judy's death hit you. I'll miss you... a lot. So will the team. You're the best left fielder around." She gave Corey's hand a squeeze and released it. "But I want you to find happiness again. Even if it's in Timbuktu."

Corey laughed as she blinked away her tears. "You sound like my parents. Grand Lake might be far, but we'll keep in touch, all right? I'll try and call you once a month." Corey held up her hand when Penny started to interrupt. "Let me get settled, make new friends, that kind of stuff. I *promise* I'll call. This once-a-month thing won't be permanent."

"As long as you don't drop off the face of the earth."

"No, I won't. I'll keep you posted on everything. I don't know how I can explain all of this other than moving seems like the right thing to do. I can feel it deep inside."

"Well, hell, when you put it that way, how can I argue? You've always been good with your instincts." Penny held up her bottle of beer. "Here's to new memories."

Corey clinked bottles with her.

Penny gave her a sly grin. "Who knows... true love might await you in the Rockies."

"Oh, now don't start that shit with me."

Penny laughed and stood up. "Come on. Let me beat your ass at pool one last time before you go."

* * *

"Mom, I promise I'll call you and dad all along the way. I'll be safe." Corey felt like her mother was squeezing the life out of her. She tried to pull away, but Vera tightened her embrace even more.

"You stop when you're tired, you hear? And no driving straight through. I'll come out there and whip your butt if you try to drive straight through."

Corey was finally able to break free from the hug. "I promise. I'm not as young as I used to be and wouldn't think of doing that anyway." Corey looked over her mom's shoulder at her dad who was blinking fast. "Dad, it's not like you won't see me again." This departure was more daunting than Corey had imagined.

"I know." He put his arms around her. "We've been used to you being close, and we're going to miss you. That's all."

"I'll Skype you, too." Corey tried to lighten the mood.

Her mother scrunched up her face. "You know I hate computers."

"But, Mom, it'll be fun."

"If you say so. I can remember when a simple phone call was the best way to stay in touch. Now, with these texting nuts and with this Sky thing..."

"Skype."

"Sky... Skype. Same thing. Sometimes it's too much for me to take in." Vera stroked Corey's cheek. "But if it means I can see you while we talk, I'll give it a shot."

"Thanks." Corey hugged her again and gave her dad a final embrace. She picked up her last box and put it in the back of her Toyota RAV4. "Once I find a place to live, I'll get a moving company to pick up the rest of my stuff. If I don't need the furniture, we can sell it off." She got into the SUV. Vera and Daniel leaned into the open window.

Corey looked toward them. "I'm glad Carrie will rent the house for now, though. I trust her. I know once I do put the place on the market, my mom, the super realtor, will work her magic." Her cousin, Carrie, had been searching for a decent rental for months and jumped at the chance at renting Corey's furnished home.

Vera waved off her comment. "Remember that when those low bids come in."

Corey keyed the ignition. "I love you both so much." It was her turn to get emotional, and she struggled not to cry.

"We love you, too," Daniel said. "Call us when you stop next for gas so we know how you're doing."

"I will." Corey backed out of her drive. She slowed in front of the ranch house. "Hope I'm doing the right thing, Judy," she whispered.

* * *

Corey arrived in Omaha, Nebraska, at 10 p.m., after making frequent stops along the way to stretch her legs. She had divided the mileage as close as possible into equal drive times. Omaha seemed like a good stopping point. She checked into a hotel and gave her parents a call. Then she took a hot shower and sat on the bed to study her map.

She ran her finger along her route. Interstate 80 led directly into Cheyenne, Wyoming. From there, she'd hop on I-25 until she hit US 34 in Colorado which would take her into Grand Lake. It'd be another 650 miles of driving.

She folded up the map and set her cell phone alarm for five. Her plan was to get to the lodge in the evening sometime. She switched off the bedside lamp and settled under the covers.

When she closed her eyes, she pictured Judy's face full of animation when they talked about this trip. Judy might not be with her physically, but Corey felt her spirit surrounding her and urging her on her journey.

Chapter 7

"Scott, I told you. Cabin eight needs some lightbulbs replaced in the bathroom. Where are you now?" Erin waited for his response on the two-way radio.

"I'm finishing up in twelve. Jesus Christ, Erin, I'm working as fast as I can."

Erin held back from firing off a smart-ass response. "Get there when you're done."

Scott, however, didn't have a problem with being a smart-ass. "Where else would I go?"

Erin set the walkie-talkie down on the front desk counter a little harder than she'd intended.

Tess came out of the office and frowned at her. "Who peed on your Pop Tarts?"

"No one."

"You look like death warmed over, and believe me, I'm being kind."

"Gee, thanks, Aunt Tess."

"If you plan on biting off all of our employees' heads this morning, why don't you go upstairs and lay down for a bit. Take a nap."

"I'm not five years old." Erin glared at her.

"Could've fooled me. This wouldn't have anything to do with the woman I saw coming out of cabin four yesterday morning, would it?"

Erin's cheeks instantly warmed.

"With that expression on your face, I'd say I hit the mark." Tess waved at a couple who greeted her as they passed by the front desk. "Why don't you take a break? I don't care where you go or what you do. Take your attitude out that door, and when you return, try to remember we're in the business of making our lodgers feel welcome. Seeing and hearing you go off on another employee isn't exactly what I'd like them to witness."

"I'm sorry, Aunt Tess—"

"I don't want to hear it. Go. I'll get Emily to cover for you. She'd be happy to step away from washing sheets this morning."

Erin knew when to keep her mouth shut. She rounded the counter to the front entrance and stepped out onto the long porch overlooking Grand Lake. As she took the stairs to the trail that led down to the lake, she tried to clear her mind. Everything felt so jumbled. Like someone had thrown her brain into a mixer and set it to Grind.

Considering how I've been acting lately, maybe that mental image isn't so far from the truth.

* * *

"Mom, I called to let you know I made it to Colorado. I'm almost in Grand Lake. I've got to go, though. I'm driving in the mountains."

"In the dark?" her mom almost shouted in her ear.

"Which is why I need to get off the phone."

Her mom released a heavy sigh. "Call me tomorrow once you've had a good night's rest."

"Yes, ma'am."

"And don't be a smart aleck."

Corey chuckled and ended the call.

For at least the twentieth time in the last one hundred miles, Corey was questioning her decision in driving at night for the final leg of her journey. She flipped on her brights. She spotted a wide area in the shoulder and pulled over, thankful there was a guardrail. Who knew how far down the drop-off was beside the road?

After switching on the overhead light, she opened the map and made sure she hadn't done something stupid and veered off course. She checked the road sign in front of her. No. Still on US 34. She laid the map on the passenger side, clicked off the inside light, and eased back onto the road. A green sign was just ahead. Thank God, she thought, when she saw, "Grand Lake 4 Miles."

Four miles driving in the mountains did not equate to four miles driving in the city. Twenty minutes later, she was parking the SUV.

She stepped out, stretched, and every bone of her body cracked and popped in protest. She was about to walk toward the lodge when she caught a glimpse of the expanse of stars overhead. She stumbled to a halt.

"Holy shit." Corey had never seen anything like it. Not even on the camping trips she and Judy had taken in the Upper Peninsula. It felt as though she could reach out and yank down a star from the sky. They seemed that close. She crossed the gravel lot to the steps leading up to Rainbow Lodge. Solar lights lit the path to the long porch.

She entered the lodge. The great room stretched for at least thirty feet ahead of her and to the right was a glassed-off area that appeared to be a restaurant. The varnished, hardwood floor was buffed to a bright sheen. Above, beams extended from one side of the ceiling to the other. A stuffed, antlered deer's head sat in a place of prominence, mounted on the front beam. To Corey's left stood a long wooden counter. An antique brass cash register which looked to be in working order, sat to the right on the corner of the counter. But modern touches abounded with the computer screen and credit card machine nearby. Corey's hopes rose when she saw a red "Help Wanted" sign taped to the counter.

An older woman had her head down as she flipped through paperwork.

Corey approached her. "Hi."

The woman raised her head and greeted her with a warm smile. "Hello. Wanting to stay?"

"Yes, ma'am." Corey gestured to the sign. "But I also need a job."

The woman studied her. "What can you do?"

Corey wasn't ready for the question and didn't respond right away.

The woman must have noticed Corey's puzzled expression. "You know… your expertise?"

"I don't know what you're looking for, but I worked with my father's construction company back home. We did a lot of remodeling and odd jobs in the area."

The woman nodded. "The position is the head of maintenance and repairs. You'd oversee two men, Scott and Eddie, except with your hire, they'd do more of the maintaining end of it and you'd focus on the repairs. Would you have a problem giving men orders?"

"Not at all. I was foreman for my dad and took the lead on a lot of projects."

"That's good enough for me." The woman reached underneath the counter and pulled out an application. "Fill this out. If you're not wanted in ten states," she said and winked, "I think we'll be fine."

Corey took the pen from her.

"I'm Tess Landers, by the way."

"Corey Banner."

"While you're filling out your application, I'll get you a place to stay. Anyone with you?"

"No, ma'am," Corey said as she wrote down her Social Security number. She filled out the rest of the sheet and handed it to Tess.

"I'll call in the morning on your references, but I usually have a good feel for these things, and I think we'll be fine. If you have a credit card, we're all set for your stay. If you're hired, though, your lodging is paid. One of the perks of working here full-time."

Corey slid her wallet out of her back pocket and handed Tess a card. As Tess was running the card, a door Corey hadn't noticed before opened behind the counter. A blonde, who bore enough of a resemblance to Tess to be family, walked over. She gave Corey a small smile as she stood at a polite distance.

Tess finished running the card and handed it to Corey. She reached down and pulled out a key. "You're in cabin five." She looked over at the other woman. "Here's my niece. Erin, I'd like you to meet Corey Banner who's a lodger but very well may be a new employee in the morning."

Erin narrowed her eyes at Corey.

Corey shifted in place, a little uncomfortable with the scrutiny.

"Are you experienced in maintenance work?" Erin asked.

Before Corey answered, Tess cut in. "It's all on this application. You'll have to excuse Erin, Corey. She's watching out for her old, senile aunt who apparently isn't capable enough of knowing a good hire when she's standing right in front of her."

After giving her aunt a glare, Erin said, "I apologize, Corey. I didn't mean anything by the question."

"Why don't you help Corey with her bags, because even though I don't see them with her, I'm sure she has some out in her car. Right?" Tess asked Corey.

"Yes, ma'am."

Erin came around the counter and led Corey back outside. Corey tried to keep up with Erin's purposeful strides. By the way Erin was stomping down the steps, she didn't seem too pleased with her aunt's attitude.

"Hey, I didn't mean to cause any problems back there," Corey said.

Erin stopped so abruptly at the foot of the steps that Corey stumbled into her. Erin grabbed her and kept her from falling. Corey felt the warmth of Erin's fingers around her forearms through her jacket.

"No, I'm the one who should apologize. Sometimes my aunt and I mix like oil and water. This was one of them."

Corey noticed Erin hadn't let go of her yet.

Erin released her and eased out of her personal space. "Which one's yours?"

"It's the RAV4 over there." Corey gestured to the SUV.

They trudged along in silence. Corey unlocked the back and lifted out two suitcases.

"Just the other one there." She nodded at her duffel bag. "I'll get the boxes, my PC, and other stuff in the morning."

Erin picked up the duffel. "Looks like you'd planned to stay no matter what. What cabin you in again?"

"Cabin five."

"You're down this path." Erin moved ahead of her.

Again, Corey had to hustle to keep up. They stopped at a small cabin with a porch. Corey fumbled in her pocket for the key. She tried to insert it into the keyhole but wasn't having much luck in the dark.

"Here." Erin held out her hand.

Corey gave her the key. Erin unlocked the door and flipped on an inside light. She carried the duffel bag in and set it by the door. She proceeded across the room and flipped on another light that illuminated a small kitchenette and dining area.

"You got a living area here." Erin pointed. "Kitchenette there." Erin led her down a small hall. She motioned to her left. "Bedroom there and another small room across the hall. You can use that as an office for your computer if you want."

Corey took everything in. It was small, yes. But it was big enough to suit her needs.

Erin leaned through a doorway and switched on the bathroom light. "And your bathroom. It's not the Ritz, but it's functional and clean." She turned and bumped into Corey who was peering in the bathroom. "Excuse me." Erin ducked her head to move past her.

Corey followed Erin to the door and onto the porch. "Thank you."

"You're welcome."

Corey tried to read her expression in the shadows.

"I guess you'll be up at the front desk in the morning to talk to Aunt Tess?"

"Yes."

"Maybe I'll see you then. It was nice meeting you... Corey?"

"Right. And it's Erin?"

Erin smiled, causing a deep dimple to crease her right cheek. "Right." She turned and disappeared into the darkness.

Chapter 8

The next morning, Erin finished dressing and descended the steps of their living quarters. She overheard another voice coming from the dining room.

"No, ma'am, I don't usually eat a big breakfast."

Erin peeked around the corner, surprised to see Corey helping Tess take food to the table.

"If you're going to work for us, and I have a feeling you will be, you need to keep your strength up," Tess said. "You're too thin."

"I've been accused of a lot of things, but being too thin wasn't one of them."

Erin raked her eyes over Corey's body. No, she definitely wasn't thin. She fills out those jeans just fine.

"Erin, honey, glad you're joining us."

Corey greeted her with a warm smile. "Hello."

"I feel like I overslept or something." Erin moved past Corey to the kitchen and poured a mug of coffee. When she came back to the dining room, Corey and Tess had already sat down. Erin stared at Corey a little too long.

Corey jumped to her feet. "Am I in your chair?"

"No, not at all," Erin said as she sat down across from her.

"There's no assigned seating, Corey." Tess shot Erin a sharp look.

Erin reached for a biscuit and slathered it with butter. "So, where are you from, Corey?"

Corey struggled with a sip of coffee before answering. "Lansing, Michigan."

"What brings you out to Colorado?" Erin pushed on.

"Good morning, Corey? And how are you?" Tess was now openly scowling at Erin.

"If this is too personal…"

"No, no. Not at all. We've… I mean… I've always wanted to

36

visit."

Erin didn't miss the slip. Her gaydar had gone off the instant she'd met Corey, but that didn't always mean anything. She thought Corey was handsome. Short dark hair with gray sprinkled throughout. Her jaws were well-defined and a small cleft in her chin made her appear even more distinguished. But her brown eyes held a deep sadness.

"You had quite a drive from Michigan to Grand Lake. How long did it take you?" Tess asked.

"I left day before yesterday and drove straight through to Omaha before stopping. Then I drove straight through to Grand Lake yesterday."

"Well, you're very welcome here. Isn't she, Erin?"

Erin met Corey's gaze, and the despair she saw almost pulled her in. It felt like she was in the presence of a wounded soul, many years older than her actual age. Which was what? Early thirties? She realized she hadn't answered her aunt.

"Of course she's welcome."

Corey's mouth twitched with a ghost of a smile. "I saw your lodge featured in an *Outdoor USA* spread about the Rocky Mountains. I decided to take a chance and come out to Grand Lake. I thought maybe I'd find a job. It might sound silly…"

"No, not silly at all." Erin felt a sudden desire to get as far away from Corey's sadness as possible. She glanced at her watch and stood up. "I need to get started on my chores."

"Why don't you take Corey around and give her the lay of the lodge?"

Erin was about to ask if they shouldn't wait until Tess checked on her references, but she caught herself. "Corey, you feel up to it? You haven't had much of a chance to eat any of your breakfast."

Corey's food was virtually untouched. She folded her napkin and placed it on the table. "I was telling your aunt I wasn't much of a big-breakfast eater."

"Follow me. It's dark, but I can show you some of the work you might be doing if you get the job." They started for the door. "We'll be back in a few, Aunt Tess."

Erin walked in front of Corey. She tried to sort out what she was feeling. It was an unsettled sensation, one she hadn't experienced in a long time. Bonnie's face suddenly came to mind. Erin stumbled in her gait.

"You okay?" Corey gripped Erin's elbow and helped her

recover her footing.

The touch was tender. Too tender for Erin to handle. She yanked free and stalked away from Corey's kindness, immediately ashamed of her reaction.

They reached cabin seven that was in need of a number of repairs. Erin unlocked the door and flipped the light switch. The overhead light illuminated Corey's face and caught her confused expression.

"I'm sorry I pulled away from you," Erin said. "You were only trying to keep me from falling."

Corey shrugged. "Don't worry about it." She waved around the room. "So, what needs to be done?"

Erin, distracted by the dismissal of her apology, tried to focus on why they were there. "Let me show you." She led Corey to the first bedroom in the two-bedroom cabin and flipped on another light. Paint was peeling off the walls. Erin pointed up at a yellow stain on the ceiling. "We had a leak during a heavy snow this winter and haven't been able to get to it."

Corey moved under the stain. "This shouldn't be too difficult." She studied the room. "And I'll have no trouble scraping and repainting the walls. If you don't mind me asking, how many employees work at the lodge?"

"Nine. With you, ten. Some of those are part-timers, though, including Scott and Eddie who'd assist you when you need them. Aunt Tess probably told you they're not too keen on repairs. They're local college students." Erin kept her tone upbeat, hoping to break the tension she felt between them.

"You seem to have faith in my background check."

Erin drifted farther into the room and stood in front of one of the walls with her back to Corey. She peeled off a paint chip and crumbled it in her fingers, brushed her hands together, and turned around. "You haven't killed anybody have you?" She tried hard to look serious.

Corey laughed. Erin loved hearing the deep timbre of her voice and decided she needed to say something funny in the future just to hear the sound again.

"A few years ago, there was an incident, but I was never proven guilty."

Erin's stomach dropped until she noticed Corey's amused expression. "Your lawyer was that good, huh?" she teased back.

"Never went to trial. I paid off the sheriff."

This time, they both laughed.

"I like your sense of humor, Corey."

Corey bowed slightly. "Why thank you, Erin."

Erin used the lighthearted moment to chance asking another question. "When we were at the breakfast table, you said something about 'we' vacationing in Grand Lake. Was there someone else?"

Corey paled.

Erin realized she'd stepped over a line. "Please forget I asked. It's none of my business. Sometimes my mouth gets me into the worst kind of trouble."

"No, it's all right," Corey said softly. "My partner, Judy, and I..." She stopped and took a breath. "We'd talked of visiting the Rockies for several years, maybe even building a cabin, but we never made it."

Two things struck Erin. First, her intuition about Corey was right—she was a lesbian. And second, she was afraid of the next words Corey would speak.

"Judy was killed two years ago in a car accident." Corey's eyes brimmed with tears. "You'd think I'd be over this by now." She bit her lower lip.

Erin took a step toward her. She felt an overwhelming desire to reach out and hug Corey, anything to take away her pain. "I'm not sure you can ever get over the loss of a spouse," she said gently. "I'm sorry I pried."

"It would have come out eventually." Corey's expression changed. "When I saw those photos in *Outdoors USA*, it hit me we never made it. I was feeling so unsettled. Like I couldn't stand to be in my own skin, you know? Have you ever felt like that?"

She nodded as Corey described exactly how Erin had been feeling lately.

"And I'd recently broken up with someone I'd been with for five months. I needed to leave. This seemed to be the place for me. I'm sure it sounds crazy."

"No. It doesn't."

"You don't think so?" Corey's expression changed to something Erin was unable to discern.

"You needed a fresh start, Corey. What better place than here? How about I show you what else needs to be fixed?"

Erin led her to the next bedroom and motioned at some missing floorboards. As she knelt down to finger the wood, Erin recognized what she'd seen in Corey's expression. Wonder. Like a child's face when she opens a present to find the gift she'd longed for, but never thought possible.

Corey accompanied Erin around to the other cabins where Erin showed her what needed to be repaired. While Erin talked and pointed to a crack in the ceiling of a bathroom, Corey thought about how easily she'd told Erin about Judy. She probably would have told her eventually, but the fact she'd divulged Judy's death so quickly after meeting Erin was a shock.

"Corey?"

"I missed what you said. Could you please repeat the question?"

"I asked if you'd like to see something spectacular." Erin checked her wristwatch and glanced at the window. "The light looks about right. You're up to speed about the repairs. Can I interest you in a little bit of magic?"

Corey was intrigued. "Lead on."

They ambled down the trail at a leisurely pace. The sky had begun to lighten with the approach of dawn. Corey followed Erin to the shore of the lake. From her vantage point, she enjoyed the gentle sway of Erin's hips.

"You okay back there?"

Corey snapped her head up and hoped the dim lighting hid her embarrassment. "I'm fine."

"We need to get to the other side," Erin said as she kept walking. "The trail leading over is pretty flat."

They crunched through the frost on the short grass until they reached the far side of the lake and faced east toward the lodge.

"Those photos didn't do this place justice," Corey said as she stood beside Erin.

"Listen." Erin's voice lowered to almost a whisper. "I swear you can almost hear the sunrise."

Corey concentrated hard, fearful that if she blinked, she'd miss Erin's "magic."

The first rays of sunlight moved toward the back of the lodge before clearing the building and the high pines behind it. Then, all the colors of the rainbow burst in a millisecond of brightness, before the sun made a full appearance, glinting off the water.

Corey gasped. "Wow."

"Pretty magical, isn't it?"

Corey no longer saw the sunrise. She marveled at the highlights in Erin's blonde hair that glowed in the sun's rays. The fine wisps caressed her temples like angel feathers.

"Don't you think?" Erin looked at Corey.

Corey realized she was staring and blinked. "It's definitely magical," she managed to say as she turned back to the sun.

"You've never seen anything like it, have you?"

She felt Erin watching her. Corey finally got brave enough to face her again. "No, I haven't."

A faint blush appeared at Erin's cheeks. "We'd better get back. Aunt Tess is probably thinking I've kidnapped you or something. Or run you off. I'm sorry again about earlier."

"You were only looking out for your aunt."

"I'm glad you understand." Erin started up the trail. "Let's see if she's found you yet on America's Most Wanted List."

"What do you know? I called your references in Michigan, and they checked out," Tess said as they entered the lobby. "Not sure if you know what you're getting yourself into, but I won't look a gift horse in the mouth. Do you still want the job?"

Erin moved past Corey to step behind the counter. She needed something between them, even a physical barrier. When she caught Corey staring at her down at the lake, she hadn't known how to react. Other than to pretend she hadn't felt Corey's intense gaze deep inside in a place she'd closed off years ago. She was used to chasing women, or being chased, consequences be damned. What was different about Corey? She pushed that question into the back of her mind.

"Yes, ma'am," Corey said. "I want the job."

"That's what I wanted to hear. And please call me Tess. Erin showed you some of the repairs you'll be doing?"

"She walked me through a couple of the cabins."

Scott and Eddie entered the lodge and were about to pass the counter when Tess stopped them. "Hey, you two, I'd like you to meet Corey Banner. I just hired her as our head of maintenance. In other words, she's your boss now. Corey, this is Scott and Eddie."

They took turns shaking her hand.

"You two don't have to worry about trying to fix anything around here anymore. Corey was a foreman for her father's construction company. Think you can handle focusing on making sure lightbulbs are replaced, furnace filters changed, and the like?"

"I can handle it, Tess," Scott said. "And, Corey, I'm glad you're on board."

Eddie spoke up. "Me, too. Let us know when you need us for anything. Erin keeps us on our toes, though."

Scott glanced over at Erin, probably remembering their latest confrontation on the two-way radios. "Speaking of which, we have to hit the other cabins and check the bulbs. Nice to meet you, Corey."

After they walked away, Tess said, "I don't think you'll have any problems with those boys. They're good local kids who've lived in Grand Lake all their lives. How would you feel about getting to work right away? We need those cabins up and running before our first big push of the summer season after Memorial Day weekend."

"If you'll show me where your tools are, I'll get started. I'm assuming there's a lumber store nearby?"

"Erin, why don't you take Corey to town? But go in her vehicle so she'll get an idea of how to find it."

"I'd be happy to. Come on, Corey."

Corey followed her as they headed out to the parking lot and slid into the front seats of the SUV.

"Make a left," Erin said when they reached the two-lane highway. She grew quiet, still grappling with her mixed feelings.

"I like your aunt."

"Hmm?"

"Your aunt," Corey said. "I like her."

"She's a gem. She has her moments with me sometimes, though."

"Telling you what to do?"

"And knowing what's best for me. Although she's mostly right." Erin didn't want to think she was right about her love life. Especially at that moment.

"Can I ask you a question?"

"I'm gay." Erin cringed in embarrassment as soon as the words left her mouth.

"That wasn't the question, but it's nice to know." Corey's voice was touched with amusement.

"I can't believe I just blurted that out."

"Think nothing of it. My question is did we miss our turn back there at the Grand Lake sign."

Erin hadn't noticed until now how far they'd driven on US 34. "Shit. We did. If you can do a U-turn…"

Corey maneuvered the SUV over into the graveled shoulder and then pointed them in the right direction.

"I know I didn't need to tell you that I'm gay," Erin said again.

"Seriously, Erin, don't worry about it."

"I figured it was only fair if I told you since you shared your story with me." That sounded lame, but Erin was unable to think fast enough for any other excuse.

"I appreciate the honesty." Corey gestured at the Big Red's Lumber sign. "Is this it?"

"If you drive around close to the front there, we can load up when we're done." Erin glanced into the backseat. "Damn. I didn't even think to ask before we left. Will the lumber fit in your SUV? If not, we can go back and get Bertha."

"Who's Bertha?" Corey asked as she pulled near the store entrance.

"My Land Rover."

"You own a Land Rover?"

Erin unbuckled her seatbelt. "Don't go getting any ideas about money. It's a 1973 tank."

"But still…" Corey chuckled.

"But still nothing. I got a nice deal on it. Bill who owns the dude ranch sold it to me for a good price. You didn't really answer my question about the lumber fitting in your SUV."

"It'll fit. What I need are smaller pieces. I'll ask to have them cut down for the floorboard. Once I measure at the lodge, I can cut the pieces to exact size."

"The lumber's in the rear of the store." Erin waved for Corey to follow her.

They talked with the clerk and picked out what they needed. As he cut the wood down, Corey said, "I think I'll wander around to get a better feel of the place." She went down the aisle of paint supplies.

Erin grabbed an empty cart and rolled it over for the clerk to stack the wood. After he finished, she headed toward the paint department to find Corey.

Corey was talking to another clerk when Erin joined her. "Joe here says he can get me all I need for paint supplies. You still want off-white for the room, right?"

"It's the most functional."

Joe left them when another customer called him over.

"You seem a little preoccupied, Erin."

"I'm fine." Erin was still questioning herself for announcing her sexuality to Corey with no prompting. Corey wasn't even her type. She wasn't a lodger or a summer hire. She'd be permanent. Which made it that much more final and that much more obvious to Erin she needed to steer clear. Besides, Corey carried too many shadows with her from Michigan.

Joe came back to them with a cart filled with a five-gallon bucket of a top-brand, off-white paint and three cans of Kilz.

"You said you knew what else you needed?" Joe asked her.

"I'll find it in the next aisle over, right?" Corey took the cart from him.

"Right."

Corey pushed the cart around the corner. She chose scrapers, edgers, three different sized brushes, and picked out a couple of rolls of edging tape. "You have tarps at the lodge?"

"I think so."

"To be on the safe side, we can grab some vinyl tenting. Works just as well, and they're ten times cheaper. Any idea of where we can find it?"

Erin pointed to the other side of the store.

"I can never get over how big these places are." Corey strode quickly to the area Erin had indicated.

They finished getting what they needed, and Erin handed her credit card to the checkout clerk.

She pushed the cart of cut lumber, and Corey pushed the other cart to the SUV. Corey opened the back doors and pulled the seats down. She then popped the trunk door. They each unloaded their supplies. Corey shut the door, and they'd almost made it to the front seats when a woman called out Erin's name.

Erin turned toward the voice. *Lee.*

"Hey." Lee trotted over. "I thought I recognized you."

Corey leaned on the top of the SUV, watching with interest.

"Forgive my manners, Corey," Erin said. "This is Lee. Lee, this is Corey Banner. She's the new head of maintenance for Rainbow Lodge."

"Nice to meet you, Corey." Lee seemed to be sizing up her competition as she gave Corey the once-over. Then she leaned in and pressed her mouth close to Erin's ear. "When can I see you again?"

Erin's face grew hot. "I don't know. Probably when I bring another lodger to the dude ranch."

Lee straightened, and a flash of disappointment crossed her face. "Not before then, huh?"

"I need to help Corey get acclimated."

"I just bet you do," Lee said, her voice dripping in sarcasm.

Erin glared at her. She opened the door and got inside. Corey did the same.

As they drove away, Corey lifted her chin at the rearview mirror. "Your girlfriend's kind of possessive."

"She's not my girlfriend," Erin snapped and crossed her arms over her chest.

"You might want to tell her that."

Erin didn't say anything the rest of the way to the lodge. After Corey parked in the graveled parking lot, Erin hopped out and started toward the lodge.

"I'll run and get the cart," she yelled over her shoulder. She had to get away from Corey, if only briefly.

Erin disappeared around one of the sheds behind the lodge. Corey pictured Lee and Erin together and just as quickly pushed it out of her mind.

Erin approached with a cart carrying a box full of tools. The handle from a saw stuck out of the pile.

"This should be what you need to get the work underway on the back cabins." Erin wheeled the cart to the trunk and set the box of tools on the ground.

Corey started unloading everything, handing the material to Erin to set on the cart. There was one piece of wood which had fallen against the back of the front seat. Corey crawled in on all fours to get to it. She'd almost reached it when Erin opened one of the back doors and grabbed the piece of wood.

Erin grinned at her. "A little easier this way."

Corey laughed. "I guess so." Rather than try to maneuver around to crawl out the rear door, she edged backwards. She checked behind her to see how close she was to the end and found Erin staring at her ass as she got ready to jump out. Erin quickly looked away and kept her head down as she tossed the wood in with the rest of the pile.

"I'll let you get to work. I should check on Aunt Tess and see what needs to be done up front." Erin wouldn't meet her eyes before she walked away. She shoved her hands into the back pockets of her jeans. Before entering the lodge, she spun partly around and waved. Corey waved back.

Interesting. Corey set the tool box on top of the pile of supplies and pushed the rickety cart with its wobbly front wheel toward the cabins.

Chapter 9

The alarm buzzed as it always did at four the next morning. Erin lay there and gathered her thoughts. She tried to remember her dream from the night before, but it stayed just out of reach.

Sighing, she shuffled off to the shower. After she dressed, she descended the stairs and paused when she heard Corey's husky voice as she talked to Aunt Tess.

"No. Only a sister. No brother."

"Who taught you how to do all the handiwork then? Your father?"

"Yes. He had incredible patience with me. I can't tell you how many projects we had to redo because of something I goofed up. Once I got the hang of it, he had me tag along on his projects. After I graduated from high school, I went to work for him full-time."

Erin smiled wistfully at the evident love Corey had for her father. Erin's dad had died five years ago. She went around the corner and saw Corey sitting with Aunt Tess at the dining room table.

Corey lifted her mug and saluted Erin. "Morning."

"Morning, Corey. Aunt Tess."

"You got downstairs earlier than you normally do," Tess said as Erin passed behind her to the kitchen.

She returned quickly with a cup of coffee, leaned against the doorway, and took a sip of it. "Don't make it sound like I'm a slacker."

"Pshaw," Tess said with a dismissive wave.

Erin grinned. "Pshaw?"

"You might be a little tardy rising sometimes, but I'm not accusing you of slacking off. You know better."

"Wouldn't want Corey to get the wrong idea of me since she doesn't know me well."

Corey stood up from the table. "I think I'll head out to cabin seven. Thanks for the coffee, Tess."

"You're welcome. You can come in anytime. We don't have very many lodgers up this early needing anything. If so, they can always use the bell on the counter to call me."

Corey left the living quarters.

"I like her," Tess said.

"She's nice."

Tess sighed.

"What?" Erin took another cautious sip of coffee.

"I think you should make an effort to be friends with her. She seems a little lost."

"Have I done anything to make it seem like I don't like her?"

"You've acted a little cold."

Erin thought for a moment. "Maybe. I'll work on it."

Tess picked up her plate and carried it into the kitchen. "I didn't make a killer breakfast this morning. Hope you don't mind."

"Nah. I'll have a couple of your biscuits."

"Too late. Corey ate the last of them."

"Oh, she did, did she? It didn't take her long to make herself at home."

Tess slammed a plate into the dishwasher with a little more force than necessary. "I am not having this discussion with you. Do me a favor and work on it with Corey, like you said you'd do."

Erin threw the rest of her coffee into the drain. She didn't need Tess to lecture her about Corey, a woman she'd only met a couple of days ago. Especially someone with baggage, attractive or not. *I don't do baggage.*

Sweat dripped down Corey's forehead and burned her eyes. She blinked it away until she could focus on the nail she was hammering into the floorboard. She took another nail out of the pouch of her leather tool belt. She lined it up and was about to raise her hammer when her cell phone vibrated at her side. She rocked back on her haunches and flipped the phone open after seeing who was calling.

Oh, crap. She's going to kill me. Her mom had left a couple of messages, but Corey had been getting acclimated and forgot to return the calls. She sat on her butt and leaned against the wall to prepare for the lecture. She hadn't even finished with her "hello," before her mother lit into her.

"I've been worried sick. You're halfway around the world—"

"Mom, I wouldn't call Colorado halfway around—"

"*Don't* interrupt me, Corey Sue."

Corey cringed at the sound of her middle name. Which she hated.

"Your father and I were thinking of calling the Grand Lake Sheriff's Department to hunt you down."

"I'm sorry, okay? I got settled in and then started on this job, and I forgot. I'm really, really sorry."

"What job?"

Corey felt a little better. Maybe she'd be successful in steering her mother away from her rant. "The owners hired me as the head of maintenance at the lodge. I've been working in the cabins."

There was a slight pause. "That's good news I guess." Another pause. "But it still doesn't get you off the hook for not calling us."

"No, it doesn't. I know those are poor excuses."

"Hold on. Your father wants to talk to you."

Corey heard her mom's muffled voice but couldn't make out the words.

"Hey, Cor," her dad said. "Your mother told me you've got yourself a job already doing maintenance and repair."

"Yeah. I'm working on the cabins here at the lodge. I'm supervising two part-time employees as well."

"Good for you. That sounds right up your alley. Listen, I'll give the phone back to your mom, but do me a favor. Do a better job of keeping in touch." Her father's voice lowered. "She's been driving me nuts."

"Will do, Dad."

"Hang on. Here's your mom."

"How do you like it there, honey?" her mom asked.

"It's beautiful, Mom. The lodge is everything I thought it would be, and the owners are nice. Tess and her niece, Erin, run the place." Corey's voice softened as she thought of Erin.

Erin stopped in the hall outside the bedroom door when she heard Corey say her name.

"Yes, they're paying me enough and my lodging's taken care of," Corey said.

Erin leaned a little closer to catch the words.

"I don't know. Probably a little younger than me, I guess." Corey voice rose. "Mom! I can't believe you're asking me if she's gay. Why should it matter?"

Erin clasped her hand over her mouth to hold in her laughter.

"Yes, she's very pretty."

Erin felt the heat of a blush working its way up her neck to her face.

"I don't know if she's attached. God, Mom, do we really need to have this conversation? I've only been here a few days. I'm not even sure she likes me." Corey grunted. "You're my mother. You're supposed to feel that way. Besides, I don't think it's a good idea to get involved even if she did like me. For one, she's my employer. For another..." When Corey spoke again, her voice was shaky. "For another, I think I'm damaged goods."

Erin heard the thick emotion behind those words and wanted to do anything to take away the pain.

"I got to go, Mom. Like I said, I promise to call sooner next time. Love you, too. Bye."

Erin waited until she heard Corey hammering before she stepped into the room. "Hey."

Corey obviously hadn't heard her as she kept hammering.

Erin moved closer and spoke a little louder. "Hey, Corey."

Corey jumped and slammed the hammer down on her thumb. "Ow! Son of a bitch!" She dropped the hammer and gripped her thumb. "Ow, ow, ow, ow."

"Oh, God, I'm so sorry." Erin knelt down beside Corey, who was leaning against the wall with her eyes squeezed shut. "I didn't mean to scare you. May I see?" Erin held out her hand.

Corey opened her eyes and stared at her, obviously debating if this was a wise move.

"I promise I won't hurt you. Please."

Corey slowly loosened her grip on her thumb. Her hand shook as she presented it to Erin.

Erin frowned when she saw the bruising. "It's already swelling." She reached out to touch the thumb.

Corey immediately jerked her hand away and cradled it to her body.

"Please let me see if it's broken."

"It's not broken," Corey said through clenched teeth. "I wouldn't be able to move it like this." She wiggled the thumb. "See?"

"Let's at least get some ice on it."

"Really, Erin. It's fine. I'm finishing up on the floor and don't want to take a break."

Erin rose to her feet and stuck her fists on her hips. "This is where I pull the employer card and say, yes, you are taking a break to get this tended to."

Corey narrowed her eyes. "You wouldn't."

"Does it look like I'm kidding?"

"Fine." As Corey struggled to her feet, Erin reached down to help her, but Corey waved her off. "No, I think you've done enough."

"All I did was enter the room and say 'Hey, Corey.' It's not like I took the hammer and slammed it on your thumb on purpose."

They stood there staring at each other until Corey cracked a small smile. "I know you didn't do anything deliberately. I got off the phone with my mom and…"

"And?" Erin wanted to see what Corey would say.

"And sometimes our conversations don't go so well."

Erin almost pushed her to admit more but thought better of it. "Come on. Let's get that iced down."

* * *

Corey followed Erin into the back of the lodge.

"Have a seat," Erin said over her shoulder. "I'll get some ice from the kitchen."

Corey looked around and found they were in the laundry room. She sat down at a table and tried to ignore the throbbing in her thumb. Erin was right. It had swelled in the limited time it had taken them to walk to the lodge. Her skin was already bruised to a deep purple, and the thumbnail was blackened as well.

"Here we go." Erin brought in a plastic bag of ice and a glass of water. She tugged something out of her pocket. "Take these."

"Erin, it's not like this is some dire emergency."

"Are you always this stubborn?"

"Depends on who you ask."

"Here." Erin dropped two pills into Corey's hand. "Ibuprofen."

While Corey downed the pills, Erin reached above the shelving over the dryer and pulled down a towel. She wrapped the towel around the bag of ice.

"Hold out your hand again." Erin made a face when she saw the thumb. "I'm so sorry."

"Hey, you didn't raise the hammer."

"No, but I guess I startled you enough to cause you to miss the nail." Erin was about to place the bag onto the thumb, but Corey flinched. "Trust me," Erin said softly.

A blue haze of need rushed over Corey as she met Erin's eyes. She felt as though the ocean tide had caught her unawares and swept her into the deep.

"Corey?"

"Huh?"

"Your hand?"

When Corey offered her hand, they still stared at each other until Erin shook her head slightly and looked away. She gently placed the bag of ice on the thumb.

"Can you hold the bag in place?" she asked. Her voice sounded hoarse.

Corey took the bag from Erin, and their hands touched. It was if a spark had flashed between them, almost like touching someone's hand in the winter after walking on a carpet. She wondered if she was the only one who felt it. She searched Erin's face, but it held no clue to her emotions.

"Um…" Erin pushed a lock of hair behind her ear. "Why don't you take the rest of the day off?"

Corey broke free from her trance. "No way. I'll humor you and ice this for an hour, but afterwards, I'm going back to work."

A slow smile crept across Erin's lips. "You really are stubborn, aren't you?"

"Come to think of it, I guess I am."

"Why don't you sit out front and enjoy the view while you ice your thumb." Erin started to leave but stopped at the door. Keeping her back to Corey, she said something so softly that Corey couldn't make it out.

"What?"

Erin turned around. "I said I like you. I apologize if I gave you a different impression." She waved her hand vaguely toward the front of the lodge in the general direction of the living quarters. "I've been kind of abrupt."

"Tess put you up to this, didn't she?"

"No. Absolutely not. I mean it."

Corey waited a long moment before responding. "All right. I'm glad you like me because I like you, too."

"Okay. Good. We've got that all settled." She backed toward the door. "Promise me you'll wait an hour before you start working again."

Corey crossed her heart. "Promise."

"I need to get to cabin three to strip the beds."

"I'll go that way with you," Corey said as she stood up.

They left the laundry room and walked side by side until they reached where Corey would take the path to the front of the building.

"Thanks for this," she said as she held up her hands.

"You're welcome. I'll check on you later today, but I'll make a loud enough entrance to let you know I'm coming."

Corey grinned. "A little warning would help."

Erin strode toward the cabins. Corey stood watching her until she went out of sight around a bend in the trees.

As Corey approached the long porch in the front of the lodge, she thought about the feelings she had when Erin touched her and their subsequent conversation. A familiar sensation stirred inside her, but she quickly dismissed it. It was nothing.

Erin waited until she was out of sight before leaning against a fir tree. Her pulse pounded in her ears. "Jesus, Erin. 'I like you'? Could you have sounded any more sophomoric?"

She slapped her forehead with her palm and continued on to the cabins.

Chapter 10

The next afternoon, Erin sat in one of the porch swings and munched on a hastily made sandwich. She frowned as the sky darkened, giving every indication of an imminent storm. She wondered what Corey was working on today. Erin had avoided her since yesterday. She even drove into town to eat in case Corey showed up at their dinner table. But she couldn't avoid her forever, regardless of the confusion that threatened to smother her. What was different about Corey? That question refused to stay hidden. Was Erin so used to jumping into bed with any attractive woman that Corey's lack of trying befuddled her?

Erin popped the last bite into her mouth. She was about to head down to the cabins when she thought it might be nice to take Corey something for lunch. Corey seemed like the type who concentrated so intently on her work, she'd forget to eat. Erin passed her aunt on the way to the living quarters.

"Storm's coming," Tess said.

"Looks like this one will be a little more intense than our typical afternoon thundershower." Erin entered the kitchen and slapped together a ham sandwich from the leftover baked ham. She wrapped it in foil and started for the back.

"Where you going with the sandwich?" Tess called after her.

"I thought Corey might not have eaten."

"I'm glad to see you're making an effort, Erin. I checked on cabin two last night. Tell her I think she's doing a fine job."

"I'll let her know."

On her way to the cabins, Erin thought she should've brought something cold to drink. Oh well. Maybe Corey had something in her cooler.

Erin rounded the corner on the trail and stopped dead in her tracks. Corey was up on the roof bent over while she hammered on some loose shingles. Her gray T-shirt was wet and clung to her torso. Her muscles rippled across her back as she brought the hammer down. It took a minute to realize Corey had spoken.

"Hey, Erin. Is that for me?"

Erin quickly recovered and walked to the side of the cabin, craning her neck to peer up at her. "I thought you might appreciate some nourishment. I pegged you for someone who doesn't eat like they should and lets meals slide by when she's busy."

Corey descended the ladder. Erin tried to force herself to keep her eyes from drifting lower, but she still managed another quick scan of her gorgeous ass.

"I hope you have something to drink," Erin said. "If not, I can go to the lodge and grab you something."

"Nope. I have some bottled water in my cooler." Corey took the wrapped sandwich from Erin's outstretched hand. "What do we have?"

"Some of Tess's baked ham left over from last night's dinner."

Corey didn't waste any time unwrapping the foil and digging in. "Aren't you going to have anything?" she said around a mouthful. She plopped into one of the porch chairs.

"Just had a sandwich."

"This is delicious." Corey reached into the cooler and took out a bottle of water. She held it up. "Want one?"

Erin took the bottle from her and opened the lid.

Corey grabbed another bottle, took a big swig of water, and motioned to the other chair. "Want to sit while I eat?"

Erin used the excuse of a rumble of thunder to tear away from Corey's dark, penetrating stare. "I think we have a storm blowing in," she said as the clouds passed over the trees. "You might want to work inside for the afternoon."

Pain skittered across Corey's tanned face. Erin tried to figure out what had caused it.

"Didn't even notice the weather," Corey said, her voice barely above a whisper. She looked up at the sky.

"You all right?"

Corey wadded up the foil and stood abruptly. She tossed the foil and her empty bottle into a trash bin that sat at the porch corner. "I'm fine. I think I'll go inside and scrape some paint. It was thoughtful of you to bring the sandwich. Thank you."

"You're welcome." Erin almost asked her if she wanted company. She was about to leave when Corey stopped her with a question.

"Do you know where I could go in town to get a good steak?"

"Mo's Tavern serves excellent steak. Best in the area."

"Can you give me directions?"

Erin spoke without thinking. "If you feel like company, I can drive you there."

"If you don't mind."

"How does six sound?"

"Perfect. I'll meet you up at the lodge."

Erin began walking away but couldn't resist. "Make sure that hammer misses your thumb."

Corey's laughter followed her up the trail.

* * *

Corey settled into the passenger seat of Erin's Land Rover. "Bertha, huh?"

"Yup. She likes her name, too."

Corey examined the worn interior with the overhead material drooping down from the dome light. "It fits."

Erin gave her a mock scowl. "You're not making fun of her, are you? Because she's very sensitive."

"Absolutely not. Seems like you drove her hard. Like a tank, as you said earlier."

"The name 'Bertha' denotes reliable, don't you think?"

"It does." As they drove, Corey took in the breathtaking views. "How could you ever leave the mountains?" She didn't realize she'd spoken the words aloud until Erin answered.

"I couldn't. I went to school at the University of Colorado and then moved back to Grand Lake two years after graduating. Although…"

Corey waited for more, but Erin's expression had changed. "Although?"

"Nothing. I thought of moving to California once."

"What's in California?"

"My ex-partner and I thought about living in L.A., but it didn't work out." Erin was talking so low, Corey had to strain to hear her over the engine. Erin's sadness draped over Corey like a burial shroud. "She left me for an artist and moved to New York."

"She was a fool."

Erin smiled sadly. "I don't know about that."

"Well, she was." Corey cleared her throat and changed the subject. "Mo's doesn't exactly sound like a great steak joint."

Erin brightened at the mention of the tavern. "Wait and see."

* * *

The darkened dining portion of the bar's interior had an eclectic array of mounted kill adorning the paneled walls. At the table where Corey and Erin sat, a ten-point deer stared out at the patrons. Erin must've noticed what drew Corey's attention.

"Mo shot the buck himself three years ago. Hasn't stopped talking about it since," Erin said.

"I'm not really big on hunting."

"Don't say that too loud. You'll get called a tree-hugger by the townsfolk." Erin's eyes sparkled in the low light of the bar. "Especially don't mention it to our server, Charlene. She's Mo's wife."

"Duly noted."

Charlene approached them with their dinners. "Ten-ounce porterhouse," she said as she set the plate in front of Corey. "And six-ounce sirloin. Steak sauce is there on the table. Anything else, ladies?"

"Another Coors Light, please," Erin said.

Corey held up her nearly empty bottle. "Me, too."

"You got it." Charlene left for the bar.

She brought them two iced down bottles of beer, and their conversation resumed around bites of steak.

"Tell me about your family, Corey."

"My parents, Daniel and Vera, still live in Lansing. I have a younger sister, Betty, and two nephews, Brady and Cole."

"How old?"

"Brady's eight. Cole celebrated his fourth birthday a month ago." Thinking about her rambunctious nephews unleashed a rush of homesickness.

"You sound like you're close."

"Betty and I have always been close. When Judy was alive, we used to watch the kids on the weekends whenever Betty needed a break."

"After she died, you stopped watching them?"

"Not completely." Corey focused on the piece of steak she pushed around in her steak sauce. "I didn't watch them as much. Judy... Judy was really good with them." She glanced up to see Erin's sympathetic expression.

"I can't imagine how difficult it was for you," Erin said gently.

Corey took a sip of her beer. "I don't think it'll ever get any easier." She hesitated before continuing. "Judy died while driving home early from work. It was storming. The state troopers said they thought her car hydroplaned." The next words caught in her throat. "It was Halloween night, and I had asked her to hurry home. Before she left, she told me she might surprise me and leave before midnight when she was scheduled to clock out." She stabbed at a piece of her steak. "I feel like it's my fault. If I hadn't pushed her, she might have stayed at work and would still be alive."

Erin reached across the table and encircled Corey's forearm with her fingers. "Oh, Corey. You can't think you were responsible. You don't know what would have happened. It was an accident."

Corey raised her head and looked at Erin through her blurred vision. "That's what everyone tells me, but I haven't been able to let it go."

Erin's hand lingered, and she made smoothing motions with her fingertips across Corey's skin. "You need to believe them because it's the truth. Sometimes there's nothing we can do to prevent these things from happening." She lowered her head to maintain eye contact with Corey. "It's not your fault."

Corey took a shaky breath and nodded, not able to speak for fear she'd really break down.

Erin gave her arm a squeeze before letting go and cutting into her steak. They remained quiet as they ate. Erin seemed as lost in her thoughts as Corey. Corey broke the silence, taking a chance on delving into Erin's past.

"What was her name?"

Erin raised her eyebrows but didn't ask Corey who she was talking about. "Bonnie."

"How long were you together?"

Erin didn't answer right away.

"It's none of my business—"

"No, you're fine. We met as freshmen in college and were together for two more years after we graduated. I came home one afternoon from work. She was boxing up her stuff. I of course confronted her. She told me she was moving to New York with some artist from Steamboat Springs. Ironically, I was with Bonnie when they met. Her work was showing at the university. They'd been seeing each other for several months after that without my knowledge." Erin took a drag of her beer. "I felt like a damned fool."

"No."

Erin stared at her. "What do you mean?"

"Like I told you before, she was the fool."

Erin quickly broke eye contact and started eating again. "Thanks," she murmured.

"You don't need to thank me for being honest."

Erin smiled at her, and with that smile, Corey's spirits lifted higher than they had in two years.

* * *

They were mostly quiet on the return drive to the lodge. Occasionally, Erin would glance over at Corey to find her with her head back on the headrest, staring up at the night sky.

Erin pulled into the graveled lot closest to the cabins, and they got out of the Land Rover.

"I appreciate you showing me where the tavern is," Corey said. "Now I know where to get an awesome steak in town."

"I'm glad you liked it." She tried to get a clearer look at Corey's face, but the darkness made her expression difficult to read.

"Well, guess I'll head to my cabin." Corey took a couple of steps to leave.

Erin acted on impulse. "I'll walk you down. It's kind of tricky in the dark, and I know the trail," she added, hastily. "Let me grab my flashlight out of the glove compartment."

They strolled to the cabins until they reached Corey's. Corey stood under the porch light.

"Thanks again, Erin."

"I enjoyed dinner." Erin was overcome with a sudden urge to join Corey on the porch and hug her. Or brush the dark hair off her forehead. *Whoa, Erin...*

"See you tomorrow maybe?"

"I should be around," Erin answered.

Corey unlocked the door and went inside.

Erin was about to leave for the lodge, but instead, she veered down the trail to the lake as she had the other night. She climbed up on her rock, lay with her hands behind her head, and stared at the star-filled canopy.

A shooting star streaked across the sky and burned out as quickly as it appeared. Erin wanted to make a wish but was at a loss as to what to wish for. She once again experienced the stirrings of something inside. Something she'd given up hope of ever feeling again. And it scared her.

There was such a vulnerability about Corey—like how she sounded when she told her mother on the phone she thought she was "damaged goods." How fragile she appeared when she told Erin about how her partner died. Erin didn't know if any of her words had pierced Corey's shield of guilt.

The image of Corey's eyes brimming with unshed tears remained burned in Erin's mind. Another shooting star flashed overhead. This time Erin made a wish for peace. Peace for Corey.

Chapter 11

The rest of the week passed with Corey not seeing Erin. She wondered about the pangs of disappointment Erin's absence caused her.

She entered the lodge to grab a quick jolt of sugar from one of the vending machines. After she fed her dollar into the slot, she punched the buttons for a Snickers bar. The arm moved excruciatingly slowly as the Snickers bar inched forward. But as the bar was about to drop, the arm snagged it and stopped its progress. It hung there suspended above the bin, as if taunting her.

"Crap." Corey jiggled the machine a little. Then pounded her fist once against the glass in frustration. "Damn it."

"I don't think the machine heard you."

Corey didn't jump at the sound of Erin's voice this time. "You never know."

Erin tugged money out of her pocket and fed another dollar into the bill slot. She punched in the numbers for the Snickers bar. Two of them fell with a loud plunk into the bin below. She reached in, snatched them up, and handed both bars to Corey.

"Here's one for now and one for later when you get a craving."

"You're a lifesaver." Corey ripped open the wrapper and munched down on the candy bar. She had to work the bite in her mouth before swallowing and saying, "Haven't seen you around."

"I've been busy running back and forth into town for restaurant supplies. I've also been holed up in the office poring over our books."

"Rainbow Lodge seems to do well."

"We're booked almost all summer."

Corey swallowed another bite. "Has Tess ever thought of adding more cabins?"

"No. There are a couple of other lodges nearby with fifty and seventy cabins, but she has no desire to expand. She's happy with the status quo."

Corey finished off the rest of the Snickers bar in quick fashion, wadded up the wrapper, and tossed it in a nearby trash can. She caught Erin's amused expression. "What's so funny?"

"I've never seen anyone devour a candy bar like that before."

"Force of habit, I guess. I used to sneak them in on quick breaks when working with my dad. He always kept me hopping, and I didn't have much time to get in a snack."

Erin nodded absently and started fidgeting.

"Everything okay?"

"Um..." Erin shoved her hands into her jeans pockets and stared at her sneakers. "There's a dance Bill holds at his ranch every month. It's coming up Saturday night. I was wondering if you might want to go."

Corey still didn't dance—or at least not well. Judy had been the dancer, just as she had from the very beginning. As long as Judy led, Corey could muddle along. But the last time had been the impromptu dance by the fire in the Upper Peninsula. She was also noting her reaction to Erin's invitation—it was if a swarm of butterflies had taken flight in the pit of her stomach.

Erin mistook Corey's hesitation as a rejection. She raised her head, and Corey saw the disappointment reflected there. "Never mind. It was just a thought." She turned to leave.

"Wait."

Erin stopped and looked at her expectantly.

"I'm not much of a dancer, but I'd enjoy your company. So, sure, I'd love to go with you."

"You would?"

"Yeah, I would." And she meant it.

"We might not see each other between now and then. I'm still on food runs into town. Meet me by Bertha at seven Saturday night, and I'll drive us over."

"What do I wear? I don't have any dress-up clothes."

"It's a dude ranch, Corey." Erin's gaze drifted from Corey's face, down her denim shirt, to her jeans below, and back up. "What you have on is fine. Just throw on a thermal shirt under that to stay warm."

A little flustered with the blatant appraisal, Corey cleared her throat. "Good to know."

"Don't wear yourself out. You need to save some strength for dancing." Erin winked and left the vending room.

Corey stood there as she let it sink in that Saturday night was giving every indication of being a date.

* * *

Erin stood in front of the mirror and brushed her hair. Should she put it in a more functional ponytail or leave it down? She fluffed it around her shoulders. Definitely down. After spritzing on her favorite perfume, Highland Lilac, she ran her fingers along her green-checked, long-sleeved cotton shirt and brushed across her flat stomach, glad the lodge kept her busy and in shape. She adjusted the collar of the turtleneck she wore underneath the shirt. She turned around and looked over her shoulder at how her black jeans fit her hips. They were tight in the butt but loose enough to allow her to move freely when dancing.

"You look very nice," Tess said from the doorway.

"You think so?"

Tess leaned against the doorjamb. "Yes." Her mouth twitched in amusement. "Who are we trying to impress?"

Erin ducked her head so her aunt didn't see the blush she was sure was evident in the light. "Nobody," she mumbled.

Tess chuckled. "Keep telling yourself that." As she was leaving the room, she said, "I'm glad you're getting to know her better."

"You're impossible," Erin shouted.

She glanced one last time in the mirror, grabbed her keys off the dresser, and left the lodge. She strode around the corner and stopped short at the sight of Corey leaning against the Land Rover. She was wearing a red denim shirt tucked into her faded blue jeans. A thermal undershirt peeked through her open collar. A worn leather belt polished off the outfit. It appeared her scuffed cowboy boots had seen some use. The overall package was... breathtaking.

Corey must have heard her approaching. She pushed off the side of the Land Rover. "Hey."

"Ready to two-step?" Erin asked as she unlocked the doors. "Seems like it with those boots."

"I bought these years ago for fun. And I wouldn't know how to two-step if my life depended on it." Corey fastened her seatbelt.

"Then I might have to show you."

They turned onto the highway.

"It's not very far," Erin said. "And we're in luck with the warm spell. Sometimes, it's in the thirties at night here this time of the year."

"I noticed, and I thought spring nights in Lansing could be cold. So, nobody minds seeing two women dancing together?"

"Ah, hell no. It's a western tradition. If there's honky-tonk music playing—and there will be with Bill and his boys on stage—there's good ol' two-stepping going on. And it don't matter who's dancing together."

"It don't, huh? Tell me, does your language revert to country when you go to these things? Because if so, I need to get in practice."

"Why yes it does, Ms. Banner. And don't you worry none. We'll get you into practice afore your Midwestern self knows what hit you."

They parked in the lot at the dude ranch and followed couples strolling hand in hand to the corrals in the back. Overhead lights draped over a stage set up to the rear. To their right, several long tables overflowed with buckets of iced beer and bottled water for those not inclined to drink alcohol.

"The gray-haired guy with the goatee and banjo is Bill Cooper," Erin said, nodding toward the stage where four men warmed up their instruments. "He owns the ranch."

"Hey, Erin. Where's Tess tonight?" An older woman with graying, auburn hair approached them.

"She's staying at the lodge and taking care of guests. Our part-time desk clerk called in sick tonight." Erin motioned toward Corey. "This is Corey Banner, our new head of maintenance. Corey, this is Midge Cooper, Bill's wife."

Midge stuck out her hand. "Nice to meet you."

"Nice to meet you, too, Mrs. Cooper."

Midge laughed. "Erin, where'd you find this one? Nobody has this kind of manners around here. Corey, we're on a first-name basis, all right?" Midge scrutinized them, as if trying to figure out if this was more than an employer showing her employee western hospitality.

Erin tugged Corey by the arm toward the beer table before Midge commenced with her game of twenty questions.

"If I remember right, you like Coors." Erin reached in a bucket and lifted out an ice-cold bottle dripping with water. She handed it to Corey and grabbed one for herself.

The band played the open notes of a fast country tune, and couples took to the dirt dance floor.

Erin challenged her. "Ready?"

Corey grimaced and held up her bottle. "Can I at least down this to get some courage?"

"Then no backing out, ya hear?"

"Oh, I hear all right." Corey sipped her beer as she watched the dancers.

Erin watched, too, tapping her toe to the beat. By the time the song ended, Corey had finished her beer.

"Nervous?" Erin asked, with a smile.

Corey opened her mouth to answer when something behind Erin caught her attention.

"Erin, how are you?"

Erin turned to see Lee ambling over. She was wearing a short jeans skirt with a denim shirt tied at the bottom over a white ribbed top. Her full breasts filled out the top, showing plenty of cleavage. She wore her cowboy hat low, cloaking her face in shadow.

"Lee. Hi."

Lee raised her chin at Corey. "What was your name again?"

"Corey," she answered with an even voice.

The two women stared at each other like gunslingers ready to draw their six-shooters in the middle of town.

"Corey and I were about to dance. She's never two-stepped before."

"Why don't you and I show her how it's done, Erin?"

Erin was about to protest, but Corey silenced any refusal. "I'll wait, Erin. Go ahead."

Lee didn't need any more incentive. She grabbed Erin by the hand and pulled her toward the center of the dance area.

"You know, you were kind of rude," Erin said as the music started.

"She's a big girl. Besides, she needs to let two pros show her the moves."

Erin didn't say anything as she concentrated on following Lee's lead. She had to give Lee this much. She was good. Erin got lost in the music, not paying much attention to who she was dancing with. She searched for Corey who had drifted into the shadows. She seemed to be following their every move. Erin couldn't tell if she was concentrating on getting the steps down or if it was something else.

The song ended, and the band quickly started on the next.

"How about another go?" Lee asked.

"No, I promised Corey I'd show her how to two-step." Erin pulled out of her embrace and walked toward Corey. "Got your courage up yet?"

Corey set her beer on a nearby table. "One-and-a-half beers gave me enough gumption."

Erin held out her left hand and Corey took it. She placed her other hand loosely on Corey's shoulder.

"Since I'll be leading, put your left hand on my arm here. You'll be able to feel which direction I'm headed when I squeeze your other hand."

"Okay." Corey lifted her head and gave a small sniff. "I smell lilacs."

"Uh… that's my perfume."

"Good. I mean it smells good."

"Thanks. Did you catch on any to the dancing?" Erin asked in a rush.

"Not much."

"First of all, don't let the experienced dancers scare you." She nodded toward couples doing fast spins around the dance floor. "I'll teach you the basics. Watch my feet at first. I'll lead. It's two quick steps forward. That's two quick steps back for you." She moved forward. "And then two slow steps. The beat is quick-quick-slow-slow, quick-quick-slow-slow."

Corey's brow furrowed, and the tip of her tongue stuck out of the side of her mouth.

God, she's adorable, Erin thought as they moved haltingly with the other dancers. Corey uttered an occasional "damn it" when her steps faltered.

"Now, don't look at our feet," Erin said.

"Are you crazy? If not, I'll fall on my ass."

"No you won't. Trust me. Raise your head and focus on me."

Corey met her eyes as another fast song drifted through the night air. The face lined in concentration had slipped away, and a much more heated expression had replaced it. This time, Erin stumbled. She quickly righted her steps.

They moved now with a smoother gait, almost as if they'd been dancing together for years. The music ended, and they stopped as the band led into a slow song. A lot of the couples left the dance floor. Erin still held Corey's right hand in her left with her other hand on Corey's shoulder.

Without thinking, she drew Corey closer and dropped her hand around Corey's waist. They swayed gently to the mournful country ballad. Eventually, Erin rested her cheek against Corey's. Corey trembled at the move. Erin wanted the song to last forever but had to settle for a few minutes of bliss in Corey's arms.

She reluctantly withdrew from the embrace when the song ended. "That was… nice."

"It was," Corey said in a soft voice. She shook her head slightly as if to regain her composure. "Do you mind if I sit the next one out? Lee's coming this way. I think she'll want to dance with you again."

Erin was about to say she didn't want to dance with another woman, but Corey had already drifted from under the overhead lights and into the darkness.

"She seemed to catch on fast." Lee reached out to take Erin's hand, but Erin turned away.

"I'm going to check on her."

* * *

Corey walked in between the corrals, away from the dance and away from the unexpected feelings she was experiencing. She put her hands on the top railing of the corral fence and lifted herself up to sit down, still trying to figure out what had happened.

"Corey?"

Erin.

She thought of jumping down and hiding behind the barn but realized how childish that would be. "Over here."

Erin moved in and out of shadows until she stood in front of her. She placed a hand on Corey's knee. "You okay?"

"I'm not sure." She kept her head down as she picked at her jeans. "I've not danced like that since... since Judy." The soft stroking of Erin's fingertips on top of her jeans made her skin feel like it was on fire.

"I apologize if I made you uncomfortable."

Corey finally raised her head. The floodlight over the barn allowed her to see the concern etched on Erin's face.

She placed her hand on top of Erin's wandering fingers. "You didn't do anything wrong." She gripped the wooden rail before jumping down in front of Erin. The move brought them close together. Close enough for Corey to smell Erin's perfume again. The soft scent of lilacs wafted over her and filled her senses. They edged even closer. Corey bent her head to bring her lips to Erin's, but a peal of laughter stopped her short. She stepped back as a couple staggered toward them, groping at each other's clothes.

An overwhelming need to leave consumed Corey like a wildfire burning through dry timber. "Would you mind taking me back to the lodge?"

Erin's eyes flashed with disappointment, but she quickly

seemed to recover. "If that's what you want," she said quietly.

They didn't talk as they walked to the Land Rover and remained silent on the drive to the lodge. After Erin parked, Corey got out and circled around the front of the Rover to join her.

"I want to apologize again for ruining—"

Erin pressed her fingertips to her lips and silenced her. "Shh." She leaned forward and gently kissed Corey's cheek. "You didn't ruin anything. Those three dances with you were worth going out tonight."

Corey touched the spot on her cheek that still tingled from Erin's kiss. "Thanks for understanding." She walked backwards a couple of feet before heading down the path to her cabin.

Erin watched as Corey moved down the soft incline. When Corey disappeared from view, she left for the lodge.

"What have you gotten yourself into, Erin Elizabeth?"

Chapter 12

Erin was beginning to feel that Corey was avoiding her. It had been over a week since the dance, and the most she'd seen of her was a wave from the distance as Corey pushed a cartful of building supplies to the cabins.

"Aunt Tess, have you seen Corey around?" Erin asked as she entered the lodge.

Tess held up an index finger while she counted money. She looked up from her task. "She came in a few minutes ago and went into the restaurant. When she came out, she was munching on a sandwich. I think she might have gone down to the lake."

Erin made her way along the trail to the water's edge. The sun shimmered brightly on the lake as several sailboats tried to catch the faint breeze blowing in from the mountains. She found Corey a few feet from "her" rock. Corey popped the last of her sandwich into her mouth and brushed the crumbs from her hands. She reached down, picked up a stone, and flung it sidearm toward the water. The rock skipped five times before sinking into the lake.

Erin walked to where Corey stood at the edge of the water. She bent down, picked up a smooth stone, and flipped it toward the lake. It skittered seven times and disappeared from view. She waited for Corey to speak. When she didn't, Erin took a chance and peered at her.

"It's good to see you, Erin," Corey said with a smile.

"I'm glad to hear you feel that way."

"Why wouldn't I?"

Erin picked up another stone and skipped it across the water. "I thought you might be avoiding me." Corey's silence answered her unspoken question. "I want to tell you again I didn't mean to make you uncomfortable at the dance." She reached for another stone, but Corey stilled her hand before she picked it up.

Erin met Corey's eyes and then dropped her gaze to her lips. She remembered their softness against her fingertips. She moved even closer, placing her hands lightly on Corey's hips.

"I don't know if this is a good idea." Corey's voice was rough with emotion.

"I won't kiss you if you don't want me to," Erin whispered. When she saw the fear on Corey's face, she stepped away and waited for her to say something. She studied Corey's profile while she stared out at the lake as if searching for her words.

"I've dated women since Judy. Like I told you before, the best I could do was a five-month relationship with a woman who wanted more. I wasn't able to give them what they needed, and I don't know if I can ever have what I had with Judy." Corey picked up a large stone, reared back, and threw it far into the lake where it made a loud splash. There was no skimming across the water this time.

Erin took hold of Corey's hand. She rubbed her thumb across the rough calluses. "How long were you together?"

"Almost six years. We would've celebrated our wedding anniversary a few days after she died. November fourth."

Erin was quiet as she watched a hawk circle above. She thought it ironic that her relationship with Bonnie had lasted about the same amount of time. But they had reacted so differently. Corey seemed to have withdrawn, while Erin had played the field. "That had to have been so hard. Did you have anyone who offered support?"

"My parents and Betty. I don't know what I would have done without them. I had friends, too, but my family was my rock."

"Do you think you can tell me about her someday?" Erin squeezed her hand so Corey would have to look at her.

"I wasn't very good at talking about her with Sandy. It's what drove us apart. It's as if I couldn't share Judy with her. Like if I did, Judy wouldn't be mine anymore. As if I'd be giving away my memories of her and never get them back." Corey kicked at a stone with her work shoe. "I know it might sound crazy."

Erin reached up and caressed her cheek. "It's not crazy. Don't ever call your feelings crazy."

"I don't know why, but with you I want to share my memories of her."

"Maybe it's because this is a new beginning for you. Maybe it's because I'm new."

A breeze drifted across the water and blew Erin's hair into her eyes. She was about to push it away when Corey brushed it aside, letting her fingers linger on Erin's cheek.

"I don't think so. You seem like a lost soul, too, Erin."

Erin drew in a jagged breath. No one had ever tapped into her loneliness. Everyone saw the happy-go-lucky woman who tried to rid her memory of Bonnie by sleeping with as many women as possible. But she did feel lost. Why was it the one person who understood her was someone who'd only entered her life a few weeks ago? Someone who wasn't ready and might never be ready to move on and love again. Someone unattainable.

"Listen, I need to go," Erin said abruptly. "Maybe I'll catch you later." She felt Corey's eyes on her back as she walked away. But she didn't stop.

"What a pair we make," Corey muttered. She slumped onto the boulder nearby and sat there for a long time, thinking about her life. Thinking about Judy and how she would've loved the grandeur of this place.

And she thought about the beautiful Erin Flannery who wrestled with her own haunted memories.

* * *

"Give me a whiskey sour, Mo, heavy on the whiskey." Erin had entered Mo's bar at ten. She'd finished doing her chores at the lodge, got a shower, and started for the stairs. Aunt Tess had given her a sharp look as Erin passed her bedroom, but Erin didn't stop to talk to her. She didn't need to hear another lecture.

She couldn't get Corey out of her mind. With any other woman, Erin would've been even more blatant in making her move and not thought twice about it. But something about Corey had stopped Erin cold. Was it the fear in her eyes? Erin couldn't figure Corey out. Hell, she couldn't figure herself out.

Mo mixed the drink and set it in front of Erin. "Do I need to be worried about you, Erin?"

"Nope. Everything's perfect now that I have this." She took a big gulp and welcomed the burn down her throat. She downed the rest of the drink quickly. "Another."

"Did you drive?" Mo asked as he mixed the drink and poured it into a glass.

Lee slid onto the stool beside Erin. "It's all right. I'll make sure she gets home safely." Lee turned to her. "How's it going, champ?"

"Just peachy." Erin grabbed her glass and tackled the drink with as much gusto as her first.

Lee waved Mo away when he asked if she wanted anything.

"You sure don't seem peachy."

"Oh yeah? If you're so worried about me, why don't you take me to your place tonight?"

"You're up for that?" Lee said with a cocky smile.

"Try me."

Thirty minutes and four drinks later, Lee kicked the door shut to her apartment above the barn. Lee grasped Erin's hair tightly as they kissed, but Erin welcomed the pain. Lee worked the buttons on Erin's shirt and pushed it open. She unclasped her bra, shoving Erin against the wall as she took a nipple into her mouth.

"Oh, God," Erin rasped. It was her turn to grip Lee's hair as she devoured her breast. A gush of wetness soaked her panties. She unsnapped her jeans, grabbed one of Lee's hands, and shoved it against her mound.

Lee pushed aside her panties and delved into her wetness. She sucked on Erin's neck hard enough to leave her mark, but Erin didn't care. Lee worked her way up to Erin's ear. "Is this what you want?" She entered Erin with two fingers while rubbing her thumb against her clit. "Tell me, Erin."

Erin strained her hips forward. She slammed her eyes shut, instantly seeing Corey's sadness that covered her face as if someone had painted it there. A sadness that threatened to break down the last of Erin's barriers and possess her very soul.

"Tell me how you want it, baby."

"Hard." Hard enough to forget Corey. To forget their conversation. To forget their shared pain.

Lee pounded into her as she reclaimed Erin's mouth.

Erin shivered at the first stirrings of her climax. Lee kept working her until Erin screamed her release into Lee's mouth. She slumped against the wall. Lee pulled her fingers out and withdrew her hand. If she hadn't been supporting Erin with her body, Erin would have slid to the floor.

Tears threatened to make an unwanted appearance. *Oh, God. Don't cry now.* She kept her face averted from Lee until she regained her composure.

"What about you? What do you need?"

Lee gave her a lopsided grin. "Nothing. I got off doing you."

Erin flinched at the words. It sounded like she was in a skin flick. But she couldn't judge Lee. Shouldn't. Hell, Erin instigated it, and she'd gotten exactly what she wanted. A quick fuck. Why wouldn't it sound like lines from a porno? After all, Erin was a co-star.

Lee made a face and touched Erin's neck. "Ooh. I think you'll have a bruise there. Sorry."

No, you're not. Erin was sobering up fast. "Can you take me to my Rover?"

Lee frowned. "I don't know. You had a lot of drinks at Mo's."

Erin straightened, snapped closed the clasps of her bra, and buttoned her shirt. "I can drive."

"Still, I'd feel better if you'd stay. Besides, we can have some more fun."

In spite of mindlessly throwing herself at Lee, a night of meaningless sex with her was the last thing Erin wanted. She didn't want to argue, so she tried for a compromise. "How about you drive me to the lodge then? I'll get someone to take me to pick up the Rover tomorrow." She shoved her shirt into her jeans and snapped them.

Lee gripped Erin's crotch. "I think you're capable of another round."

She willed her body not to react. She placed her hand on Lee's and firmly pushed it away. "No, I think I need to go home. Remember I get up at four."

Lee sighed. "Jesus, do you have to be so dedicated to your job?"

Now, Erin was growing irritated. "I do. I would've thought you'd know that by now. I co-own the lodge, and my aunt deserves enough respect that I don't drop the ball." She thought of the irony. She was conscientious about her job but obviously didn't give a damn about her personal life.

"All right. Come on."

She followed Lee out the door and down the stairs to her car. They didn't speak on the drive to the lodge. Erin put her hand on the door handle as Lee was slowing to a stop.

Lee rubbed the inside of Erin's thigh. "Can I see you again soon?"

Erin wouldn't look at her. "I don't know."

"You don't know?" Lee asked in an incredulous tone. "I gave you what you wanted, hell, what you begged for, and you don't know?"

"Lee, grow up," Erin snapped.

"Shit, just get out of my car."

Erin pushed the door open. Before she slammed it closed, Lee got in her parting shot.

"I don't think she wants you, Erin."

"Who?"

Lee glared at her. "Don't even pretend like you don't know who I'm talking about." As soon as Erin shut the door, Lee tore out of the parking lot, spraying gravel along the way.

Erin craned her neck to the sky, and a wave of dizziness assaulted her. Obviously, she wasn't as sober as she thought. She walked along the path to the front of the lodge on her way to the living quarters. She had her head down as tears slid down her cheeks. She was so damn lonely. She rounded the corner and slammed into Corey. Erin staggered backwards, stunned. Corey gripped her arms to keep her from falling.

"God, Erin, I didn't mean to run into you."

Erin raised her head. The light streaming down from the lodge allowed her to see Corey's rugged face and dark eyes that were full of concern.

"Hey, are you okay?" Corey gently touched her cheek.

With Lee's taunt still ringing in her ears, she acted on instinct. She grabbed Corey's wrist and pulled her against her body.

"No, I'm not okay. But you can make it better." Erin crushed her mouth against Corey's and thrust her tongue inside. *God. Yes. This is who I want to kiss.* She moaned when she felt Corey begin to respond. She grabbed Corey's hair and tugged her even tighter. Her nipples hardened as she pressed into Corey's. At first, she didn't notice when Corey tried to pull away. But then Corey pushed against her shoulders with both hands.

"Wait," Corey gasped.

Erin staggered backwards. "What's wrong?" She reached for Corey again.

"No, Erin. You've been drinking."

"So? You didn't seem to mind."

"Well, I do." Corey's gaze dropped to her neck. Erin quickly pulled her shirt collar higher.

Corey's expression morphed into an unreadable mask. "Do you need help going upstairs?"

"No." Erin pushed past her. "If you don't want me, then fine. It's not like I can't get other women." She stumbled as she started up the stairs, but righted herself and continued on her way. She didn't know why, but she chanced a glance over her shoulder at Corey. She stood at the bottom of the steps with her hands shoved into the front pockets of her jeans. "It's late, Corey. Go to bed."

With slumped shoulders, Corey turned and started walking up

the path to the cabins.

Erin immediately regretted her actions and harsh words. "Damn it. Corey! I'm sorry!"

But Corey kept walking.

As Erin entered the lodge, she tried to erase Corey's hurt expression from her mind. Her pile of regrets was growing.

Chapter 13

Corey tugged on a hooded sweatshirt before she left her cabin. The early morning temperatures had dropped into the thirties. Having endured Michigan winters, she was used to cold temperatures, but facing the cold during summer months was a new thing for her.

She thought she'd take a hike around the lake. The moon was providing enough light for her to see the trail. But when she approached the front of the lodge, the sight of the porch reminded her of her encounter with Erin and the state she'd been in late last night. She still couldn't believe she'd first responded when Erin had come on to her. It was obvious that not only had Erin been drunk, but she also was in pain. She wondered if Erin knew how lost she was—at least to Corey she seemed lost. Corey remembered the same kind of pain reflected back at her when she stared in the mirror on the mornings after Judy's death. Raw, unadulterated misery no kind words or charitable acts could soothe away.

Erin had obviously been with someone last night. And it was just as obvious, at least to Corey, that person hadn't helped matters.

She debated about going up the steps and talking to Tess over a cup of coffee. Not about Erin, necessarily, but about anything and everything. Tess reminded her of her mom, and she needed to feel connected to home.

Corey took the plunge and headed up the stairs. She pushed the door open and was relieved to see Tess already behind the counter, shuffling through paperwork.

"Corey, haven't seen you for a few mornings," Tess said with a big smile. "Why don't you come in the living quarters and have some breakfast with me. I've been waiting for Erin to get up, but she lost her window of opportunity."

Corey let the comment about Erin slide. "A cup of coffee sounds fine, Tess."

"Oh, now, stop it. You're too damn skinny as it is."

Corey still didn't know what Tess saw when she looked at her body. "I don't think I'm skinny at all."

"It's my prerogative to say you need some meat on those bones, and I say you do."

Corey followed Tess into the living quarters. Tess fixed scrambled eggs and bacon, and they sat down to eat.

"What do you think of my niece?" Tess asked as Corey was taking a bite of eggs.

Allowing herself time to swallow, Corey bought more time by taking a sip of coffee. "I think Erin is very nice."

"That's not what I mean and you know it."

Corey set her fork down and thought how she needed to tread through the minefield of this conversation carefully. "She *is* nice. I also think she might be a little lost. I believe Erin's still mourning the loss of her partner to another woman."

Tess held her cup with both hands and peered at Corey over the rim. "You're very perceptive."

"Maybe. I think it's a pain we share. It's a little more transparent to me." She wasn't about to mention last night's incident to Tess. She was glad, though, that Tess didn't push to talk about her own sadness. Corey didn't think she was quite ready to tell her story again.

Tess's soft face filled with compassion, as if she knew there was something more. "I don't mean to cause you discomfort, dear. I'm trying to understand my niece. I thought you might be able to give me some perspective. Can you be her friend? Because I think she needs one now more than ever."

Erin paused at the bottom of the stairs when she heard Tess's question.

"Yes. I'd like very much to be her friend. I don't know how she'd care for it, though."

Tess gave a harsh laugh. "Don't you worry about any snit fit Erin might have had. She's stubborn sometimes when it comes to her feelings."

Erin made a little more noise than necessary walking through the doorway from the stairs.

She barely acknowledged them as she passed by on her way to the kitchen. "Aunt Tess. Corey." She returned with a cup of coffee and sat down across from Corey.

Tess gave Erin's neck a pointed stare. "You look like hell."

"And good morning to you, too, Aunt Tess." Erin shifted

uncomfortably in her chair, knowing they'd just finished talking about her. And she couldn't even meet Corey's eyes after her behavior from the night before. Even though the coffee was hot, she made short work of finishing her cup. "I'm walking into town to get Bertha. Do we need anything from Sam's?" she asked about the town's only twenty-four-hour grocery store.

"I don't want to know how your Land Rover got left there, do I?" Tess's gaze dropped to Erin's neck again. "Although I think I have a pretty good idea. And it's still dark out. I don't think it's too smart to be walking around in it."

Tess's cutting remarks snapped the last of Erin's nerves. "You know what? I'm twenty-eight-years old. I don't need any lectures from you."

She barged out of the lodge. She practically sprinted to the highway on her way to town, angry with herself for crying.

"Fuck!" she yelled as she slapped at the tears rolling down her cheeks.

She took care to watch where she was going, even though she was stomping along like a soldier at boot camp. Traffic was almost nonexistent at this hour, so it surprised her a few minutes later when a set of high beams flashed on the road beside her. She turned around and shielded her eyes against the glare to try to identify the vehicle. The SUV slowed to a stop, and the passenger-side window powered down. The dashboard light allowed Erin to make out Corey's face.

"Need a ride?"

Erin stood there for a few seconds, tossing the offer around.

"I promise I won't lecture you."

Erin stepped up into the SUV and shut the door. She put her seatbelt on but said nothing. They churned up the short miles on the way to town. She finally broke the uneasy silence. "First, I want to say I'm sorry about last night. I'm sure you think I'm horrible."

Corey glanced at her before eyeing the road again. "No, I don't. I'm not going to say you didn't upset me, but I definitely don't think you're horrible."

"Even after what I did to you?"

"I told you earlier last night I think you're a little lost like me, and we all handle death differently."

"Death?" Erin asked incredulously.

"Judy's was a physical death, but you went through the death of a relationship. There are different stages of grief for both. I think you're still in the anger stage."

Turning in her seat to face Corey, Erin asked, "What stage are you in?"

Enough time passed that Erin didn't think Corey would answer.

"Maybe a little denial with my own stage of guilt thrown in."

"But isn't denial the first stage?"

"You know the stages?"

"Don't seem so surprised, Corey. I took psychology in college. I'm familiar with the Kübler-Ross model."

"According to my therapist, there's not necessarily an order to the stages. But I've been stuck in sort of a loop. I get through them all, even acceptance. Then a bad dream about the night she died will start the whole thing over. My therapist thinks it's my guilt holding me back. Once I let the guilt go, he thinks I'll really start healing."

Erin touched Corey's arm. "He's right, you know." Corey tensed and then relaxed against her fingers.

"You'd think after two years I'd be over it."

"I think when you're ready, it'll happen and not a day or a minute sooner. Don't be so hard on yourself."

They both remained silent as the sound of the tires filled up the void.

"She was thirty-seven, three years older than me, when she died." Corey's voice was hushed and low as if she were afraid to disturb the air between them. "We were introduced at a softball game."

Erin stayed very still for fear that Corey would stop talking.

"I thought she was handsome and sexy. But it was much more than a physical attraction. She had a gentleness that drew everyone to her. Everybody wanted to be Judy's friend. It's like she exuded this positive energy. It practically glowed." Corey smiled sadly. "Maybe that's why it hurt even more to see her life snuffed out like that. When a vitality like hers leaves the earth, a gaping hole is left behind."

The dashboard light caught the shimmer of moisture in Corey's eyes.

"That gaping hole became my heart. With the help of therapy, my family, and friends, I've been able to fill it some. But I don't... I don't know if I'll ever feel complete again." Corey blinked, and the tears rolled down her cheeks. She dropped her right hand off the steering wheel to the console between them.

Erin reached for her hand and held it, letting the time slip by as they neared town. When they entered the outskirts, she said, "I'm parked at Mo's." She heard the roughness in her voice, not admitting to herself until then how much Corey's words had affected her.

Corey parked next to the Land Rover. She twisted to face Erin. "Thanks for listening."

"No, thank you for sharing." On impulse, Erin leaned over and kissed her cheek. She got out and slid inside the Rover.

Corey drove away, and Erin sat in darkness for a long time. She lowered her head and said a silent prayer for Corey's healing... then added one for herself.

Chapter 14

"Hey, Mom. You look nice. Did you do something different to your hair?" Corey scooted closer to the computer screen.

Her mom fingered her hair. "Fannie thought I should try something different. You like it, huh?"

"I do. Fannie's trying some bold new things at the shop."

"How are you, Corey? You seem tired."

She was tired. Since she'd talked to Erin two weeks ago, she'd had more dreams about Judy. But they weren't of the night she died. Some were snippets of their life, like rapid shutter shots from a camera. Others, the dreams which stayed with her long after she awakened, were the ones in which she knew Judy had died, but they still talked, laughed, and loved as if they had a future together. She wasn't sure what her subconscious was trying to tell her.

"I've been working on the cabins. One in particular has taken a lot of my time."

"Need any advice?" Her dad poked his head in front of the webcam.

"I should've paid more attention when you laid tile, Dad. I was always so busy with other parts of remodeling, I never caught on."

"It'll get easier once you get the hang of it."

"I'll say my goodbyes now, Corey, because I can tell you and your father are about to have a serious conversation. I love you."

"Love you, Mom. I miss you."

"Miss you, too, sweetheart. You get some rest."

Her father sat in front of the webcam, and they talked about the ins and outs of laying tile. Eventually, her father signed off.

Corey checked the time and saw it was nine. She grabbed a bottle of water from the fridge, pulled on a sweatshirt, and sat on the front porch stoop. She listened to the sounds of the crickets and frogs. An occasional "hoot" from an owl drifted down from some nearby tree. A rustling along the path to her cabin got her attention.

Erin smiled as she drew nearer. "Hey, stranger."

"Hi, Erin." Corey patted the porch.

Erin sat down beside her. "Aunt Tess said you've been busy with cabin seven. Something about tiling the kitchen?"

Corey took a sip of her water. "Want me to get you a bottle?"

"No, thank you."

"Funny you should ask about cabin seven. Had a conversation with my dad about tiling about thirty minutes ago. It was never my strong suit while I worked with him. He gave me some good pointers, though."

"That's great. I've been trying to keep up with the lodgers. Lord, they're demanding sometimes."

"But you love your job."

"Yeah, I do." Erin rubbed her palms up and down her thighs. "Um, listen. I've managed to get this Saturday off. One of the part-time college students is more than happy to earn some extra pay. And Aunt Tess doesn't mind. In fact, she was all for it since—"

Corey rested her hand on Erin's knee to slow her down. "What is it?"

"Would you like to join me on a day trip to Steamboat Springs? It's about a two-hour drive. They have antique and specialty shops, but I'd really like to visit some of the art studios. If you don't want to go because of the other night, I'd understand." She stared down at her feet.

"Like I told you, I'm over that, okay? The trip sounds like a fantastic idea. I can even drive, if you like."

Erin raised her head. "Are you saying you don't trust Bertha?" she asked, her voice full of mock indignation.

"I didn't say that, did I? I know how sensitive you are about your Land Rover." Corey bumped shoulders with her.

"Damn right I am. She and I have been through a lot together."

"I have no qualms with you driving us to Steamboat Springs. Especially since I haven't a clue on how to get there."

Erin stood up and stretched, causing her sweatshirt to ride up and reveal a flash of tanned and toned flesh. Corey was temporarily mesmerized. She looked up in time to catch Erin's knowing smile.

"Seven too early for you?" Erin asked.

"Nope."

"Good. Don't know if we'll see each other between now and then. If not, meet me by Bertha at seven. Make sure you wear comfortable shoes because I plan on us doing a lot of walking."

Erin trudged up the gentle incline of the path then pivoted and gave Corey a small wave.

Letting the sounds of the night serenade her, Corey closed her eyes, took a deep breath, and felt unexpected relief that the face greeting her in her mind wasn't Judy's.

* * *

A sense of comfort settled over Erin at the familiar sight of Corey leaning against the Land Rover. Corey grinned at her, causing Erin to misstep. *She looks so happy to see me.*

"Ready for our grand adventure?" Erin asked.

"Yup." Corey picked up a small cooler at her feet. "Brought a couple of waters and sodas."

"Perfect." Erin held up a bag. "Tess made us some breakfast sandwiches."

They settled into their seats, and Erin steered them onto the highway.

"We take 34 until we hook up with US 40 right outside of Granby, which will take us into Steamboat Springs."

"Want to eat now?" Corey asked.

"How about we stop in town first on our way through and get a coffee to go at Gerry's Diner? I don't know about you, but I could use some pick-me-up."

"You'll never hear me refuse a cup of coffee."

After they'd stopped for the coffee, they hit the road again. Corey took their breakfast sandwiches out, handed Erin one, and tore into hers with gusto. "Oh, my God. Your aunt is the best."

Erin bit into her sandwich. "She certainly has her good points."

They merged onto US 40, began the drive west, and eventually veered north. They chatted about how quickly the weather changed in the mountain elevations. Corey grew quiet.

Erin thought she'd drifted off to sleep only to notice she was staring at Erin intently.

"What is it?" Erin asked.

"You told me a little bit about her, but what was Bonnie like?"

The question took Erin by surprise considering how lighthearted their conversation had been earlier. She brought her attention back to the road.

"That's kind of a loaded question." Erin tried to stall for time.

"If you don't want to talk about her…"

"No, no. I do." Erin tapped her fingers rhythmically against the steering wheel while her mind drifted to her ex. "Bonnie and I met at an intramural basketball game the summer after our first year at the University of Colorado. I was there to watch a friend's team play. Bonnie was a forward on the other team." Erin smiled at the memory of Bonnie in her uniform, her short blonde hair drenched in sweat.

"A good memory?"

"Yes. Despite what happened later, meeting her was a good memory. We had a lot of them for almost six years. We were roommates until we got an apartment together our junior year when we moved off campus. After we graduated, Bonnie took a job at a Boulder graphics company. I worked as an assistant manager at a hotel in town."

Erin thought about that time in her life when everything seemed so promising. So perfect.

"Like I told you before, one weekend we went to an art exhibit at the university. They were showcasing artists from the state. Beautiful landscape paintings. And abstract. This one particular abstract with lots of primary colors caught Bonnie's attention. If you asked me, it looked like something a grade school kid would do. I said the same thing to Bonnie. She got pissed off at me and told me I didn't understand art." Erin remembered how much Bonnie's comment hurt at the time. "The artist approached us and introduced herself. Megan Reynolds." Saying the name out loud still put a bitter taste in her mouth.

"I didn't see what was going on at the time and didn't recognize the signs. Bonnie would say she needed to work late. It kept happening more and more frequently. I think I didn't want to see, you know?" She blinked a few times to keep away the tears. "The day I came home to find her packing most of her stuff, I think she was hoping she'd escape without a confrontation. We had it out after I asked if she was seeing anyone. The pathetic thing is, I probably would've forgiven her if she'd come back."

Corey touched her leg and gave it a gentle squeeze. "You loved her, Erin. There's nothing pathetic about loving someone."

Corey's look of sympathy eased some of Erin's pain.

"Did you ever see her again?" Corey asked.

"No. Never heard from her again, either."

"There's been no one serious since then?"

Erin smirked. "I think you got the answer to your question the one night I ran into you in front of the lodge."

"Don't you think you deserve to be happy, Erin?"

Erin met her eyes. "I could say the same to you."

* * *

They made it into Steamboat Springs shortly before ten. Corey immediately fell in love with the quaint shops and art studios.

Their shoulders brushed occasionally as they strolled down main street, window shopping. Erin would touch her arm to point out something in a shop. The warmth of her touch would linger long after Erin moved on.

They ate outdoors at La Hacienda, a Mexican restaurant. Erin ordered a sampler platter, while Corey chose the chimichanga plate.

"Most excellent," Corey said after she took her first bite.

"Glad you like it. I usually eat here when I pop into town."

The sun highlighted Erin's hair and made her blue eyes appear almost hypnotic. Corey ignored her food as she watched Erin eat.

"I thought you said you liked it?" Erin waved her fork at Corey's plate.

"I do. It's good." Corey went back to her food. When she raised her head again, she caught Erin looking at her.

"I'm having a lot of fun," Erin said.

"Me, too. So, where to next?"

"I'd like to hit this western wear store and then a couple of the art galleries. I think I read there's an exhibit of local artists at this one studio I'd like to visit."

They finished their meals and entered the western apparel store. Corey headed for the boots, while Erin went to the shirt rack. After going through three boxes of boots, Corey settled on a black pair. She asked the clerk to hold them at the checkout while she searched for Erin. She found her in front of a mirror. The deep blue western shirt she had on was amazing on her, hugging her body and showing off her full breasts.

Corey didn't realize she was staring until Erin met her gaze in the mirror. A flush hit her cheeks, and some time passed before Corey could speak.

"I think you should buy it," she was finally able to rasp out.

"You do?"

"It looks fantastic on you."

"Thank you," Erin said softly.

They purchased the shirt and boots and deposited them in the Land Rover before taking in the art galleries. After perusing two galleries, they entered the gallery that housed the exhibit.

Erin moved down one wall while Corey went down the other. She tilted her head a couple of times as she tried to figure out what exactly she was seeing. She eventually met up with Erin in the rear of the gallery. All of these paintings seemed to be by the same artist. She leaned over to see the artist's signature and froze. Megan Reynolds. Beside her, Erin was as white as a ghost.

"Do you want to go?" Corey asked. She'd barely gotten the words out of her mouth when she spotted a blonde woman stepping toward Erin and slowing to a halt behind her.

Please don't tell me that's who I think it is.

"Erin?"

Seeing the panicked expression on Erin's face was enough confirmation for Corey.

Erin closed her eyes, opened them, and slowly turned around as if the very move caused great physical pain. "Bonnie."

"I thought it might be you from behind, but I wasn't sure. You look… you look fantastic."

Corey shifted closer. She wanted to put her arm around Erin in a protective embrace but didn't know how Erin would react.

"I see Megan's exhibiting here," Erin said in a flat tone. In fact, her entire demeanor had changed, with her expression now devoid of emotion.

"They wanted some local artists who had sold well in New York. The last time Megan showed in Colorado—"

"I remember the last time Megan's work showed in the state. You don't need to remind me."

Bonnie's mouth set in a tight, straight line. "I'm sure I don't." She seemed to notice Corey for the first time.

"This is my friend, Corey Banner. Corey, this is Bonnie Templeton."

"Hi." Corey held out at her hand. Bonnie barely grasped it and let go.

A woman with long dark hair walked toward them. Erin immediately tensed beside her.

The woman flashed a bright grin. "Bonnie, who are your friends? Wait, isn't this Erin? I think I remember meeting her at my exhibit at the uiversity."

Corey wanted to smack the smirk off the woman's face.

"Yes, and her friend…"

This time, Corey didn't hesitate in putting her arm around Erin's waist and pulling her close. At first, Erin stiffened but quickly relaxed into her embrace.

"Corey Banner. I wish I could say Erin has told me about you two, but I seem to be at a loss. How do you know one another?"

Bonnie's face fell. Corey felt Erin's body shaking slightly, probably in an effort to keep from laughing.

"Erin and I used to be together years ago," Bonnie said, her voice clipped and edgy. "This is my partner, Megan Reynolds."

"Huh. Never mentioned you." Bonnie looked as if she wanted to hit her, but Corey wasn't finished. "Reynolds... Reynolds... Oh? These are your paintings?"

"Yes." Megan said the word with an inflection at the end, as if waiting for Corey to comment.

Corey squinted at the paintings, cocked her head, and pursed her lips. "Interesting." She gave Erin a little squeeze. "Ready to hit the other gallery you talked about, honey?" Erin didn't say anything, so Corey squeezed her waist a little harder.

"Yes, sweetheart. Let's get there before they close."

"Nice to meet you both," Corey said. "Good luck with the exhibit." She grabbed Erin's hand and led them out of the gallery. They turned the corner onto another street before they burst out laughing.

"Oh God, Corey. You were perfect. Especially the part about me never talking about either of them." Erin wiped away tears.

"I loved the expression on Bonnie's face. I thought she wanted to punch me."

They eventually quieted. Erin closed the distance between them and before Corey knew what was happening, she cupped Corey's face and gave her a soft kiss on the lips. It was so different from their first kiss. She wanted it to last longer, but she held back from making it more than what she thought Erin was offering—a kiss of gratitude.

"Thank you," Erin said. "I never knew what I'd do if I saw her again. I didn't even consider there'd be a possibility of them being here, obviously. I thought she only showed her work in New York after they moved."

Corey caressed Erin's cheek. "I'm sorry she hurt you, but she'll never hurt you again. Not every woman is Bonnie Templeton, Erin. You need to believe that."

"I'll try."

* * *

They drove back late in the afternoon. Erin felt a closeness with Corey that hadn't been there before they shared this special trip. The way Corey jumped to her defense at the gallery had touched Erin more than she wanted to admit.

The sky darkened the way it usually did at this time of the day. The typical late afternoon storm. A clap of thunder rumbled overhead, and thick raindrops splattered the windshield. Erin flipped on the wipers. In an instant, the light rain became a deluge. Erin switched the wipers to high.

"These things blow in so fast. It's like our winter storms." Erin noticed Corey wasn't answering. She glanced over at her and was startled to see Corey's face covered in a fine sheen of sweat. She reached over and touched Corey's leg. She quivered under Erin's fingertips. "Hey, are you sick?"

Corey shook her head slightly.

"Is it the weather?"

When Corey didn't answer, Erin switched on her hazard lights and pulled onto the shoulder. She put the gear in park and grabbed Corey's hand. "We're all right. We're safe. I promise."

Corey held onto her hand as if for dear life. They sat there as the rain pounded the roof of the Land Rover. Occasionally, a bolt of lightning would flash in the sky. After ten minutes, the fierceness of the storm dissipated and the rain dwindled to a drizzle. When the sun poked through the clouds, Corey released Erin's hand from her tight grip.

Erin hesitated in asking but needed to know. "Didn't you tell me it was storming the night Judy died?"

Corey nodded. Her lower lip trembled. "I'm so sorry you had to pull over," she choked out.

"Oh, honey, don't apologize." Erin reached across the console and put her arms around Corey as her shoulders shook with sobs. "Shh. I'm here. Nothing's going to happen to us." She patted Corey's hair until her sobbing subsided.

Corey straightened and swiped at her wet cheeks. "I can't drive in storms. I think about Judy and shake uncontrollably. I'm sorry you had to see—"

"I told you there's no reason to apologize, and I mean it. I'm only glad I was with you." She brushed Corey's hair off her forehead and let her palm rest against her cheek. "It seems we faced some of our demons today. We can only get stronger, don't you think?"

Corey's smile was tentative. "We can try."

Erin's earlier words echoed back to her, and she returned the smile. "Right."

Erin shifted into drive. As she merged onto US 40, she let it

sink in that she'd kissed Corey again and called her "honey."
All in one day.

Chapter 15

Flecks of paint flew up from Corey's scraper and coated her sweat-drenched arms. She was still working overtime to get cabin seven ready. Although Tess or Erin had never pushed her, she didn't want to let them down when this could be one more cabin filled with lodgers.

She was glad she had hard labor to try to clear her mind of the weekend before. The day at Steamboat Springs had been full of highs and lows. She'd enjoyed Erin's company and their day in the town. But she also remembered the encounter in the gallery and how protective she'd been of Erin.

Corey paused in her scraping, feeling the softness of Erin's lips against hers once again. Then the storm. Erin had been so supportive and kind.

"And she called me 'honey.'" Corey wondered if Erin was even aware of what she'd said.

After their outing to Steamboat Springs, Corey hadn't felt so alone. It was as if they'd connected on a higher level. She noticed it when she'd see Erin at the lodge. Erin and Tess had invited her to dinner three times last week, which she'd gladly accepted. She'd be talking to Tess only to turn to find Erin watching her.

A yearning was growing deep inside of Corey. A yearning to get to know Erin even better.

She'd called Penny during the week to see how things were in Lansing. At first, she wasn't going to tell her about the trip to Steamboat Springs, afraid that Penny would make more out of it than what it really was. Which was what, exactly? Corey finally decided to tell her. Penny had been quiet for a few seconds before pressing Corey to tell her every little detail about Erin and the trip. Then, she'd cautioned Corey to be careful. Corey smiled when remembering the conversation. Penny always had her back.

She returned to her scraping and hummed along with the tune on the portable, paint-splattered radio Erin had loaned her. She was listening to a station playing seventies music. The song ended and jumped right into "Cool Change" by the Little River Band. Corey had always loved the song, but today she found she related even more to the lyrics about needing a change in her life.

She worked into the early afternoon before stopping since it was a Saturday. After going to her cabin to take a quick shower, she headed to the lodge.

Tess was talking with a lodger when Corey entered. She waited until Tess had finished.

"Corey, it's good to see you. Are you joining us for dinner tonight?"

"I probably will."

"You look exhausted. You're not working on a Saturday, are you? You know you *are* allowed to take time off," Tess lightly admonished.

"I'm finished for the day. I want to get number seven ready for you."

"It's not like we're paying you a huge salary. Why don't you go down to the pool? Or the lake? Enjoy this weather."

A dip in the lake sounded like fun. "Is there a swimming area at the lake, or does it matter?"

"It's best to stay on this side," Tess said. "There's a more gradual incline. Don't go out too far, though. It drops off about twenty yards out."

"I'll keep that in mind." As Corey was about to push through the door, Tess called out to her.

"You might find Erin down there. She left a little earlier in her bathing suit."

An image of a bikini-clad Erin burned into Corey's brain, leaving her dry-mouthed.

Corey went to her cabin and changed into her suit but covered it with shorts and a T-shirt until she got to the lake. She walked by the pool and didn't see Erin among those enjoying the sun. She continued down the path, a little apprehensive about what she'd find when she got to the end.

She heard splashing, so she slowed her pace. As she came to the clearing, she saw Erin the instant she raised up and left the water.

No, she wasn't wearing a bikini, but the one-piece red suit she wore cut high up on the sides, showing a long expanse of tan legs. Her nipples pebbled against the wet material.

Sweet Jesus.

Erin still hadn't seen her as she lowered her head while she dried her hair.

Corey wasn't sure of the proper protocol to announce her presence without startling Erin at the same time. She was considering her options as her gaze traveled up those legs to Erin's breasts and then to her face. She held back a gasp when she realized Erin was staring at her.

In a casual move, Erin draped her towel around her neck and covered her breasts.

"Going in?" Erin asked, gesturing to Corey's towel.

"Uh... yeah." She was suddenly self-conscious about removing her shorts and shirt, so she didn't stand there long and overanalyze the situation. She whipped off her shirt and yanked down her shorts to reveal her own one-piece, much more conservative than Erin's.

Erin's heated gaze followed her every movement.

Trying for nonchalance she didn't feel, Corey asked, "How's the water?"

"Perfect. The sun's warmed it to just the right temperature."

Corey waded into the water until she was waist deep. When she faced the shore again, Erin had spread out her towel on the rock and was leaning back on her elbows, watching her.

"How long have you been swimming?" Corey called out.

"An hour. I was about to head up to the lodge."

When Erin didn't say any more, Corey hoped it meant she stayed because of Corey's arrival. She swam out to where she thought the drop-off started. She tried to stand up and was barely able to keep her head above water with the tips of her toes on the bottom. She swam parallel to the shore but not far from where Erin lay. After some time, she stepped out of the water and grabbed her towel to dry off. Erin lay stretched out on the rock and appeared to have fallen asleep. Corey finished toweling off and enjoyed the view, thinking Erin was unaware of the scrutiny.

"Nice swim?" Erin asked with a little quirk of her lips.

"Ah, you're awake." Corey spread her towel out and sat down next her, accidently brushing against Erin's warm skin. She trembled at the touch and tried to ease the pounding in her chest. She finally recovered enough to turn away from the sun glimmering off the lake and meet Erin's eyes. "I don't think I told you how much I enjoyed last Saturday."

"Even with the drama of meeting up with my ex?"

"I could ask you, even with my meltdown on the way home

with the storm?"

"It was still a good day." Erin sat up. "In fact, I was going to ask you if you felt up to another outing."

Corey was overcome with a rush of happiness at the thought of spending more time with her. "I'd love it. Where to this time?"

"It's a secret," Erin said in a hushed voice.

"A secret."

"Yes."

Corey reached over and tickled Erin's side. "Come on, you can tell me."

That brought a peal of laughter from Erin. "Stop!" She fell back as she tried to block Corey's hand.

Corey leaned over her and tickled the other side. "Tell me where."

In between squeals, Erin gasped, "If you don't stop, we won't go."

"Oh, all right." Corey stayed where she was, propped up on her hands on either side of Erin.

Erin was breathing hard. She looked up at Corey, desire evident in her light blue eyes.

Corey swallowed. She tried to think of something to say since she felt an overwhelming urge to kiss Erin. "I... I think I'll go to my cabin. I told my parents I'd Skype them today."

"Yeah, I need to get back to the lodge anyway."

Corey quickly stood up and grabbed her towel. "I'll see you, Erin."

As she took a few steps up the trail, Erin called after her. "Next Saturday works then?"

She spun around to face her. "I trust you, so I'm up for whatever you have in mind."

"Good."

On her way to her cabin, Corey thought about what she'd just said. She did trust Erin. It was a scary, yet exhilarating feeling.

* * *

"You have got to be shitting me, Erin."

"I shit you not, and remember you said you trusted me."

A man with curly dark hair waved at them. "Erin, glad to see you made it this morning."

Corey thought maybe they were going on another daytrip when Erin met her at her cabin at four-thirty. She'd told Corey to dress in layers, which made it even more intriguing.

"Hey, Greg." Erin strode toward him as he supervised a crew filling a colorful hot air balloon. Painted, white-capped mountains spread across one side of the balloon and loomed over them like the real Rockies. "I see you're about ready to launch." She waved at another man who was assisting the crew. "Hi, Donnie." She motioned Corey closer. "Corey, this is Greg Dobson and his partner, Donnie Walters. They're the owners of Mountain High Flights."

Greg and Donnie shook Corey's hand and hugged Erin.

"You ready to have some fun?" Greg asked.

Corey looked up at the massive balloon. "I'm not sure I'd consider this fun."

"That's right. Erin said you're still a virgin." Greg grinned. "You won't be much longer." He turned to Erin. "You know we don't launch until after we eat our croissants and have a champagne toast."

Eating was the farthest thing from Corey's mind with the thought of going up in a hot air balloon. Her stomach was queasy enough as it was.

"You don't look so good," Erin said as she touched her arm. "If this is something you don't think you can do…"

"I'll try it, but I sure as hell don't want to eat anything before we go up."

"You at least have to drink a champagne toast. It's a tradition."

"I think I can handle a little champagne."

"Then let's have some, shall we?"

They joined Greg and Donnie at a table where Greg filled four flutes with champagne.

"To a memorable flight full of awe and wonder of the nature around us," he said as he held up his glass.

They raised their glasses and drank, and Donnie hustled over to the balloon.

The butterflies in Corey's stomach fluttered their wings even faster as the flame shot up inside the balloon with a loud hiss.

"Ready?" Greg asked.

As ready as I'll ever be, Corey thought.

Donnie and the rest of the crew held the basket steady as Greg climbed in first using the footholds on the side.

"Corey, why don't you get in next since Erin's done this before and can help you?"

Corey followed his lead and clambered in. She held her hand out for Erin as she climbed in beside her. Corey immediately grabbed hold of the side of the basket with a white-knuckled grip.

"You said you trusted me." Erin's voice cut through Corey's fear. "Keep looking at me, Corey."

The sound of Greg firing up the balloon caused Corey to jerk. Erin put her hand on top of Corey's. The basket shifted beneath them, but she maintained eye contact. The longer Corey stared into her eyes, the more lost she became as the first rays of the sunrise shone on Erin's face.

Time seemed to stand still. Just as at the lake, she was overwhelmed with the sudden need to kiss Erin. Corey dropped her gaze to Erin's lips and let go of the basket. She ran her thumb along Erin's mouth, remembering the gentle kiss they'd shared in Steamboat Springs. She bent her head and moved closer.

Erin was lost as she relished the touch of Corey's lips against hers. *We're kissing again. Really kissing.* And it was as magical as she thought it would be. It was so different from the rushed kiss the night she'd thrown herself at Corey. Erin felt as if a door had opened to a new world, and if she took the chance and stepped through the portal, she'd finally find true happiness.

She pressed her body against Corey's. She lifted her hand to the nape of Corey's neck and ran her fingers through the fine hairs there. They took their time, their lips melding together in what felt like the most natural thing in the world. As if this was where Erin belonged. Here. In this woman's arms.

Suddenly, the basket jerked, and they pulled apart.

"Sorry about that," Greg said. "We hit air pockets on occasion. Nothing major, though."

Corey held the sides of the basket in a death grip, but she kept her focus on Erin.

Erin touched her fingers to her mouth, still tasting the champagne from Corey's lips. *What was I thinking? She scares me so much.*

Corey's dark eyes questioned hers, but Erin couldn't speak.

"I'm… I'm sorry," Corey said.

"No, don't apologize. I think I got a little carried away with where we are and, well…"

The basket dipped again. Corey grabbed one of the crossbars overhead. She swayed when she gazed below them. "Oh, my God."

Erin was glad for the distraction of being hundreds of feet above the earth. "Magnificent, isn't it?"

The green below them was almost too beautiful to behold. At

least Erin thought so. She watched Corey's expression transform to one of awe.

"You can see the Great Divide," Greg said as he pointed below them. There was a noticeable gap in the tree line to their right.

Greg directed the balloon over Grand Lake.

"The lodge seems so small, doesn't it?" Corey asked.

Erin was unaware of her surroundings, her focus entirely on Corey and the childlike wonder emanating from her face. When she turned to face Erin, tears were rolling down her cheeks.

"I keep thinking how much Judy would've loved this."

The words stung like a slap to Erin's face. A slap of reality. If Erin hadn't had doubts about the rightness of the kiss, Corey's statement hammered it home how wrong she'd been to allow the kiss in the first place. Throwing herself at Corey was one thing— she was drunk that night, after all. Now? This meant so much more. Before Erin said anything, Corey gently grasped her arm.

"But I'm glad I'm here with you, Erin."

Corey was quiet the remaining hour of their trip which gave Erin time to think. Greg set them down onto an open field. They bounced a couple of times before coming to a stop. He'd already radioed their coordinates to the launch crew who were waiting for them at the site. After they climbed out of the basket, Erin looked anywhere but at Corey. She even stood with Greg and talked with him about the flight. Corey glanced their way a few times. Erin forced herself to focus on her conversation with Greg. She knew she couldn't face Corey yet.

Another SUV drove up, and they climbed into the back. Erin stared out at the passing scenery all the way to the launch site. She thanked Greg again before they got into the Land Rover and drove toward town.

After Erin parked the Land Rover at the lodge, Corey got out and waited for her. "Thank you again for a beautiful day, Erin." She stared at her feet. "About the kiss, I want to tell you that it was…"

"A mistake. I know. Corey, I think we should just be friends. Anything else would be… well, it would be complicated. Don't you agree?"

When Corey raised her head, Erin saw something flicker across her face that looked very much like hurt. But as quickly as it appeared, it was gone.

"Sure. Hey, I'm tired. I'm not used to getting up at four like you are. I think I'll take a nap before I tackle some more work today."

"Corey, you don't need to—"

"The balloon ride is something I'll never forget. Thank you again." Corey turned abruptly and walked toward the cabins with her head down.

Erin ran her fingers through her hair in frustration as she watched her leave. It was best for both of them that they stop this thing before it had a chance to go any further.

Then why do I feel like I've lost something precious?

Chapter 16

"Fuck!"

Aggravated, Corey ripped up the tile when she realized she hadn't measured it right for the corner of the cabinet. She cast a brief look over her shoulder at the dwindling stack of tile behind her. She couldn't afford to make too many more mistakes. "Goddammit."

She mentally brushed off her irritation and measured the area again.

"This better fucking fit," she muttered as she tore off the paper on the back. Her language was the first to go when she was frustrated—with her work and with her life. Kneeling down, her brow furrowed in concentration, she was about to fit the tile into place when someone spoke behind her.

"Hey."

Startled, Corey didn't get the tile aligned properly. She tried to lift the piece up, but the heavy coating of glue made it stick solidly. A piece of the tile broke off. "Well, fuck!" She whipped her head around and glared at Erin. She was dressed in cargo shorts and a green T-shirt with the lodge's logo over her left breast. She looked fantastic. Damn it.

Erin grimaced. "It seems I've caused another accident."

Corey struggled to her feet. Her protesting muscles made it known she'd been on the floor too long without a break.

"What do you want?" Corey said, more sharply than she intended. But the broken piece of tile was fresh in her mind, as well as the hot air balloon outing and the subsequent brush-off conversation in the parking lot. It was Friday. She'd been avoiding Erin and Tess all week, choosing instead to go to town and grab some food supplies to make her own lunches and dinners.

Erin shifted in place. "Um, Aunt Tess sent me down."

"Why?"

"She wanted to know if you're doing all right. And that you're not wasting away to nothing. Her words, not mine."

Corey leaned over and picked up another piece of tile. "Tell her I'm fine."

Erin stepped closer. "She wanted to ask you up for dinner tonight. She said to tell you you're always welcome but for me to remind you."

Corey ran her fingers over the pattern on the tile, not wanting to face Erin. "Tell her thank you, but I think I'll drive into town to get a steak tonight."

Erin moved even closer to stand in front of her. She touched her shoulder. "Please don't shut us out."

Her shoulder tingled at the touch, but she still didn't raise her head. "I'm not. I've been busy with getting this floor done."

"Corey, look at me."

She finally met Erin's eyes.

"I think I know what this is about. I didn't mean to hurt your feelings Saturday. It's just—"

Corey cut her off. "I understand. You don't need to explain it all again."

"No, I think I do. I'm your employer. If this didn't work out, it would make it extremely awkward for us to be around each other. I think maybe we got caught up in the balloon ride, the scenery... the trip to Steamboat Springs was emotional. I think it's best if we stop anything before it starts and stay friends. Don't you?"

Corey wanted to tell her that was a lot of thinking on her part. What about feelings? And what she felt had nothing to do with Erin being her employer. It had everything to do with a part of her heart opening up that she'd shut off two years ago. She'd shut it off with the thought she'd never open up again to any woman. But Erin had given her a glimpse of sunlight through the trees. Corey had reached for those rays of sun only to have them slip through her fingers.

Erin's face was hard to read. Corey tried to school her own expression before responding.

"I want to be your friend," Corey said. "Very much." She hoped her voice didn't give away her longing for more.

Erin smiled. "Good. I don't want to lose you. As a friend, I mean. I don't want to lose you as a friend."

"You haven't, and you won't." Corey motioned at the tile. "I need to get back to this. My goal is to finish by this afternoon."

"Dinner tonight at the lodge?" Erin said with a hopeful inflection.

Corey needed to work through the emotions she was feeling.

She knew she'd be facing Erin almost daily. Well, if she didn't avoid her like she had been this week. She might as well start tonight. Despite her misgivings, she said, "I'll be there."

Erin shoulders sagged in obvious relief. "I'll let Aunt Tess know she can prepare another plate. See you later then. Around six?"

"I should be finished by then."

Corey watched Erin until she left the cabin. She scrubbed her hand over her face. She picked up another piece of tile, determined more than ever to make it fit. Her personal life felt in such disarray. She wanted to at least get her job right.

* * *

Erin checked out her reflection one last time and tried to ignore the inner voice asking her why it mattered how she looked. As she reached the bottom of the stairs, she stopped at the sound of another voice.

My mother.

She braced herself before coming around the corner. Aunt Tess and her mom sat at the table, talking over their cups of coffee. Erin noticed the table was set for four. Crap. Of course her mother was there for dinner.

"Erin Elizabeth." Her mom rose and hugged her. "I know it's impossible, but you seem to have grown."

"Mom, I'm not a teenager any more. Five-seven's as tall as I'm going to get."

Her mom brushed her hair away from her face. "I thought since you didn't drive down to visit me in Denver, I'd make the trip to Grand Lake."

Erin wondered how long she was staying.

"Only the night, darling," her mother said, as if reading her mind.

No matter how much her mom annoyed her, she didn't deserve to think Erin was unhappy to see her. "I'm glad you're here."

"Good." Her mom led her to a chair at the table and sat down across from her. "Fill me in on how you're doing."

Erin shot her aunt a look.

"Kate, let me get the poor girl a cup of coffee before you grill her." Tess left for the kitchen.

"Same old stuff, Mom. Working hard at the lodge to stay on top of things." Erin kept her hands under the table tightly clasped together as she waited for the question about her love life.

Her mom took a sip of coffee. "You haven't met anyone new?"

How does she still have this effect on me, Erin wondered. I feel like I'm in high school and late returning home from a date. "No, not really."

Katherine cocked her head. "That doesn't sound very definite."

Tess set the coffee mug in front of Erin and sat down. Erin hoped her aunt would help her out, but seeing Tess's smug expression, she knew she wouldn't be coming to her defense.

There was a knock at the door.

Erin jumped to her feet. "I'll get it."

She hurried through the living room and opened the door. Corey stood there, her hair obviously damp from a shower. Erin had to ball her hand into a fist to keep from running her fingers through it.

"Come on in." Erin stepped aside for Corey to enter. As they walked toward the dining room, Erin lowered her voice. "Fair warning. My mother's here. It's a surprise visit, because trust me, Aunt Tess would've told me she was coming."

Corey came to an abrupt halt. "Is it okay that I stay for dinner?"

"It is absolutely okay." Erin gripped Corey's elbow and urged her forward until they entered the dining room. "Mom, this is Corey Banner, our new head of maintenance. Corey, this is my mother, Katherine Flannery."

"Mrs. Flannery, it's a pleasure to meet you," Corey said as she extended her hand.

"Oh, my, such good manners you have. And it's Katherine. May I call you Corey?"

"Of course."

"Would you like a cup of coffee, Corey?" Tess asked, already rising to her feet.

"Yes, thank you."

"How long have you been at the lodge?" Katherine asked. "I've not spoken with my daughter in some time."

"Almost two months, I believe."

"Where are you from? I can't quite place your accent." Katherine moved aside for Tess to place plates of food on the table.

Erin thought of helping her aunt but worried about leaving Corey alone to face her mother's inquisition.

"Lansing, Michigan."

"What brought you to Colorado?"

Corey squirmed, and Erin gave her a sympathetic look.

"I've always wanted to visit the state. I saw Rainbow Lodge in a photo spread and got the idea about staying here. I was lucky enough Tess and Erin had a job at the lodge that matches my skills."

Tess sat down. "Kate, I think you can stop with the questions at least while we eat." She motioned at Corey to pass her plate and forked a chicken breast onto it.

Erin passed around the other plates of food and poured ice water from a pitcher into their glasses. Soon they were enjoying a very tasty dinner.

As the food diminished on their plates, Katherine must have taken it as her cue to ask some more questions. "You have family back home?"

"Yes, ma'am." Corey told her about her parents, sister, and nephews.

"Boyfriend?" Katherine asked.

Erin immediately choked on her sip of water. Corey patted her back. "You all right?"

Erin nodded. Eyes watering, she recovered enough to swallow and take another sip. "Mom, that's none of your business."

"I'll answer, Erin. No boyfriend, Katherine. How about you?"

Once again, Erin had a mouthful of water. This time, she spewed it on her plate.

"Lord, Erin, can't you control yourself?" Katherine said.

Dabbing her mouth with her napkin, Erin glared across the table at her. "I was about to ask you the same thing."

Katherine turned back to Corey. "I am seeing someone, but I wouldn't exactly call him a boyfriend. More like an acquaintance." She must have noticed Erin's reaction. "I haven't told you because we don't share the details of our love lives. Besides, as I said, this doesn't constitute a love interest. Charles and I are friends who've gone out a few times."

"Charles?" Erin asked. "Charles Fredericks? Our next door neighbor?" A surge of anger rose up inside Erin, and she tried to tamp it down.

"Yes, Charles," Katherine said evenly. "Margaret's been gone for two years now. Your dad passed away five years ago. There's nothing wrong in our dating, Erin."

With her mother's rebuke, Erin was ashamed of her reaction. Despite their differences, her mother was entitled to be happy.

"I'm sorry, Mom." She reached across the table for her hand.

"It's all right. But remember, I loved your father as much as you did."

Erin lowered her head.

Corey patted her leg under the table.

Erin's breath hitched at the compassionate expression on Corey's face. When she turned back to her mother, Katherine was watching them intently. It was as though she were attempting to crawl inside Erin's brain to pry out some honest answers.

Corey cleared her throat. "Well, I think I need to get a good night's sleep. I only have a few more tiles to lay in cabin seven, but they're tricky ones. I'll probably have nightmares tonight."

They all laughed as Corey rose to her feet.

"It was nice meeting you, Katherine. Tess? Another wonderful meal. Thank you."

"You're welcome, Corey. Don't forget you have a standing invitation to eat with us every night."

Corey headed for the door with Erin trailing behind. As Corey reached for the doorknob, Erin touched her hand.

"Thanks for coming," Erin said. Then she mouthed, "Sorry about my mom."

"It's okay," Corey mouthed back and then said aloud, "Thanks again for having me."

"Like Aunt Tess said, you're always welcome."

Corey smiled once more before leaving.

Erin was lost in thought as she approached the dining room. Tess had already cleared the table. Katherine had her arms folded across her chest. *Uh-oh.*

"Is she gay?" Katherine asked.

Erin heard Tess's laughter from the kitchen.

"Mother, does it really matter?"

"I take it that's a yes."

"Yes, Corey is gay." Erin remained standing behind her chair. She gripped the wood a little tighter and waited for the inevitable.

Katherine's expression softened. "I like her."

Erin was glad she held the chair so tightly because her legs had weakened, and she needed something to support her. "You do?"

Katherine stood up, stepped around the table, and kissed Erin's forehead. "Yes, I do." She stroked her cheek before saying loudly, "Do you need any help, Tess? I know how you always hated me in your kitchen."

Tess appeared at the doorway. "I have it in hand. Why don't you two go in the living room and visit? I'll be out soon."

Katherine sat down in the chair beside the couch, while Erin took a seat in the chair across from her.

"Why does it surprise you that I like Corey?"

Erin shrugged. "I don't know. You've never shown much interest in..." Erin realized what she was about to say and stopped.

"In someone you're dating?"

"But we're not dating."

"There seems to be something between you."

"It's complicated."

Katherine settled back in her chair. "Why don't you try me? I might surprise you with some of my wisdom." The living room lamp caught the bemusement on her face.

"Corey was with someone for six years, but she was killed in a car accident two years ago. I don't think she's ready to move on."

"Have you asked her?"

Erin jerked at the question. "No."

"And why not?"

Erin slumped in the cushion of her chair. "Who are you, and what have you done to my mother?"

"What do you mean?"

"Normally, right about now, you'd be telling me about some guy who I might be interested in dating."

Katherine stared down at her folded hands. "I should have been supportive from the beginning. It's just that..." Her voice trailed off.

"Go on."

"Mothers always want what's best for their daughters. We don't like to see you have any additional hardship in your life. I thought your gay lifestyle would add even more stress. And life can throw you for a loop all on its own without added stress piled on top of it."

"It's not a lifestyle." Erin tried to keep from snapping but failed miserably.

"Oh, I know that now." Katherine tapped her finger on her knee before continuing. It was her mom's habit right before firing off a difficult question. "Tell me this. Are you happy?"

Erin realized it had gotten very quiet in the kitchen. She was fairly certain her aunt was listening in the doorway. Besides that, Tess had asked her the same question months ago.

She went with her same answer. "I'm happy enough."

"What does 'happy enough' mean?"

"It means I see women, and it's casual."

"Is 'casual' a euphemism for sleeping around?"

"Mom!" First Aunt Tess, and now her mother.

"Well, is it?"

Erin found a sudden interest in a loose thread on her jeans.

"Erin Elizabeth, I would think I brought you up better than this. What happened?"

Erin tried to keep her chin from quivering. "Bonnie Templeton happened. She left me for another woman."

"Bonnie... Wait. Wasn't she your college roommate?"

She met her mother's vivid blue eyes, so like her own. "She was my partner."

"I didn't know."

"When I came out to you, she wasn't part of my life anymore."

Katherine moved to the cushion at the end of the couch closest to Erin. She placed her hand on Erin's knee. "You should have told me. I would have listened. I'm not heartless."

Erin saw her mother's tears and looked away. Katherine gently squeezed her knee until Erin faced her.

"Now you're afraid to take chances when someone special comes along. Am I right? Because Corey seems pretty special."

Erin debated about not sharing what had happened last Saturday, but she wanted her mother's comfort just as she did as a child. "I took Corey on a hot air balloon ride last Saturday. When we got in the air, she... she kissed me."

"And how is that bad?"

"It is when the next words out of her mouth were she wished Judy, her partner who'd died, had been there. It was a huge reminder she's not gotten over her."

"What else did she say?"

The question took Erin by surprise. "What do you mean what else?"

"I'm sure the conversation didn't end there."

Erin remembered Corey's next words. She'd temporarily blocked them out as if Corey had never spoken them.

"She said she was glad she was there with me."

Katherine smiled. "See? She enjoyed being with you."

"Mom, it's not that simple."

"And I think you're finding excuses not to take a chance at love."

Erin still couldn't believe she was having this conversation with her mother. Her mother who'd call to fix her up with the sons of any number of her friends.

"I don't—"

Katherine interrupted. "Please promise me you won't give up on her, honey."

"I won't promise. But I'll see where it goes. It's the best I can do." Erin still had serious doubts that anything would ever happen to deepen her friendship with Corey—to take it to that next step beyond friendship. But for now, she was hoping to appease her mother.

Katherine waited a few seconds to respond. "All right. I can accept that if it's the best you can do."

Erin decided to turn the tables. "So, what about you and Charles?"

An adorable blush broke out on Katherine's cheeks. "We're simply dating."

Erin couldn't help it. She had to tease. "Do me a favor and let me know what his intentions are."

Katherine smacked her leg playfully. "Oh, I will." She stood up. "Give your mother a hug."

Erin wrapped her arms around her in a tight embrace. "I love you, Mom."

"I love you too, honey."

Tess chose that moment to enter the living room.

"Kate, why don't you go on up to the guest room and get some rest. I had Scott put your bags there. Denver's a long drive, even if you're planning on staying until tomorrow afternoon. I know you must be tired."

"Thank you. That sounds like a wonderful idea." She patted Erin's cheek. "I don't think I've told you lately how proud I am to call you my daughter." Before Erin could respond, Katherine headed toward the stairs. "I'll see you both in the morning."

Still in shock, Erin watched her until she was around the corner and out of sight.

"I think your mother has done some growing up, don't you?"

"I guess she has."

"You all right, honey?"

Jumbled thoughts banged together in Erin's mind like so many pots and pans. "Oh, I'm fine. I think I'll go to bed, too. I'm pretty tired."

As she ascended the stairs, she mulled over her mother's advice about Corey. "If it were only that easy," she whispered.

Chapter 17

The next week, Corey drove into town for more supplies at the hardware store. As she got out of her SUV, she heard firecrackers going off in the distance. She passed a man who was loading up his truck.

"They're doing a dry run for the Fourth on Saturday," he said.

"Excuse me?"

He nodded in the general direction of the lake. "Fireworks are Saturday night. I noticed your license plates and thought you might be wondering."

"Oh, right." Corey had been so preoccupied lately, she'd forgotten about the holiday.

"They're pretty spectacular, the biggest in Colorado, actually. Everyone gathers around the lakefronts, either on Grand Lake or over at Shadow Mountain Lake. The whole day is a lot of fun in town with barbeques and such." He offered his hand. "Fred Travers."

"Corey Banner. I'm the head of maintenance at the lodge."

He scratched his beard. "Right. I heard Tess hired someone. How's it panning out?"

She didn't respond right away as a lot of things flew through her mind, including the magic of the sun glowing on Erin's face the morning of the balloon ride.

"That bad, huh?" he teased.

"No, no. Tess is great. Erin, too. I'm very happy to be working there."

"Good to hear. If you see Tess, tell her I said hi. Maybe I'll see her… I mean, maybe I'll see all of you in town Saturday."

"Maybe you will. I'll give your message to Tess."

"I'd appreciate it." He closed up the back of his truck and drove away.

As Corey picked up her order of supplies inside the store, her mind drifted to their conversation about the fireworks. Did she even want to chance another outing with Erin? Especially since Erin had made it so clear she only sought a friendship? Dinner was one thing. A day-long celebration was another. She thought about it. Friends went on outings together. Maybe she should look at it that way.

She laughed at herself as she pushed her cart to the front of the store. *Right.*

* * *

Erin flipped through *People* magazine for the second time. The pages mostly held photos of sexy, unattainable women along with an article on the "World's Most Beautiful Woman." She sighed.

"You've sighed five times in the past thirty minutes. What's wrong?"

Erin jumped at the sound of Tess's voice behind her.

"God, Aunt Tess. Don't sneak up on me like that."

Tess greeted one of the lodgers with a friendly hello and then said, "My dear, I've been standing at the counter for the past hour. You're so self-absorbed, you didn't notice. Let me try again… what's wrong?"

What's wrong, Erin wanted to say, is my mother seems to have my love life all figured out, when I'm confused as hell.

"You know it doesn't have to be this difficult, Erin."

"What doesn't?"

Tess didn't answer. She didn't have to.

"You're inviting her to go with us to the Fourth celebration on Saturday, aren't you?" Tess arched a gray eyebrow. "And don't ask who."

"I don't know. She seems to like to work on Saturdays."

Tess frowned, obviously remembering something. "Didn't you go on an outing with her to Steamboat Springs on a Saturday? And didn't you take her on a hot air balloon ride on a Saturday morning?"

Busted.

"Yeah, but—"

"Forget it. I'll ask her myself."

"Ask who?" a husky voice said. Corey approached the counter.

"Speak of the devil. Erin and I wanted to know if you'd like to go to the Fourth of July festivities with us Saturday."

Corey glanced at Erin, then back at Tess. "I'd love to join you. I was about to ask if you were going. Oh, Fred Travers says hello, Tess. And he hopes to see you Saturday."

Tess nodded and started shuffling papers together on the counter as if it were the most important task in the world.

"Fred Travers, Aunt Tess?"

"We're friends, young lady. I haven't seen him in a while. It'll be fun to catch up." Tess promptly moved down the counter to tend to some lodgers.

"So Tess and Fred?" Corey said with a smile.

"Never knew it until now. I mean I've seen them sit with each other at functions, but I never put it together."

"That's sweet." Corey watched Tess interact with a couple and their children. "I like seeing her happy."

Sometimes she's says the kindest things.

"Did I say something wrong, Erin?"

"Hmm?"

"You had a funny expression on your face."

"Oh, it's nothing."

Corey stared down at the counter. "If you feel uncomfortable with me going on Saturday, I understand. I still have work to do, and it's not like I haven't seen fireworks before."

Erin's throat constricted as she realized Corey would give up a chance at some fun. She didn't think about it. She reached across the counter and touched Corey's fingers that were restlessly rubbing the wood grain. Corey met her gaze.

"I'd like you to join us. We're still friends, and friends can have fun together, right?"

"Right."

"You'll enjoy the afternoon with us and later the fireworks. Tess usually sits on the porch here at the lodge to watch. It's kind of cool. She switches off all the lights outside and in the great room, plus the ones by the pool down below. That way, you only focus on the fireworks."

"Cool," Corey said, using Erin's word. "Well, I'd better get going on cabin eight. I have a lot of stripping of paint to do before I Kilz that God-awful color. Whose idea was it to paint the interior baby puke green?"

Erin nodded toward Tess. "Ask her."

Corey laughed. "No, thank you. I value my job. I'll talk to you later."

Corey pushed past the lodge entrance. Through the large windows overlooking the porch, Erin followed Corey's progress. Her hand trembled in mid air as she reached for *People* magazine to put it with the others stacked on the counter. She tried to ignore the effect Corey still had on her. A trip to her rock by the lake sounded like a good idea to help clear her mind.

* * *

Corey stood in front of her closet, debating what to wear. She flipped through her shirts, occasionally lifting one out to hold it against her body while she stood in front of the mirror.

"Oh, for God's sake, Corey," she said, disgusted with her indecisiveness. "When did you become a femme?"

She yanked one of her favorite shirts off a hanger, a well-worn Detroit Tigers T-shirt with Justin Verlander's name and number on the back. She tossed it on her bed. Then took out a pair of khaki cargo shorts from her dresser and laid them next to the T-shirt. She scrutinized her ensemble.

"Perfect."

She went to the bathroom and flipped on the shower. She was about to strip when her cell phone rang. She thought about letting it go, but she had a sneaking suspicion it was her mother. They hadn't had their weekly phone call yet. She checked the number and smiled.

"Hey, Mom. How are you?"

"Doing well. Hadn't heard from you this week, so I thought I'd try to catch you on a Saturday. Although from what your dad told me, you do work on the weekend. You're not burning yourself out, are you? I remember how you were when you worked with him."

"I never feel like I'm burning myself out. I think Dad passed on his love of creating things, even if it's stripping and repainting a room." She thought about the week's arduous task. Yes, it had been a lot of work, but she still savored the feeling she got when it was completed.

They chatted for a while, with her mom filling her in on how Betty and the boys were doing. Corey had only talked to her sister a few times all summer. Betty typically was immersed in her sons' summertime baseball and soccer games. This summer was no different.

"Your father would like to speak to you."

Corey heard the muffled exchange of the phone on the other end.

"Hey, Cor. How's it going out there for you? Still enjoying your job?"

"I am. This place has been a perfect fit." She knew what would make it even more perfect, but Erin had clearly laid down the parameters of their friendship.

"Corey?"

"I'm sorry, Dad. Did you ask me something?"

"I asked if you allowed yourself to have some fun. I remember how you were when you worked with me. You could be single-minded to a fault."

"You'll be happy to know that today I'm going with Tess and her niece to the Fourth of July celebration in town. The fireworks are later."

"Is this niece the one your mother told me about? What's her name? Erica?"

"It's Erin. Mom talked about her?"

"You know your mom."

Corey knew her mother all too well. She heard her voice in the background.

"Give me that phone, Daniel."

"Oops. Guess I stepped in it now, huh?" her dad said, obviously amused with the situation. "Here's your mother again."

"What's this about Erin?"

Corey rolled her eyes. "It's no big deal, Mom. We're all heading into town for the Fourth."

"It's not a date?"

Corey had to bite her tongue from saying she only wish it were. "No, not a date."

"Oh." The disappointment in her mother's voice seeped through the phone.

"Speaking of which, I'd better get ready. I'm meeting Tess and Erin at the lodge. We're driving into town together."

"Have fun."

"Love you, Mom. Tell Dad I love him."

"I will. I love you and miss you."

"Miss you, too. I'll talk to you next week."

Corey ended the call. As she stepped into the shower and under the spray, her mother's words played over again in her head. Maybe one day, Erin would get past her fears and let Corey in.

* * *

Erin lost track of what Tess was talking about. Once she saw Corey leaning against the Land Rover, her mind went blank. Corey wore a pair of dark-shaded sunglasses and had her head tilted toward the sun. She had one leg propped on the front bumper while she rested her hand against the hood. Erin allowed herself the pleasure of simply enjoying Corey's tan, well-muscled body. Because of the way she was leaning, Corey's T-shirt tightened against her breasts.

"Earth to Erin. Did you hear a word of what I said?"

"Huh?"

Tess looked where Erin was staring.

"Never mind." Tess walked over to the Land Rover. "Corey, aren't you the handsome one."

Corey brushed her fingers over her shirt. "I don't think this is anything special."

"I do. Seeing you out of your cargo pants without a hammer in your hand is special as far as I'm concerned. Wait. You don't have any tools anywhere on those shorts, do you?"

Corey laughed. "No, Tess. I'm ready to kick back and enjoy the day with you both." She addressed Erin for the first time. "Hey."

Erin felt inexplicably shy. "Hey," she said softly. With Corey's dark glasses, Erin wasn't sure, but she thought Corey was staring at her legs. She'd picked out a pair of white shorts that showed off her tan and a navy blue V-necked T-shirt. As she was leaving her bedroom, she'd hesitated at the doorway before going to her jewelry box to take out her favorite earrings—a pair of small, sterling silver hoops she'd bought in one of the shops in town.

"You look very pretty, Erin," Corey said in a quiet voice.

"Thank you. Like Tess said, you look very handsome."

She and Corey stood rooted to the spot, not making any move toward the Land Rover. Tess patted Erin on the shoulder on her way to the passenger door. "Let's get this show on the road, shall we?"

Corey inhaled the smells around them as they ambled along Main Street. It was intoxicating. She glanced over at Erin who was listening to something Tess was saying. *Not as intoxicating as Erin.* She stopped in front of a stand selling barbequed pork sandwiches. "I don't know about you, but I'm starved."

They'd been perusing the various booths set up in front of the storefronts. The town had erected barricades, which allowed people to walk freely down the middle of the street.

"Bill's pork sandwiches are legendary in these parts," Tess said.

Corey hadn't noticed the owner of the dude ranch was the man doling out the food until Tess pointed him out. The white chef's hat he was wearing had covered up his ponytail.

"Hey, Tess. Good to see you. It's not the same if you don't visit our booth every year."

"Wouldn't miss it for the world, Bill. Give me one of your sandwiches with some fries. And don't be chincy on the meat."

He chuckled as he prepared her sandwich. "I've never shorted you in all the years I've known you."

"You know I love to give you grief. It's a tradition." Tess motioned to Corey to come forward. "I think Corey's ready to try your recipe, too. Erin? What about you?"

"Absolutely. Can't go wrong with Bill Cooper's barbeque." She turned to Corey. "Bill's won some regional barbeque competitions."

Corey pulled out her wallet to give Bill her money. Tess stopped her. "My treat."

Corey knew better than to argue. "Thanks, Tess." She took the offered plate of food and waited for Tess and Erin to get theirs.

"Let's go to Midge's for her homemade lemonade." Erin pointed at the next booth.

Bill flashed a big smile. "That's right. Keep it in the family."

After they each purchased their cups of lemonade, they found an empty picnic table in a grassy park area nearby. Tess sat on one bench and Erin on the one facing her. Corey hesitated for a few seconds before sliding in next to Erin.

Corey took a bite of her sandwich. "Oh, my God. This is delicious." It was also messy as the barbeque sauce dribbled down her wrist, but she didn't care.

"What'd I tell you?" Tess said.

They were quiet as they ate. Erin paused before taking another bite. "You can always tell how good the food is if no one's talking."

"Amen to that," Tess said.

Corey was so busy enjoying the barbeque that at first she didn't notice Tess had stopped eating. She was looking at something behind Erin.

"Erin, I hoped I'd find you here."

Corey shifted to see Lee hovering over Erin's shoulder.

"Hi, Lee." And that was all Erin said as she returned to her sandwich.

"Would you like to join me later to watch the fireworks?"

Corey held her breath as she awaited Erin's response.

"That's very nice of you, but no. I'm watching them with Aunt Tess and Corey."

"You sure?"

"Yes. I hope you enjoy the fireworks, though."

Lee waited, but when Erin didn't say anymore, she left. When Corey turned around to the table, Erin was staring at her but quickly started eating again.

Tess waved at someone. "There's Fred. I'm going to leave you two." She stood up from the table. "Have fun." Corey didn't miss the squeeze she gave Erin's shoulder as she passed her.

"You could've gone with her, you know," Corey said as she pushed a French fry through her ketchup.

"Now, that wouldn't have been a very polite thing to do, would it?"

"Well, I don't know…"

Erin brushed her fingers against Corey's arm. "I want to watch the fireworks with you, especially since this will be the first time you've seen Grand Lake's. They're spectacular."

Corey tried to tamp down the giddiness that bubbled inside her, knowing Erin preferred to be with her. "I look forward to it."

The rest of the afternoon passed quickly. When Erin didn't think she could take another step on her sore feet, she sought out Tess to ask about heading back to the lodge.

"You two go on. Fred and I want to take in some more of the stores." Tess had her arm linked with his.

"Can you bring Aunt Tess back to the lodge then, Fred?"

"I'd be honored." He beamed at Tess.

Why didn't I ever see this before, Erin wondered. Without thinking, she took hold of Corey's hand. "Let's head to the Rover." After realizing what she'd done, she tried to appear casual as she released her grip.

On the drive to the lodge, they chatted about the various stores they'd visited.

Corey rubbed her stomach. "I don't think I could eat another bite of anything."

"It was worth it, though."

Corey grinned. "Damn right it was."

They entered the parking lot, and Erin switched off the engine. "If you don't mind, I think I'll take a shower, and I might nap a bit before the fireworks."

"A nap sounds good, doesn't it?"

"Want to meet me in the lodge around nine?"

"I'll be there." Corey got out of the Rover and headed for her cabin until she was out of view.

A tingle of excitement rushed through Erin as she thought of the night ahead. "Calm down, silly. It's only fireworks."

Erin stood on the porch watching another firework explode over the lake. It was the testing before the big show. She heard someone coming up the steps.

"Hey, Erin. Sorry I'm a little late. Got caught up in talking to my friend Penny in Lansing."

Corey appeared refreshed as if she, too, had showered. She'd changed into some faded jeans and a sweatshirt with "Banner's Construction" stitched on it.

"A good friend?" Erin tried to appear nonchalant with the question and wondered why it was so important to her how Corey answered.

"Yeah. We've known each other for about ten years. We met playing softball and hit it off right away. She's been bugging me about when I'm coming home to visit."

"Are you planning to go back soon?"

"No. She knows I'm not. She just likes to torment me." Corey stepped across the porch and looked through the lodge windows. "Where's Tess, by the way?"

"She's getting changed. Fred's coming up to sit with her. I thought we'd go to the lake to watch the fireworks."

Corey's face lit up. "Oh, wow. I bet they're something to watch down there."

Corey's childlike exuberance over the simplest things never ceased to amaze Erin. "Let's head on down. Remember that big rock down there? I think of it as my own, and I don't want anyone else staking it out."

They kept quiet as they descended the trail to the water's edge. Thankfully, no one else was nearby. Most people had camped out on the beach farther down the lake. Voices and laughter drifted over the water. Erin sat down on the rock, and Corey joined her.

She was comfortable enough with Corey that she didn't feel the need to fill the silence. She relaxed in the moment as she listened to the lapping of the water against the shore. A firework shot to the sky, went off, and lit up the lake. The sound reverberated against the surrounding mountains.

"Damn, that was loud," Corey said.

"The amazing sound is another fun thing about the fireworks here. They should start in a minute. I think that was their last test."

As soon as the words left Erin's mouth, fireworks exploded above them. A multitude of colors bathed the pitch blackness of the night sky. She quickly immersed herself in the show.

Corey took in the brilliant display of pyrotechnics above them and marveled at the colors reflecting off the lake. It was as if there were two skies filled with exploding fireworks, the one above joining the mirrored one below.

"This is so cool, Erin."

"It is, isn't it?"

She gazed at Erin and took in her radiant expression. Bright blues and reds bathed Erin's face. Like before, when she'd shared her first dance with Judy, Corey knew in the very depths of her soul that this was a defining moment. She valiantly tried to hold back her tears, but one trickled down her cheek.

Erin turned to her then and let out a small gasp as the fireworks continued to explode overhead. She stared at Corey's lips and raised her gaze to meet her eyes. Unlike their hot air balloon trip, Corey waited for Erin to make the first move. She reached out to Corey's cheek and caught another tear with her thumb.

Something shifted deep inside Corey. She wanted to speak but wasn't able to over the lump in her throat. So she lived in the here and now, in this precise moment, without a thought of tomorrow. How could she think of tomorrow with the vision beside her?

They looked up at the start of what had to be the finale. The cacophony of sound rained down upon them, making speech impossible. Corey was glad… because she had no words.

Chapter 18

Corey entered the lodge the next day, not certain she wanted to see Erin. The night before had been intense—enough that she thought a little distance between them might not be a bad idea.

"Corey, good to see you," Tess said. "Are you joining us later for dinner?"

"I'm not sure. I thought I'd go on a hike on one of the trails. I've been meaning to make the time, but I've been pretty busy."

"Erin said it's coming along on cabin seven. I know we left you with a lot of work to do on that one."

"I'm enjoying it. I finished with the tiling earlier this morning. I need to double-check the roofing. Then I think we're good to go."

"You don't need to be working on Sunday, young lady."

"Yeah, I know. I usually don't, but I had planned on doing the work yesterday." She held up her hand to stop Tess from interrupting. "Don't get me wrong. I wouldn't have traded yesterday and last night for anything."

Tess pointed at a rack of brochures. "Pick up one of those on the top right. It has the trails listed around us with the degree of difficulty on each of them. I don't know how much hiking you've done."

"I'm pretty experienced. I used to hike with Judy in the UP." Corey grabbed a brochure.

"UP?"

"Upper Peninsula in Michigan."

"I bet it's beautiful there."

"Yes, it is." Corey opened the brochure on the counter to the array of trails with elevations.

"You'll find it's as gorgeous on this trail," Tess said. She tapped the brochure. "I think this one is moderate in difficulty, plus it takes you to an overlook with a magnificent view. You'll need to drive to the trailhead, though."

"You've sold me on it."

"Hang on. Let me give you some directions." Tess tore a sheet of paper from her tablet and scribbled, even drawing pictures of the mountain and lakes. "You want to drive into town until you're heading for the eastern shore of Shadow Mountain Lake, which is on the other side of Grand Lake. Take a right past the marina launch and take this road to the end. That's the trailhead, and you'll see signs marking the trail. It'll take you up to the Shadow Mountain Overlook Tower which is well worth the climb."

Corey folded up the directions and picked up the brochure. "Sounds like it's just what I'm looking for."

"Be sure to take plenty of water and rest along the way if you need to. You might have hiked at home, but not with these elevations." Tess glanced at the clock on the wall. "I think you have plenty of time to get up there before the afternoon thundershower hits."

"I should be fine, and I'll pack some extra bottles. Thanks for your help, Tess."

Corey returned to her cabin. She put some energy bars and bottled water into her makeshift backpack that had seen better days. She ran her fingers over the worn canvas as she remembered the last time she'd used it. She closed her eyes and saw Judy ahead of her, grinning at Corey and taunting her for lagging behind.

"Time to make some new memories," she said aloud and hefted the pack on her shoulders.

Corey leaned against a tree to get her second wind. She took a drink of bottled water and ran the back of her hand across her forehead. It was warm out, but the blanket of trees helped cut down on the heat.

According to the last marker, she had another mile to reach the tower. She took out an energy bar and quickly finished it off. She shoved the bottle and wrapper into her backpack, slung the pack over her shoulders, and kept climbing.

Two women passed her, hand in hand. They smiled and lifted their chins in her direction. There hadn't been many people on the trail, which pleased Corey. She craved some time alone to sort through her emotions.

A break appeared in the pines, and the stone-based tower loomed ahead. From what she'd read in the brochure, it was built as a fire tower by the Civilian Conservation Corps during the early nineteen thirties. Happily, no one seemed to be in the vicinity.

After taking one more brief rest for some water, she set her foot on the bottom step. The observation deck was on the third level. Her thigh and calf muscles strained in protest with each step, but she continued, undaunted.

When she reached the observation deck, she leaned over to catch her breath as a little light-headedness hit her. Tess hadn't been wrong about the elevation causing her some problems. Corey was thankful she'd stayed in good shape from working with her dad's construction company and at the lodge. She steadied her breathing until the white dots cleared from her vision. She approached the railing... and immediately was breathless again, but not from the altitude.

The observation deck offered a three-hundred-and-sixty-degree view of the lakes below and the surrounding mountains. In the distance, snow dusted the high peaks. Just like from the basket of the hot air balloon, the Great Divide was clearly visible. Corey followed the flight of a bird high above. She squinted to get a better view and saw the distinctive white hood and wide wingspan. It was her first glimpse of a bald eagle.

She leaned against the wooden railing and inhaled the scent of the pine trees. She thought about Judy and how she would've loved to see this. Then she remembered her words on the balloon ride. Corey had told Erin the same thing. And how that must have sounded to Erin. Erin's distance now made more sense. Although Corey had said she was glad to be there with Erin, she'd still reminded Erin about Judy.

Hope sparked in Corey's heart.

* * *

Erin waited for her aunt to hand off the key to the lodger. After he picked up his bag and walked away, she asked, "Have you seen Corey? I went to the cabins to ask if she wanted to drive into town for lunch, but I couldn't find her."

"She left around ten for a hike up Shadow Mountain. She told me she'd done some hiking in northern Michigan. I thought she'd be okay."

Erin looked up at the clock, alarmed when she saw it was two. "I think I'll head up there and see if I can catch her on the way back down."

Tess opened the small fridge behind the counter and pulled out several bottles of water. "Take these with you. I know you've been up there enough to know your way around, but I don't want you without water."

"I'll go grab my small backpack."

Thirty minutes later, Erin was on the trail. She tried to quell her anxiety. Yes, Corey had hiked before in Michigan, but it wasn't quite the same as taking a trail up a mountainside in the Rockies.

As she trudged up the incline, the image of Corey's expression from last night flashed into her mind. Erin had almost kissed her, but thankfully, the finale had started. At least Erin thought she was thankful for the interruption.

* * *

A thunderclap rumbled overhead. Corey didn't know how long she'd stood there alone. She'd been so captivated with the view, she hadn't noticed the darkening clouds.

Her thoughts drifted back to the first time she'd met Judy on the softball field, to the walks they took as they discussed their dreams, to their quiet talks in front of the fire at home. To the way Judy's face would be awash with passion when they made love. And to Judy's mischievous grin before she left for work the last day Corey had seen her alive.

Corey had a choice to make. She felt it as certain as she sensed the coming of the storm. Did she want to cling to her guilt about something she had no control over? Did she want to squash any chance at happiness by holding on to the past?

For two years, she'd mourned the woman she'd planned to spend the rest of her life with. But fate had taken Judy from her.

She lifted her face to the sky as the first drops of rain caressed her cheeks. "Judy, I know you're there. I love you, but I have to move on. I've met someone. I really like her." Corey smiled. "I think you would, too. She thinks I'm not ready, but... but I think I'm falling for her."

The rain picked up in intensity and another rumble of thunder rolled overhead. No flash of lightning followed. A heavy downpour flowed over her like a baptism of her soul that cleansed the way for a new beginning. A beginning as fresh and white as the snow on the distant peaks.

"I'm ready to dance again, baby."

As Corey spoke the words, a rainbow appeared over Shadow Mountain Lake, stretching from the water below up to the heavens above. Overwhelmed, she wept. She wept for the love she'd shared with Judy. And she wept for the future that lay before her.

Erin stood unnoticed behind Corey on the third floor of the observation deck. She'd made record time and reached the tower in a little under two hours. Corey had been talking when she had taken the last step, but the only thing she could make out through the noise of the rain was "Judy." Her heart went to her throat when she saw Corey crying.

She isn't ready to move on. More than ever, Erin knew her decision not to take their friendship to the next step was the right one—despite the growing feelings she had for Corey and especially the strong desire she'd had to kiss her again last night. She tried to remain quiet, but one of the floorboards made a loud creak under her feet.

Corey turned at the sound behind her, surprised to find Erin there. Surprised and a little shaken. Yes, she was falling for Erin, but seeing her after what she'd just experienced was too much, too soon.

"I didn't mean to intrude," Erin said as the rain began to let up.

Corey leaned over and wiped at her cheeks with the bottom of her shirt. "You didn't."

Erin gestured toward the sky. "I was worried. I figured you forgot about the afternoon thundershowers. I didn't want you to be caught up on the mountain."

Taking one last look at the fading rainbow, Corey lifted her pack onto her shoulders and walked to Erin. "Thank you. You're very kind to think of me."

"Are you sure you're ready to go? Like I said, I didn't mean—"

Corey touched her arm. "You didn't intrude. I'm ready to go if you are." She followed Erin down the steps.

"It'll be a little tricky on the trail after this rain. Let me go first, all right?" Erin said over her shoulder.

Corey didn't mind at all since it afforded her an opportunity to watch the sway of Erin's hips all the way down the four-plus miles.

They didn't do a lot of talking. Corey was going over in her mind what she'd say to Erin once they had the opportunity to be alone. Maybe they'd go to their spot on the lake. Erin seemed to draw as much comfort from the place as Corey did.

The trip down didn't take nearly as much time as the trip up. When they reached the parking lot, Corey put her backpack in the rear of her SUV. Erin threw hers on the passenger seat of her Land Rover.

"Do you want to follow me to the lodge?" Erin asked.

"Okay. I can probably find it, but I'd rather not risk getting lost."

Corey trailed behind Erin's Land Rover until they rolled to a stop beside each other in the lodge's graveled lot.

"I have to take a shower and dress in some dry clothes," Corey said as she got out of her vehicle.

Erin fingered her T-shirt. "Looks like I should, too."

Corey's gaze dropped to Erin's chest and to the outline of her breasts against the wet fabric. She raised her eyes and realized from the look on her face, Erin had noticed her scrutiny.

"You coming up for dinner later?" Erin asked.

Corey thought about it and decided she needed a little distance between the two of them before she saw Erin again. She wanted to get the words right to say what was in her heart.

"I think I'll take a rain check." Corey laughed. "Literally, I guess. Hey, if we can have some time alone this week, I'd like to talk."

"Everything all right?"

"Oh, yeah. Nothing's wrong."

"How about tomorrow?"

It was a little sooner than Corey wanted, but it didn't matter. "Tomorrow's fine."

* * *

"Tomorrow" soon became the following Sunday evening. Tess and Erin had a large influx of lodgers during the week that occupied their time. As Corey took care of the cabins and drove into town for supplies, she only saw Erin in passing.

At almost seven, she finished cleaning up and putting her tools away after replacing a leaky faucet. Like she told Tess, normally she didn't work on Sundays. But she felt pressed to get the job done as quickly as possible for the lodgers. She went to her cabin and took a shower while thinking about what she wanted to say to Erin. It was almost eight when she headed to the lodge.

She walked along the lit pathway and slowed when she heard voices drifting down from the porch. One voice was Erin's. The other was another woman's. Low and throaty. Corey came around the corner and stopped when she saw Erin standing beside a tall woman with short, dark hair. Lean and lanky, she was almost androgynous in her appearance. But there was a definite feminine softness about her face.

Erin spotted Corey. "Corey, hi. I'm sorry we haven't been able to get together this week. It's been crazy checking in all the lodgers and making sure we have everything we need."

The woman gave Corey a frank, appraising stare.

"Anna, this is Corey, our new head of maintenance. Well, not really new anymore. She's been with us since spring. Corey, this is Anna."

Corey stepped onto the porch and took Anna's outstretched hand.

"I'm hoping that means cabin four is all ready for me since Corey probably kept things running all summer," Anna said.

"Yes. Everything's up to snuff." Erin wouldn't meet Corey's eyes.

"Good. I have especially fond memories of that cabin, don't you, Erin?"

In the dim light, Corey saw Erin's cheeks redden.

"Come on," Anna said, "why don't you take a break and walk me there? I don't think I remember the way." She slid her fingers down Erin's arm and took hold of her hand.

Corey's stomach lurched. If it hadn't already been obvious Anna was more than a friend, she'd sealed it with the intimate move.

Anna picked up her bag and tried to tug Erin down the porch steps, but Erin held her ground.

"I'll set some time aside tomorrow evening. We can talk then, Corey."

"Oh, I don't know," Anna said with a smirk. "You might be a little busy tomorrow night, Erin."

The conversation she'd hoped to have with Erin was something Corey didn't even want to think about anymore. She moved to the stairs. "Don't worry about it. It wasn't that important."

Erin gently gripped Corey's forearm. "You sure? It seemed important to you."

Corey managed a weak smile and glanced at Anna. "Not anymore." She pulled free from Erin's grasp and brushed past her on her way into the lodge.

Erin resisted the urge to follow Corey. She had an overpowering feeling she'd missed a momentous opportunity. But Anna dragged her down the pathway toward the cabins.

"Come on, you," Anna said breathlessly. "I can't wait to get behind closed doors."

Erin allowed Anna to lead her into the cabin. As soon as they entered, Anna dropped her bag and pushed Erin against the door. Her lips sought out Erin's for a hard, bruising kiss. Erin tried to get lost in the embrace. To feel a spark of desire... anything. But there was nothing. She broke away from Anna's mouth. "Why don't we save this until tomorrow night?"

"You're kidding, right?" Anna made another move toward Erin, but Erin pressed her palm against her chest.

"I'm pretty tired, and it's been a rough week."

Anna straightened. "You're not kidding," she said evenly.

"You have to be a little tired after flying into Denver from Chicago and driving a rental to Grand Lake." Erin slid around her to stand at a safer distance.

Anna reached for her hand to pull her close again, but Erin resisted.

"Is everything okay with you?" Anna asked.

"Just tired, like I told you." Erin moved toward the door. "Why don't you get settled tonight? Come up to the lodge in the morning, and I'll have breakfast with you in the restaurant." Erin could've invited her to breakfast in the living chambers, but opening her home to Anna was much too intimate—at least for Erin.

Anna picked up her bag and flung it onto the mattress. She opened it and started hanging up clothes in the small closet.

"I don't know when I'll be up in the morning," Anna said in a tight voice.

"Whenever it is, ask my aunt to hunt me down if you can't find me. I'll make time to sit with you." Anna didn't say anything. "Anna?"

"Whatever. See you tomorrow." She kept her back to Erin.

Erin slipped out of the cabin and exhaled a sigh of relief. Why, she wasn't sure. She'd only been sure she wasn't ready to share any more than a kiss tonight, and that had been pushing it. With the way the summer had played out as she battled with her tumultuous feelings about Corey, she'd forgotten about Anna's visit. It was a shock when Erin saw her at the counter, ready to check in.

She was about to go up to the lodge but was afraid Corey might still be there. She attempted to shake her unease at why she didn't want to see Corey and descended the trail to her refuge by the lake.

* * *

Trying unsuccessfully to forget the image of Erin holding hands with Anna, Corey entered the lodge. She hadn't had dinner yet. She'd been so busy working that she'd lost track of time. As she approached the restaurant, the manager shut the doors and flipped the Open sign to Closed. Tess's voice stopped her as she was about to leave.

"Not had dinner?"

"No."

Tess addressed the young woman who was also behind the counter. "Think you can handle things, Emily?"

"Sure thing."

"Come on, Corey. I'll rustle you up something."

Corey almost declined but thought better of it. She followed Tess into the living quarters.

"Sit down at the table. Roast beef sandwich sound good?"

Corey's stomach rumbled in answer.

Tess chuckled. "I take that as a yes." In no time, she had a sandwich prepared. She added a dill pickle to the side and set the plate in front of Corey, along with a bottle of Coke.

"I was thinking I'd head into town for dinner, but your cooking is much better." Corey took a bite and washed it down with a sip of Coke.

"How are things going with the cabins?" Tess asked.

"They're coming along. Now, it's more or less me keeping up with the maintenance. Scott and Eddie have helped with that end of it."

"And how are you and my niece?"

Corey stopped chewing. Tess was studying her and was probably awaiting an honest answer. She swallowed and took another sip of her Coke. She stalled by wiping her mouth with her napkin and fiddled with the napkin as she answered.

"Erin and I are good. She's been very nice in helping me when I have any questions about one of the cabins."

Tess stood up and went into the kitchen. She returned with a mug of coffee. "Did you want some? I didn't even ask and assumed a Coke would go with your sandwich better than coffee."

"The Coke is fine."

Tess stared at her over the rim of her mug. She waited a few more seconds before speaking again. "I wasn't asking how she was helping you out. I was curious again as to how you felt about her personally."

Corey's pulse sped up when she realized Tess wouldn't quit

pressing. "I like her. A lot."

"Good. I'm glad."

"But I don't think she feels the same."

Tess took another sip of coffee. "I've noticed the way she looks at you, Corey. I think there's a definite interest there. You seemed to have a good time at the fireworks celebration, and you've gone on a couple of outings with her. That has to count for something."

"Forgive me for asking, but aside from her being your niece, why is this so important to you?"

"Because Erin's been lost the past few years. When I see the two of you together, she seems to have righted herself. And I think you've had a hand in that."

"It's really not up to me. She's seeing other women."

"I'm assuming you're referring to this Anna person who checked in this evening?"

Corey nodded.

"If my memory serves me well, Anna visited last summer. Erin gets involved with women who are unavailable. They're here one day and gone the next. The woman down at the stables I've seen her with seems like another one who's only interested in sex."

Corey choked on her next sip of Coke. The carbonation burned her throat and traveled all the way up to the inside of her nose. Tess went into the kitchen for a glass of water and handed it to her. Corey first got her breath before she took a few drinks of water.

"I see you and Erin have the same ailment with drinking," Tess said with bemusement. "Did you think I wouldn't notice the looks between you two? I'm surprised you didn't burn holes into each other."

"I'm sure you did notice. I'm a little surprised with your candor, I guess."

Tess tapped her fingernail against the table a few times. "You seemed lost yourself when you first arrived."

"I was." This time, Corey was ready to tell her story. From the night she'd first arrived, Tess had put her at ease, as if she'd known Tess all her life.

"I lost my partner, Judy, to a car accident. She died two years ago." The words were still difficult to say, but to Corey's surprise, she didn't feel the overwhelming sadness she had before. Yes, the sadness was still there, but it was if it were in a different layer of her heart. As if part of her had healed. She thought back to last week on the observation deck and realized that was precisely what had happened.

Tess reached across the table and touched Corey's hand. "You have my deepest sympathy."

"Thank you."

"I have to be honest with you, though."

"Honest about what?"

Tess gave her a sheepish look. "I was eavesdropping on a conversation my sister was having with Erin. Erin shared your story with her. But I never wanted to approach you about it. I wanted you to feel comfortable enough to tell me on your own."

"Erin was talking to her mother about me?" Corey wasn't sure how to take the news.

"Maybe the better way to put it is Kate was firing questions at Erin the night she stayed over."

"I seem to remember her interrogation skills." *Hell, she'd give seasoned FBI agents a run for their money.*

"May I ask if the reason you moved to Grand Lake was because of your partner's death?"

"I needed to find a new home. One where I didn't feel as though I was running into Judy's memory everywhere I turned."

"And are you healing?"

Corey smiled. "Yes, I am."

Tess patted Corey's hand. "Good, good. Erin has her own reasons for feeling lost. I don't think it's my place to share them with you."

"I know what they are, Tess."

"She's told you that much?"

"She has." Corey hesitated. "In fact, I thought we were moving past her fears, but she's withdrawn. Almost as if she's afraid of something."

Tess leaned her elbows on the table and gave Corey an intense look. "Will you do me a favor? Will you not give up on her? She's different with you than she's been with the other women. I can tell she cares about you. Deeply. She's still a little mixed up, but I know my niece enough to know eventually she'll come to her senses."

"I can only hold up my end. Erin has to make the effort to meet me halfway."

"I have a very good feeling she will."

Chapter 19

Erin arose early the next morning, earlier than her normal four-thirty wake-up time. She showered quickly and tried to scrub the conflicting feelings from her body... like soap and shampoo would do the trick.

"Yeah, right," she muttered as she toweled off. She dressed in a pair of jeans and a short-sleeved polo shirt. Tiptoeing down the hallway past Tess's room, she descended the stairs and brewed a fresh pot of coffee. As she reached into the cabinet for a mug, a voice startled her from behind.

"Is there a reason you're up earlier than usual?"

Erin jumped and spun around. "God, Aunt Tess. You really have to quit sneaking up on me."

"Pour me some while you're at it." Tess headed into the dining room and sat down.

Erin handed Tess her coffee and sat across from her. She took a cautious sip from her mug.

"That Anna woman seems familiar. Her name sounds familiar, too. Didn't she visit Grand Lake last summer?"

"Yeah." Erin wondered where this line of questioning was leading.

"Wasn't she the one who wanted to experience the 'Wild West'? I think those were her words."

"Yes." Silently, Erin hoped that'd be the end of it.

Instead of more questions, Tess quietly drank her coffee. It was worse than if she'd continued her interrogation.

"I want to get an early start on washing those loads of linens in the laundry room." Erin stood up and took her mug into the kitchen. She drained the rest of the coffee and set the mug in the dishwasher. "Have a good morning, Aunt Tess," she said and walked toward the front door.

"Erin?"

Erin waited.

"Is there anything you want to talk about?" Tess asked.

"No."

"You'd tell me if something's bothering you, right? I hope we're close enough you know we can always talk."

Erin went back to her and leaned down to kiss her cheek. "Yes, ma'am. I love you enough to talk to you. But please give me a little time. I'm not even sure myself what's wrong."

Tess brushed Erin's hair away from her face. "When you figure it out, come see me."

"I will," Erin said softly.

She grabbed her jacket before leaving the lodge but instead of going to the laundry room, she veered toward the lake. It was still dark. The half moon cast an eerie white glow across the placid water. Erin settled on her rock and hugged her knees to her chest.

Until Corey Banner came into her life, Erin thought she was in control. She made no commitments. She saw whom she pleased, glad when the woman would leave town within the next day or two. Yes, Lee wasn't a lodger, but Erin had a feeling she'd be gone when fall rolled around. It was rare that any of the summer hires stayed much past Labor Day when the early snows sometimes hit.

Corey was different. She was here to stay. But she felt out of reach as well. She still mourned her partner. That much was evident in the words Corey spoke and in her actions—especially when Erin interrupted her solitude on Shadow Mountain last Sunday.

Erin was falling for Corey just as sure as she thought it was a big mistake. Tears settled on her eyelashes, and she blinked them away.

"It's so unfair," she whispered.

*　*　*

Corey waited in the morning to go to the lodge for breakfast at the restaurant. Tess had gotten her used to big breakfasts, but the last person she wanted to see was Erin. Her gait faltered when she saw her sitting at a table with Anna. Watching the two of them together made it even worse. She hurriedly found a table in the far corner, safely out of view.

She ordered eggs and bacon and tried to ignore the churning of her stomach. When her breakfast arrived, she felt settled enough to eat. She was about to take her last bite of scrambled eggs when someone approached into her peripheral vision and stood over her.

"Hey," Erin said.

Corey reached for her orange juice and washed down the food. "Hey."

"When did you get in the restaurant?"

"About twenty minutes ago."

A look of hurt passed across Erin's face as she checked around the dining room. Corey noticed only two other tables were occupied. She guessed what Erin was thinking. Why hadn't Corey stopped by to say hello?

Anna walked over to stand next to Erin.

"Hello again," Anna said. "Cody, right?"

"Corey."

"Sorry." Anna appeared anything but sorry. She put her arm around Erin's waist in a possessive move. "Guess you'll go back to repairing the cabins after you're done."

Erin seemed annoyed with the statement. "I need to get up to the front desk."

"But I thought we could hang out some before you get caught up in your work," Anna said with a touch of irritation.

"I have a job, Anna."

Corey was watching the exchange with interest. She wanted so much to ask Erin why she put herself in these situations. But it was fruitless to ask a question she already knew the answer to.

Erin ignored Anna as she turned back to Corey. "What are you working on today?"

"Another leak. Cabin ten's kitchen sink. Tess told me this morning the lodgers drove to Steamboat Springs today. I thought I'd get the work done while they're out of the cabin."

At the mention of Steamboat Springs, a slow grin made its way across Erin's mouth.

Corey couldn't help but grin back, knowing Erin was remembering their outing in the town.

Anna hugged Erin a little tighter to her body. "Why don't you at least walk with me to my cabin before you return to your reservations or whatever it is you do?" She didn't wait for Erin's answer as she grabbed Erin's hand and led her toward the door. "Have a nice day, Cody."

Before they were out of earshot, Corey heard Erin say, "Her name is Corey. Why are you being such a bitch?"

The pipe under the kitchen sink didn't stand much of a chance against Corey's anger and frustration. Seeing Erin with Anna, even though it most likely wasn't serious, was another reminder of Erin's fear of any kind of commitment. Which pissed her off more. Even if Corey wasn't the one Erin wanted, she should give someone else a chance—someone more worthy than a woman out for only one thing. "Fucking bitch," she muttered as she thought about Anna.

"How's it going under there?"

Corey jerked at the unexpected intrusion and banged her forehead against the pipe.

"Goddammit!" She slid out from under the sink and rubbed the spot on her head. A slight bump had already formed. She glared up at Erin. "What *is* it with you, huh?"

Erin took a step back. "I... I didn't mean to sneak up on you."

Corey saw Erin's hurt expression and regretted her reaction. She sighed. "I didn't mean to snap at you." She struggled to her feet.

"Let me see." Erin motioned for her to bend over.

"I'm fine, Erin. Really."

"Please?" Erin's brow was furrowed with worry.

Corey bent her head slightly.

"Where does it hurt?"

Corey pointed to the spot under her bangs.

Erin pushed Corey's hair aside and with a tender touch, probed the area. "I think you should ice this." She kept gently brushing her fingers through Corey's hair.

Corey flinched but not because it hurt. Her skin tingled where Erin touched her. Erin's fingers running through her hair felt good. Too good. She grasped Erin's hand to stop the motion. "I think I'll survive."

Erin dropped her gaze to Corey's mouth. With a quick head shake, she put some distance between them.

"Did you need something?" Corey asked.

"Uh, yes. I'm going into town for lunch. Did you want to come?"

"What about Anna?"

"What about her?"

Corey twisted the wrench in her hands and looked away. "I don't think it would be a good idea."

"But—"

"You have to decide what you want," Corey said. "And until you do, I need to keep my distance."

"I could say the same thing to you."

"What do you mean?"

"What do *you* want, Corey?"

"Erin, there you are." Anna stood in the doorway with her hand on her hip. "I've been searching for you. How about we get lunch?"

"Give me a minute," Erin said.

"Come on—"

Erin snapped her head around. "I said give me a minute. Please wait outside." After Anna huffed off, Erin turned back to Corey. "What do you want?" she repeated.

"What I want and what I can have are two different things." Corey raised her chin toward the front door. "Anna's waiting."

Erin hesitated as if she expected Corey to say more. "We still need to have that talk."

Corey didn't respond as Erin left her feeling as cold as the wrench she twisted in her hands.

* * *

Erin strode up to Anna who was leaning on a pine tree.

"Jesus, Anna. Couldn't you wait until I was done?"

"You looked like you were ready to kiss her."

"Even if I was, which I wasn't, what would it have mattered? It's not like you have any say-so."

Anna looked like she was about to say more but must have thought better of it. "True. Forget it." She held out her hand. "Come on. Let me take you to lunch. Or better yet, why don't *you* take me out to eat. I think I deserve a free lunch after waiting."

Erin stifled the urge to roll her eyes, but she took Anna's hand. She glanced behind her at the cabin. Corey stood on the porch, still holding the wrench. Erin tried to ignore the tingling in her stomach knowing Corey had been watching her. Corey waved the wrench in a little salute before heading into the cabin.

After lunch in town with Anna, Erin returned to work. On one of her last tasks for the day, she ran a lodger to the dude ranch. When she returned, it was already five. Anna had asked her for dinner as well. She'd told her it depended on how tired she was, and she was beat.

"Hey you," Tess said as Erin moved behind the counter. "Why don't you go on up and get a shower and try to take some downtime. You've been on the go nonstop today. Maybe you and Corey can go out?"

"I told Anna if I felt up to it, I'd have dinner with her tonight." Erin didn't miss Tess's scowl. "Aunt Tess, it's not like she's staying much longer."

Tess mumbled, "One week with that woman is long enough."

"I heard you," Erin said as she entered the living quarters. She couldn't help but feel the same.

It was seven when Erin and Anna left for dinner at Mo's Tavern. The waitress seated them at the same booth she'd shared with Corey. Erin was lost in thought and didn't realize Anna had asked a question.

"You said something?" Erin said, taking a sip of her beer.

"Would you like to stay with me tonight?"

"I don't know ..."

"Come on." Anna stroked Erin's forearm with her fingertips. "I didn't come all this way to ride horses and view the scenery. I've already done all that. What I'd like to do is have some time with you. Get reacquainted. I thought we had fun last summer. Didn't you?"

"Yes, I enjoyed it." Erin wanted to tell her things had changed. *She* had changed. But had she? She pushed her food around her plate with her fork, not really having much of an appetite.

"You've not fallen for the butch at the lodge, have you?"

"Why would you say that?" Erin asked defensively.

"Maybe it's the way you look at her. Hell, earlier I thought you were going to kiss her, remember?" Anna sat back in her chair. "She doesn't seem like your type, though. Besides, didn't you tell me you were only out for a good time? I'd think it would get messy dating someone you see everyday—especially an employee—only to have it not work out."

"Let's drop it, okay?"

Anna held her hands up. "Okay with me."

Erin snatched her check off the table. She fished out her money and paid the bill. "Come on. Let's go."

On the drive to the lodge, Anna kept glancing her way. They drove into the lot and parked. When they got out of the Rover, Anna rested her forearms on the roof of the vehicle as she stared at Erin on the other side. "So?" she asked.

"It's dark. I'll walk you to your cabin." Erin leaned into the Land Rover and grabbed a flashlight out of the glove compartment.

When they made it to cabin four, Anna stepped up onto the porch and tugged Erin with her. "Come on. Let's have some fun."

Erin reluctantly followed Anna to the door. She gave Anna a quick kiss but wasn't fast enough to keep Anna from yanking her inside. The instant the door closed, Anna was all over her. Her hands seemed to be everywhere, and everything was happening too fast. Way too fast.

"Slow down," Erin mumbled against Anna's lips.

Anna wasn't listening. She pressed her mouth against Erin's neck, then up to ear. "Tell me this isn't turning you on, and I'll stop." Anna cupped Erin's breasts in her hands and ran her thumbs against her nipples until they became taut peaks. Erin moaned. "I thought so." Anna pushed up Erin's shirt and bra and captured one nipple in her mouth.

Erin throbbed with the contact. Before she even knew what was happening, Anna had unsnapped her jeans and pushed her hand inside.

"Oh, yeah, you're turned on all right." Anna stroked her finger against her panties. Erin jerked her hips.

"Wait," Erin said. "God, wait." But Anna had slipped into her wetness and rubbed her thumb against her clit. With a few efficient strokes, Erin was coming.

"That's it. I've got you." Anna kept her hand in place until Erin pulled it from her jeans. "Feels like old times, huh?"

Erin didn't respond because the image burned in her mind was of Corey's dark eyes, full of hurt, asking her what she was doing. She hurriedly fastened her jeans, thinking about the last time she was in this position with Lee. She mentally shook her head.

Anna yanked her forward by the waistband. "Don't tell me you're done."

Erin pried Anna's fingers free. "I never should have started."

Anna's expression darkened. "What is your problem? Like I told you, I didn't come to Grand Lake to enjoy the scenery. I came to be with you. When I called to make reservations, you seemed excited."

Suddenly, the cabin didn't have enough air, and the walls felt like they were pressing in on her. Erin's heart hammered against her chest. Sweat broke out on her forehead. "I need to get out of here." She pushed past Anna and out the door. In her hurry to get away, she didn't see Corey coming up the trail.

"Erin? Are you all right?" Corey gently gripped her arms.

The door to the cabin opened. Anna stood silhouetted against the interior light. "I enjoyed our date, Erin. You can come to my cabin anytime," she said in a seductive tone before going back inside and shutting the door.

Corey released her. "I thought you were upset about something.

Guess I was wrong." Corey turned in the direction of her cabin.

"Hold on, Corey." Even though she and Corey had done nothing more than kiss, she still felt guilty. Because there was something going on between them—something that scared her.

"Don't worry about it." Corey lifted her chin toward the doorway where Anna had been standing. "I get the picture. You don't owe me any explanation." She took a step again to leave. Erin grasped her arm.

"It's not what you think." The incredulous look Corey gave her made her wince at her own words. "I mean, it is—"

Corey slipped free from Erin's grasp. "Like I said. You don't owe me anything. I'm tired. I have a lot of work to do in the morning."

Erin watched Corey walk away with her shoulders hunched over, her hands shoved in her jeans pockets.

"Damn it." Erin glared up at the door to Anna's cabin, tempted to march up there and tell her off. But she knew it was useless. It wasn't like Anna was lying. And that's what bothered her the most.

Corey kicked at a stone in the path, not caring that her big toe throbbed in protest. Why would she think Erin would be interested in someone like her? Someone who was permanent. Someone who wouldn't fly in for a quick night in bed and leave in the morning.

She entered the cabin and went to the refrigerator for a beer. She twisted off the cap on her way out to the porch and took a big gulp. It was dark, but she was able to make out the lights from the lodge blinking through the trees as the branches swayed in the wind. She first pictured Erin in the lodge. But she won't be there, Corey thought. She'd be down at the lake. Although Corey was angry, she saw the confusion play across Erin's face when she tried to deny what had happened with Anna.

Corey thought of stomping down to the lake and having it out with her, once and for all. Instead, she took another sip of her beer, leaned her head against the porch chair, and tried to sort through her emotions.

Erin followed the trail up to the lodge. She'd been at the lake for an hour after her confrontation with Corey, and she was cold.

"Hi, Lizzie," she said to the petite blonde behind the counter as she entered the lodge.

"Hey, Erin."

"Been quiet?"

"Typical for a Tuesday night… slow."

"Let us know if anything comes up you can't handle. You have the number to our residence."

When Erin went inside, she found Tess sitting in the living room, working a crossword puzzle. If Erin didn't know better, she'd think Tess was waiting up to talk to her. After her serious discussion with her mother, Erin wasn't ready for yet another confrontation.

"How was your date?" Tess asked as she set the paper aside and removed her reading glasses.

Erin shrugged her shoulders. "Nothing special." She took two steps toward the stairs.

"Why don't you tell me about it?"

Shit. "What do you want to know?" Erin said as she sat down in a chair across from Tess.

Tess studied her for a long moment. "You seemed to be getting along with Corey. And now this Anna comes into the picture."

"Aunt Tess, I told you she's only here the week. She'll be leaving Sunday morning."

"What are you so afraid of?"

Erin bit her lower lip.

"You used to do that as a child when you thought you were disappointing me," Tess said.

"It's nothing against Corey, but there's something about her…"

"What is it that bothers you?"

Erin rose to her feet and went to the window that overlooked the lake below. It was cloudy, but the clouds were moving fast, causing the moon to glint sporadically on the water. She felt like the water. Like the clouds were her moods, changing in shape as they raced through her veins.

"Erin?"

"She has so much baggage." *So many shadows…*

"And what about you, Ms. Samsonite?"

Erin spun around. "You know, it's a good thing I love you so much." She folded her arms across her chest.

"Lose the defensive posture, Erin Elizabeth, and tell me I'm wrong about *your* baggage."

Erin was about to argue with her, but Tess was right. Who was she to judge Corey?

In the silence, Tess said, "It's time to quit running, honey. It's time to heal."

Erin surprised herself by choking up at the gentleness in Tess's voice.

Tess stood up and held out her hand. "Come here." Tess led her to the couch and took Erin into her arms.

Erin allowed herself to get lost in the soft caresses of her hair, in the murmuring, "It's okay to cry." Which is what Erin did. She cried. She cried for the past few years. For the cynicism that seemed to rule her life. For the lack of faith in initiating anything resembling a commitment. She let her aunt soothe away the pain.

"Corey really likes you. Can't you see that?" Tess said. "I think you're putting up a wall between you and happiness. Happiness that's only a few feet away, right outside the door."

Erin sat up and wiped her cheeks. "She wants to talk to me."

"I'll ask you again, what are you afraid of? Tell me."

"That I could fall in love again."

Tess smiled. "And this would be bad?"

"But Bonnie—"

"Not every woman is Bonnie, Erin. You need to quit thinking they are." She laid her hand over Erin's heart. "Remember when I told you someone would come along to fill that space in here?"

Erin nodded.

"Corey might be that special woman. But you'll never know unless you open yourself up for love again. If not, you're going to feel empty for the rest of your life. Like something's missing. Something essential that will complete your world." She caressed Erin's cheek. "Give her a chance."

"I'll try," Erin said quietly. She thought of something. "We saw Bonnie and her lover when we went to Steamboat Springs."

"And you didn't tell me? Wait, you don't seem upset. I don't remember you being upset when you got back, either."

She told Tess about Corey and how she handled the situation. After she finished relaying the scene in the art gallery, Tess was wiping away tears of laughter. She sobered up enough to say, "You'd better have that talk with her or I will for you."

Thursday, Erin was on her way to find Corey when Anna called to her from behind.

"Hey, glad I found you," Anna said. "Haven't seen you since Tuesday night. You haven't been avoiding me, have you?"

"I've been busy."

"I saw a flyer up at the lodge. Apparently, there's a dance Saturday night at the dude ranch. That'll be my last night. Want to go with me?"

Erin looked up the path toward the cabins. "I don't think so."

"You know, I have every reason to be pissed off about flying all the way to Colorado to visit you and have you act like I'm the last person on earth who you wanted to see." Anna moved closer and stroked Erin's arm. "You told me you remembered all the fun we had last summer."

Erin snatched her arm away. "Things have changed."

"It's Corey, isn't it?"

"And you didn't help things Tuesday night."

Anna shrugged one shoulder. "You can't fault me for trying. Does she even know?"

Erin was about to give her more grief about Tuesday night but stopped. Who was she to judge when she wasn't that much different from Anna? "Corey knows. We've been meaning to have a talk, but it hasn't happened yet."

"Then go out with me one last time for the heck of it," Anna said. "I only want to dance with you. Would it be so bad?"

Erin had wanted to ask Corey, but she thought she at least owed it to Anna to go to the dance with her. She'd be leaving Sunday, and that would be the end of it.

"I'll come by your cabin at seven Saturday night. We can go in the Rover."

"Thanks." Anna leaned over and placed a light kiss on her lips.

Corey took a break and chugged some water as she stood at the window of cabin eight. She stiffened when she saw Anna and Erin kissing. She didn't realize how hard she was squeezing the bottle until water shot out of the lip like a fountain.

"Fuck." Corey wiped her wet hand against her jeans. Not wanting to see any more, she focused on her job.

She rhythmically sawed on a two-by-four until a small piece broke off and she had the size she needed to fix part of the floorboard. She took her tape measure out of her tool belt and made sure she had the right length. She set the piece into the open slot. She raised her hammer but stopped when she caught a shadow out of the corner of her eye.

Erin was leaning against the doorframe.

Drops of sweat ran down Corey's temple into her eyes. She wiped them away. "Glad I spotted you this time. I'm running out of things to hurt."

"Wouldn't want that to happen again."

Corey stood up from her kneeling position. "Did you need something?"

"Bill Cooper's having another dance Saturday night."

Corey thought she knew what Erin was about to ask. The shared kiss between Anna and Erin was still fresh in her mind. "If you're asking me to the dance, I think I'll sit this one out. Besides, I think Anna would love to go with you."

"She's going, but it's only because that's her last night at the lodge. It doesn't mean anything," Erin said in a rush.

"I'm sure you don't need me around then." Corey twisted the handle of the hammer so hard she was surprised it didn't disintegrate into sawdust.

"But—"

"Besides, I have some more work I need to get done before Monday when the next lodger is scheduled for this cabin." Corey tried not to let Erin's crestfallen expression get to her.

Erin nodded once. "I understand you have to finish your work. But you still owe me that talk."

"Erin—"

"No, Corey. This you can't get out of." Erin pivoted on her heel and left Corey standing there unable to voice any further objection.

Corey lost her concentration after Erin's visit and gave up fixing the rest of the flooring. She went to her cabin, took a shower, and headed up the trail to eat at the restaurant.

"Corey! You're just in time for dinner," Tess said as soon as Corey entered the lodge.

"Hey, Tess." Corey waved toward the restaurant. "I think I'll eat there, but I appreciate the offer."

"Come on. It'll be me and you. Erin's gone into town." Tess put her hand on the young blonde's shoulder behind the counter. "Lizzie, it's all yours for a little over an hour. Can you handle it?"

"No problem, Ms. T."

"Corey, you're with me." Tess didn't even bother to see if Corey was following her. She was already entering the living quarters.

"Guess I don't have a choice," Corey said under her breath, but apparently not low enough for Lizzie.

Lizzie grinned. "Nope. Once Ms. T has her mind made up, you're done for."

When Corey entered, she heard Tess banging around in the kitchen.

"How does a warmed up roast beef sandwich sound to you?

With a dill pickle? You liked it before," Tess said loudly.

Corey stood in the kitchen doorway. "Sounds fine."

"Why don't you grab the lemonade out of the fridge? There are glasses up in the second shelf from the bottom." She pointed to the cabinet.

Corey took down two glasses and got the pitcher of lemonade. They took everything to the table. Tess went into the kitchen and brought back a loaf of bread and a large cutting knife. She sliced some pieces, setting two on Corey's plate and two on hers.

They were quiet for a while as they took their first few bites. Corey was wiping her mouth with her napkin when Tess broke the silence.

"You going to Bill Cooper's dance Saturday night?"

"No. I'd like to keep working on cabin eight and get it ready for Monday."

"Corey, the couple won't be in until Monday night. Erin said you were almost done."

Corey thought it interesting Erin had told Tess, as if she was trying to find another way to get her to the dance. "Oh, she did, did she?"

"She also said you didn't want to go to the dance."

Corey sat back in her chair but didn't respond.

"You do know this Anna woman is leaving Sunday morning, don't you?"

"Where are you going with this?"

Tess gave her a stare. "I think you know very well where I'm going with it. But since we've had this conversation on more than one occasion, I'll drop it."

"Tess, I hate to sound like a broken record, but I don't think Erin's ready for anything serious."

"Do you always give up so easily?"

"Not usually, but watching her with Anna this week pretty much reinforces why it's such a bad idea we get together."

"Good Lord. If I could get the two of you together in the same room again, I'd bang your heads together. You're both so pig-headed."

Corey was about to object, but Tess cut her off.

"Tell you what. Let's not even argue over Erin. You'll be my date Saturday night. If you turn me down, you'll hurt my feelings."

And this was the other way to get Corey to the dance. She threw her hands up in the air. "How can I argue with that?"

"You're right. You can't."

Chapter 20

Corey stared at her reflection in the long mirror behind the bathroom door. She'd never even bothered to use it before. And now, she wasn't sure why she cared about her appearance.

Oh, you know why you care.

She tucked a soft denim long-sleeved shirt into a pair of black jeans—ones that Judy had always said made her look hot. *Judy.* Somehow, it seemed sort of right that she wanted to look as good for Erin as she did for Judy. She grabbed her leather belt from the bed and threaded it through the belt loops. When she ran her fingers through her hair, a little more gray peeked through with each pass. She always thought she'd earned the gray, so why color it?

The last few nights had been warmer than usual. Tonight was no exception, so she left her sweatshirt behind. At a little after seven, she walked up to the lodge to pick up Tess. Tess was leaving the living quarters as Corey entered the lodge. For the first time since Corey had arrived, Tess had let her gray hair fall to her shoulders. Normally, Corey wasn't fond of long hair on older women, but with Tess, it was elegant. Corey felt transported to a time when women let their hair grow long, regardless of their age. Tess wore a jeans skirt that fell well below her knees. She also had tucked in a blue-checked cotton shirt and polished the outfit off with a turquoise-studded, silver belt.

Tess brightened when she spotted Corey standing by the door. "Well, you're quite the sight."

"You're looking good yourself," Corey said with a grin.

"Do you feel like driving? Or we could take my old station wagon."

Corey held up her keys. "I can drive. No problem."

From the number of vehicles in the parking lot, the dance already appeared to be in full swing. The only place left to park was in the grass next to the graveled lot.

"I can drop you off closer and then park," Corey said.

"You don't mind? I would argue with you, but I'm not used to wearing these boots."

"I don't mind at all." Corey let Tess off by the path leading to the dance area. She heard Bill Cooper's band playing a lively tune as Tess opened the door and shut it. She parked the SUV and began the long walk toward the music.

As before, a string of lights encircled the crowded dirt dance floor. Corey heard Tess calling her name. She walked over to where she was standing with Midge Cooper.

"Glad you could make it again, Corey. Tess tells me you've been working hard at the lodge," Midge said.

"Just doing my job."

Midge laughed. "If you added a 'ma'am' after that sentence, I swear I'd need to see your badge, Marshal Dillon."

"Oh, now, Midge, don't go harassing her for having more manners than everyone here put together."

Embarrassed, Corey sought out a quick exit. "I think I'll grab a beer. You want anything, Tess?"

"Not right now, thank you."

Corey lifted a Coors Light from the bucket of ice and twisted off the top. She watched the dancers, not even trying to kid herself into thinking she wasn't searching for Erin.

And there she was in the middle of the dance floor, two-stepping with Lee. She smiled at the obvious joy that lit up Erin's face while she danced.

"Looks good out there, doesn't she?"

Corey recognized Anna's voice behind her. She didn't want to acknowledge her question, but did anyway. "She always looks good."

"Care to dance?" Anna held out her hand and gave her a cocky grin.

Oh, what the hell.

"I'm not very good at this," Corey said as Anna led her into the throng.

"It's like riding a bike or having sex. You need to climb on the seat or the woman, and it'll all come back to you."

Hearing Anna mention sex immediately brought up an unbidden and unwanted image of Erin with Anna. Corey tried to concentrate on the dance steps and push all the other stuff out of her mind.

"See?" Anna said. "You're doing fine."

Corey had to admit she was holding her own despite having

only recently learned how to two-step from Erin. She got caught up in the music and didn't feel someone staring at her right away. Then the feeling became so overwhelming she raised her eyes and immediately locked gazes with Erin.

Bill and his band segued seamlessly from the fast song into the intro of a slow tune. A woman who favored Midge Cooper enough to be her daughter stepped up to the microphone and sang the opening lines of Patsy Cline's "Crazy." Erin said something to Lee before approaching Corey.

Anna glanced over her shoulder at what had caught Corey's attention. "Wonder who she's cutting in on?" She didn't try hiding her sarcasm as Erin drew nearer.

"Do you mind, Anna?" Erin never looked away from Corey.

"Somehow, it doesn't surprise me," Anna muttered. "Be my guest."

Erin held out her hand. Corey allowed her to lead them farther onto the dance floor, and Erin took her in her arms. As the soft lyrics flowed through Corey's veins, she pressed even closer to Erin's body.

"Renee Cooper has a fantastic voice, doesn't she?" Erin said into Corey's ear. "Maybe this could be our theme song."

Corey leaned back and caught the amusement on Erin's face. "You think so?"

Erin drew her close again. "According to Aunt Tess, we're both crazy for fighting this attraction. Because it *is* an attraction. Tell me you don't feel it."

Corey felt it all right. Every place Erin's body touched hers was laced with energy. "Yeah, I feel it."

They danced to the rest of the song in silence. When it ended, Erin didn't speak but tugged Corey along with her.

"Where are we going?" Corey asked.

"Remember our talk? I think it's high time we have it."

"But what about Anna?"

Erin glanced over her shoulder at the dancers. "Do you honestly think she'll miss me?"

Corey looked back. Anna and Lee were wrapped around each other, oblivious to anyone around them.

"I don't think she'll have a problem getting a ride, either," Erin said.

Corey stuttered to a stop. "Wait. I brought Tess to the dance."

"I'll take care of it." Erin walked over to Tess and Midge. "Aunt Tess, do you mind driving the Rover back to the lodge?"

Tess gave them a knowing smile. "Not at all."

They were quiet during the drive, each seemingly lost in thought. After she parked, Corey keyed off the ignition. The ticking of the cooling engine kept time with the beating of Erin's heart.

She looked at Corey. "So?"

"Let's go to my cabin."

With each step, Erin tried to formulate in her mind what she wanted to say. When they reached the cabin, Corey sat down on the porch step. She patted beside her. Too keyed up to stay still, Erin launched into a nervous habit... she paced.

"I have to say this to you. You've scared the shit out of me ever since you arrived, Corey. You're easy to fall for, but you're so out of reach."

"Why do you think I'm so out of reach?"

"Because of how you still feel about Judy."

Corey stood up. "Yes, I still love her. I'll always love her. I'll not deny that, but—"

"You can't let yourself love again, can you? I saw you up at the lookout, and I heard you."

Corey appeared puzzled for a moment, but then her expression changed. "You were there when I was crying?"

Erin nodded.

"I was telling Judy I was moving on. I was letting her know I was falling for you."

Erin's pacing came to an abrupt stop. "What... what did you say?"

Corey caressed her face. "I'm falling for you."

"You are?"

"But I need to say something to you before we take this any further. When are you going to let Bonnie go?"

Erin stepped away from Corey's touch. "I've let her go."

"Damn it, Erin, you know what I mean. I'm not starting something with you if you're only looking to have fun. Because that's not what this is about to me. When are you going to stop running?"

Erin almost argued with her. She wanted to tell Corey she didn't know her at all. But Corey knew her better than every one of the women she'd been with since Bonnie shattered her life.

"Jesus Christ, you scare me, Corey."

Corey smiled. "You already said that."

"I... I don't want to run anymore."

Corey touched Erin's cheek. "I'm right here."

Erin grabbed Corey's shoulders and yanked her forward. She captured Corey's mouth, thrusting her tongue inside. When Corey responded and met her stroke for stroke, Erin moaned. She jerked Corey's shirt from her jeans and ran her fingers under it until she touched the solid muscle of Corey's stomach. Corey trembled at the touch. She tore her mouth away and hurriedly led Erin up the stairs and into her cabin. She slammed the door behind them and pushed Erin against it, shoving her thigh between Erin's legs.

"God," Erin gasped.

Corey pressed her mouth against Erin's neck, nibbling and licking as she unbuttoned Erin's shirt. One button proved to be stubborn. Corey growled in frustration and ripped open the blouse. Erin heard the buttons bounce on the hardwood floor but thought of nothing else as Corey unsnapped her bra and freed her breasts. She writhed with pleasure when Corey brushed her thumbs across her nipples as she continued her assault on Erin's neck. Afraid she'd come from that simple act alone, Erin stilled Corey's hands.

"Corey, slow down."

Corey didn't seem to be listening because she lowered her head and captured a nipple in her mouth.

"Oh, God." Erin felt the beginning stirrings of her orgasm. *Not like this.* She grasped Corey's head and gently pulled her up. Corey's pupils had darkened in desire. "I need this as much as you do. You can't believe how incredibly wet I am right now, but I want to feel you against me. All of you."

Corey's breath caught as her face flushed in arousal. "Yes."

They undressed, each watching the other as every article of clothing hit the floor. Erin moved closer and rubbed against Corey's nipples. Corey groaned.

"Your body is just like I pictured it," Erin whispered into her ear.

Corey urged Erin toward the bed. She pulled the covers aside and gently pushed Erin down. She lay on her side and placed a light kiss on Erin's forehead, then her cheeks, while she caressed her breasts until Erin's nipples had hardened almost painfully. A part of her wanted this slow burn. The other part screamed for release.

Corey trailed her fingers lower until she rested her hand between Erin's legs. As Erin was about to beg Corey to touch her, Corey lowered her mouth to Erin's breast and spread Erin's folds apart. She dipped her fingers into her wetness and moaned against Erin's breast.

Erin gripped Corey's head and tugged her even tighter against her nipple. She raised her hips to urge Corey on. Corey released her breast from her mouth and met Erin's eyes.

"I'm going to touch you now," she said hoarsely. She rubbed her thumb against Erin's clit as she entered her with two fingers.

Erin tensed in glorious anticipation while Corey stroked her higher and higher. The bed shifted as Corey threw her leg over Erin's and straddled her thigh.

"You're so wet, Corey. Come with me. Please." Corey moved in time with the rhythm of her hand. "Like that. Oh, God. Just like that." Corey quickened her pace, and Erin lifted her hips in perfect motion. Erin gripped Corey's shoulders and felt the strain of Corey's muscles. Watching the pulse throb in her neck, Erin said, "That's it, baby. Come with me." Erin trembled with the first stirrings of her release but tried to hold off until Corey joined her. It was too much. She exploded into her orgasm with Corey tensing against her leg. Corey cried out and collapsed onto the bed.

Time passed with their heavy breathing the only sound in the room.

"Let me hold you," Erin said softly. Corey shifted into her arms. Minutes passed as the night noises outside the cabin intruded into their quiet. Corey's breathing had grown shallow, enough for Erin to think she'd fallen asleep. She tried to move into a more comfortable position. Corey tightened her hold on her waist.

"Please don't leave me."

Erin brushed Corey's hair off her forehead. "I'm not going anywhere, sweetheart."

Corey awakened from a deep sleep. Erin had shifted onto her side during the night. Corey was curled around her body. Her arm rested against the swell of Erin's breasts. Arousal pounded through Corey's veins as she remembered the love they'd made for hours. She nuzzled Erin's neck and dropped her hand between Erin's legs. Erin murmured in her sleep but didn't wake up. Corey dipped into Erin's folds and smiled when she found she was already wet. She brushed against Erin's clit, her smile widening when Erin moaned and opened her legs. Corey stroked her until Erin's legs tightened and she clamped them together, trapping Corey's hand. She finally relaxed and turned to face Corey.

"You sure know how to wake a girl properly," Erin said and gave Corey a light kiss.

Corey fingered Erin's hair and let it drop to Erin's shoulders.

"You're so beautiful." Erin tried to lower her head, but Corey tipped her chin up, leaned down, and kissed Erin again. "You better get used to hearing that."

"And I've thought you were handsome since the first minute we met." They both sighed at the same time. Erin giggled. "I'd say we feel the same way about tonight."

"If it's that you don't want it to end and you hope it's the first of many more to come, then, yes. I feel the same way."

Erin propped herself on her elbow and stared down at Corey. "This isn't a one-time thing for me. I wouldn't have made love with you tonight if I thought it would be like the other nights I've shared with women. It means everything to me. *You* mean everything to me."

"I told you I was falling for you," Corey's voice caught. "Erin, I—"

Erin placed a slender finger against her lips. "That's enough for now."

A twinge of disappointment hit Corey, but with what they'd shared tonight, she felt it was only a matter of time before she'd say the words.

Corey lay on her stomach with one leg drawn up toward her chest. The pale light of dawn crept under the drawn blinds—enough to awaken her. She trembled at the memory of last night's shared passion. She reached to touch Erin but found only a rumpled sheet and slight indentation where Erin had laid.

At first, a sick feeling hit the pit of her stomach with the thought Erin had left during the night. But the smell of freshly brewed coffee gave her hope. Corey slid into her jeans and searched for her shirt. She soon discovered it was missing. *I can guess where it is.* She went to her closet and slipped on another one. Buttoning it as she walked down the hallway, she opened the screen door and was relieved to see Erin in one of the chairs, sipping a cup of coffee.

Erin craned her neck to look back at Corey. "Hey, sleepyhead."

"Hey." Corey leaned over and gave her a light kiss. She sat down in the other chair and eyed Erin's shirt. "It looks good on you."

Erin fingered the material. "I hope you don't mind me borrowing it. It seems my shirt got a bit damaged last night."

Corey chuckled. "Nope. Don't mind at all, although you are quite fetching without one." She picked at her jeans, afraid to bring up what troubled her.

Erin reached over and grabbed her hand. "Everything okay?"

Knowing she needed to be honest for this to work, Corey took the plunge. "I thought you'd left." A squeeze of her hand made her look at Erin.

"I told you I wouldn't leave." A sad smile creased Erin's lips. "I'm sure it'll take more than one night to have you trust me. You have every right to doubt me. I don't exactly have a good track record."

Corey chose her words carefully, trying her best not to bring "love" into the equation. "But I *do* trust you. I think I let some of my insecurities get the best of me. I never thought I'd feel like this again."

"I'm sure this is different than Judy."

From her expression, Corey thought Erin was feeling just as insecure. She cradled Erin's hand in both of hers. "Yes, it is different." Erin tensed, so she quickly continued. "But it doesn't mean I don't have the same depth of feeling for you." She thought for a moment. "It's like flipping a page in a romance novel and finding the author has written even more passion between the two characters. It builds and builds until you feel you might burst from the emotion. What I felt for Judy stays with her. What I feel for you is a new beginning. As it should be."

What Corey wanted to shout to the universe was, "I love you, Erin Flannery!" But she knew Erin wasn't ready.

Erin didn't speak for the longest time. Corey thought maybe she'd said something wrong. She opened her mouth, but Erin stopped her.

"That's the most beautiful thing anyone has ever said to me." Erin drew Corey to her and gently kissed her. "Thank you."

Corey caressed Erin's cheek with her fingertips. "You're welcome."

Chapter 21

"You don't need to worry about Aunt Tess." Erin almost laughed at the look of terror on Corey's face.

They'd taken showers—separately because they knew they'd never leave the cabin, otherwise. While they were dressing, Corey fretted about what Tess would think with Erin showing up wearing Corey's shirt.

Erin bumped shoulders with her as they headed up the path to the lodge. "Remember she's the one who's been pushing us together."

"I guess," Corey mumbled.

Erin grasped her arm to stop her from walking any farther. "Hold on."

Corey stood in front of her.

"Corey." Erin ducked her head so Corey had no option but to meet her gaze. "I'm falling for you, too. Tess will see it on my face the second we walk into the lodge. You have to trust me on this, too. Do you?"

"Yeah."

"All right then. Let's go face the music... or at least Aunt Tess." Before Erin pushed through the front door of the lodge, she said, "She's not working out front today." Emily was talking to a customer at the counter when they entered. "Hello, Emily, having any problems this morning?"

"It's been pretty quiet. Oh, Anna McIntire checked out this morning and wanted me to give you this." Emily reached under the counter and handed Erin an envelope.

She opened the envelope. Anna thanked her for the stay and for Lee. They'd connected last night. Surprisingly, she wished Erin good luck with Corey. Erin wadded up the note and tossed it in the wastebasket on their way into the living quarters.

"I guess I was right about Anna and Lee," she told Corey. "She did wish us luck, though."

148

Corey snorted.

Erin laughed as she opened the door. "Aunt Tess?" There was no answer, but there was banging coming from the kitchen. "Must be fixing something."

Corey wiped the palms of her hands against her jeans. "Man, I feel like a teenager bringing a girl home after a date."

"Relax."

Tess glanced at them as she moved around the kitchen. "I see you've made it to the land of the living. Hungry?"

Smelling the frying bacon made Erin realize how famished she was. Corey's stomach growled.

"I'd say you are. Erin, why don't you finish frying the bacon? I'll make us some scrambled eggs. Do you want any eggs, Corey?"

"Yes, ma'am."

Tess gave her a sharp look. "We're back to ma'am, are we?"

"N-no."

"Good. You can set the table."

Tess and Erin finished preparing the eggs and bacon. They brought everything out to the table where Corey waited. Erin and Corey dug in and didn't speak until they finished. When Erin looked up from dabbing her mouth with her napkin, Tess was staring at her.

"What's wrong?" Now it was her turn to get nervous.

Tess's gaze dropped to Erin's shirt. "I seem to recall that shirt. Except the last time I saw it, Corey was wearing it."

Erin tried to will the full blush from rising up her neck and infusing her cheeks, but she knew it was a lost cause. Corey fiddled with her napkin and kept her head down.

"No need to be embarrassed, Erin. Corey's a keeper."

Corey slumped back in her chair. "Oh, thank God."

"Did you think I would suddenly change my mind?"

"No," Corey said. "At least I hoped not."

Erin questioned Corey with a raised eyebrow.

"Tess had a conversation with me about the two of us. More than one, actually."

"You too, huh?" Erin said. "Why were you worried then?"

Corey didn't say anything.

Tess took over. "I'll answer for her. Saying I wanted to see the two of you together, and having you show up this morning after a night of mad, passionate sex, are two different things entirely."

"Aunt Tess!"

Corey dropped her head in her hands. "Dear God."

"Oh, grow up, you two. You think I don't know what's going

on?"

Erin started to answer, but Tess held up her hand.

"I don't want to know the details. But seeing you both happy?" Tess beamed at them. "It makes me happy." She stood up and gathered their plates. "You go have some fun today." She pointed the plate she was holding at Corey. "And you. No working."

They headed to the front door.

"What do you feel like doing?" Erin said.

Corey put her arm around her. "I could think of a few things."

"I could, too, but how about we try an outdoor activity?"

"What I'm thinking of can be accomplished outside."

Erin laughed. "I'm sure it can be, but let's not give the lodgers a free show." She snapped her fingers. "Hey, I have the perfect idea. But we need to change into shorts and tank tops. We'll be cooler that way."

"This isn't exactly what I had in mind," Corey grumbled, feeling her muscles strain as she pulled the oar through the water.

"Buck up, Ms. Banner. It's a gorgeous day. Temp's in the upper seventies. Sun is bright. Oh, and we got out here well before the afternoon rain."

Corey rested the oar on top of the canoe. "Renting a canoe? This is your brilliant idea?"

Erin raised her face to the sun. "Seems pretty brilliant to me."

Corey became distracted as she enjoyed the view before her— and it wasn't of the mountains. Erin had draped her long, tan legs in front of her. Corey's eyes traveled from that tantalizing sight up past the curve of her breasts to the slight dimple in her right cheek that Corey still ached to press her lips to. The line of her neck drew Corey to the hint of cleavage below. She looked up to find Erin staring at her.

"If you keep ogling me like that, you can paddle us right back to shore."

"Ogle? Really? Ogle?"

Erin poked Corey's knee with her bare foot.

"I can't help it, Erin. I'll never tire of saying this—you're so beautiful."

Erin's expression grew pensive.

"What's wrong?" Corey said.

"Other women have told me they thought I was beautiful. I never really believed them."

"Even Bonnie?"

Erin nodded. "I always had this twinge of doubt when she'd tell me, like she was angling for something from me. Like she'd said it before to other women. I should've followed my instincts. But I believe *you*. Not because I think I'm beautiful, but because you make me feel that way—with the way you kiss me, the way you touch me, the way you look at me. I feel cherished."

Corey had to kiss her. She stood up to move closer. Erin grabbed the sides of the canoe as it tilted precariously. Corey tried to right her balance, but the more she tried, the more the canoe tipped. With one last rocking motion, the canoe capsized. They landed in the water at the same time with a big splash. Corey pushed to the surface and searched frantically for Erin. Erin emerged on the other side of the upside-down canoe. Her long blonde hair clung to her face. She pushed the wet strands out of her eyes and glared at Corey.

"You never, ever, *ever* stand up in a canoe. Didn't you go canoeing in Michigan?"

"A few times when we went camping."

"Did you ever stand up in the canoe?" Erin's voice continued to rise with each word.

"Uh, no." Corey tried to stifle her laughter, but it bubbled up inside her until she couldn't hold it in.

"What's so funny?" Erin edged her way around the canoe to Corey.

"You're..." Corey started laughing again. "You're so adorable, looking like you do while you're pissed at me."

"Adorable, huh?" Erin looked like she was trying not to smile.

"Absolutely adorable."

"You're not so bad yourself." She brushed Corey's bangs out of her eyes and kept her palm pressed against her cheek. Each holding onto the canoe with one hand, they shared a heated stare. They used their free hand to pull each other together in a rush. Their bodies crashed together, and their lips locked in a frenzied kiss. They broke apart at the same time.

"I don't know about you, but I'm feeling wet for other reasons," Corey managed to rasp out.

"How about we get this canoe righted and return it to the rental shop? Your original plan for the day is looking better and better."

"Couldn't agree more."

* * *

The week was a busy one for Erin. A large number of lodgers were coming and going. The phone never stopped ringing. She disappointed a lot of out-of-state callers with telling them Rainbow Lodge shut down September fifth, the Friday before Labor Day weekend. Coloradans knew better than to try to book there after that date, but those who lived out of state thought nothing of the impending snow season. She directed them to a sister lodge in Steamboat Springs that was open all winter for skiing.

She was frustrated she'd not been able to see Corey much during the week. Erin had stayed overnight a couple of times, but they'd both been too exhausted to do anything except fall asleep in each other's arms. She smiled. Actually, that was a comforting feeling.

"What are you smiling about?" Tess said as she came to the counter.

"Nothing." Erin went around the counter and made a show of straightening the brochure rack.

"I'd say 'nothing' just walked through the door." Tess turned to a couple who'd stepped over to ask a question.

Corey strode toward the front desk. Erin had to restrain herself from literally jumping in her arms.

"Hey, Erin."

"Hey, yourself."

They linked their fingers together in a brief exchange of intimacy.

"Just finished another phone call with Penny, by the way." Corey leaned one elbow against the counter.

"Yeah?"

"Kind of a serious conversation, too."

Erin at first was worried but then caught the twinkle in Corey's eyes. "It was, was it."

"Yup. It's pretty serious when I'm talking about the amazing woman in my life."

Erin couldn't keep from smiling. "What did she say?"

"She said she couldn't wait to meet you. I know you'll really like each other." Corey edged closer and looked like she was about to kiss her.

Tess walked up to them. "You two have any plans for the weekend?"

Erin took a step back and was about to answer no, when Corey spoke.

"As a matter of fact, we do."

"We do?" Erin asked.

"Yup." But Corey didn't offer any more.

"Would you like to fill me in?"

"Nope."

"Oh, come on. I need to know what to prepare for."

Corey squinted and tapped her chin with her index finger. "If I recall, someone didn't give me any clues about a surprise."

"Yeah, but—"

"Nope," Corey repeated. "You're not getting it out of me."

Erin stepped closer and whispered in her ear. "I bet I could get it out of you tonight."

Corey leaned into her and whispered back, "I'd love to have you try."

Erin tingled at the sexual innuendo.

Tess walked over to them. "You know I would tell you two to get a room, but I don't think I need to."

"No, you don't." Erin tugged on Corey's hand. "Speaking of which, I should be over around eight tonight. Then you have to suffer through my interrogation tactics."

"Can't wait." Corey winked at her. "Need to get some tools out of the storage shed, but I wanted to drop in to see you."

"Glad you did." She watched as Corey exited through the back.

"You've got it bad, girl," Tess said.

"I do, Aunt Tess, I do." And it felt good. It felt like love.

*　*　*

Exhausted, Corey fell back onto the bed, her body covered with a light sheen of sweat. "God, you're amazing."

Erin leaned on an elbow and ran her fingers between Corey's breasts. "You stole my line." She bent over and gave Corey a lingering kiss. "Have I told you how glad I am you came into my life?"

"Not in so many words, no."

Erin tapped her chest. "Well, I am."

Corey held Erin in her arms as she thought of their first meeting. "You couldn't convince me of that when we first met. You didn't seem happy to have me working for you. In fact, you kind of intimidated me."

Erin looked up at her. "I did?"

"You weren't too pleased with Tess hiring me. At least you gave me that impression."

"I'm overprotective of her. She can be too trusting sometimes, and you have to admit, yours was a rather quick hire."

"Oh, so now you're saying I'm not qualified." Corey tried to sound hurt.

"There was the matter about your arrest in Michigan."

"I *told* you the charges were dropped. Don't you believe me?"

"I believe you. Because I can't imagine someone this kind"— Erin kissed her shoulder—"giving"—she trailed her kisses to her breast—"and the best lover in the world could possibly be an axe murderer." She lowered her head to Corey's nipple.

"Erin?"

"Hmm?"

"I'm still not telling you about your surprise."

Erin released her nipple with a soft pop. "You are such a shit."

Corey grinned at her. "What happened to 'kind,' 'giving,' and 'the best lover in the world'?"

Erin flipped onto her side to face the other way. Corey brushed her fingers against her back, but Erin shrugged her off.

"I'm not talking to you," Erin said.

Corey lowered her hand to cup Erin's butt cheek. "Oh, really?" Erin squirmed with her touch. Corey tested the waters some more by dipping between Erin's legs, pleased to find her wet. "Your body seems to be doing a lot of talking."

Erin rolled onto her back and opened her legs. "What... oh, God... what's it s-saying?"

"That you're not ready to go to sleep yet."

Erin grabbed Corey's hand and pushed it into her wetness even harder. "Then why don't you put me to sleep?" She arched her back as Corey entered her.

"Well, now that you ask so nicely..."

* * *

Erin followed Corey outside of Mo's Diner.

"I enjoyed the meal. Was this my surprise?" Erin tried not to sound too disappointed.

"I don't think this would be much of a surprise, would it?" Corey got into the SUV.

"I didn't want to sound bitchy," Erin said as she shut her door.

Corey keyed the engine.

"You're *still* not going to tell me?"

"Erin, I swear. Are you like this around your birthday?" Corey checked both ways before turning onto Main Street.

"You'll find out soon enough. It's in October. I'm even worse at Christmas, by the way."

"Thanks for the heads-up."

Erin let the conversation settle between them. What they'd said to each other in so many words was they wanted a future together. She wondered whether Corey noticed the same thing.

They continued out of town for about thirty minutes. Erin glanced over at Corey, who was pensive, but she didn't interrupt her thoughts. This whole evening felt right. She didn't need to have Corey address their future yet.

They turned down a familiar road, but Erin was puzzled. "Why are we going this way?"

"You'll see."

When they arrived at the same clearing, Erin knew what her surprise was. Greg, Donnie, and their crew were busy readying the balloon.

"But Greg only flies in the morning," Erin said.

Corey grinned as she put the SUV in park. "He made an exception for us."

They got out and headed over to the group.

"Hey, Erin and Corey. Ready for something new?"

"Greg, are you sure you can do this?" Erin was skeptical.

"You doubt the incomparable Greg Dobson?" He clutched his chest. "You wound me with your lack of faith."

"God, what an ego," Donnie muttered.

"Oh, hush, hon. You know you love me." Greg slapped him on the shoulder as he walked by.

"Yeah, yeah." Donnie went to a table once again set up with four flutes and a bottle of champagne. He poured the champagne into the glasses.

"I didn't think you could fly at night," Erin said.

"Check your watch there, missy."

Erin glanced at the time. "It's seven."

"We'll go up now for an hour. Sunset is at 8:30. We'll land while we can still see, but we won't miss a gorgeous sky." He pointed to the west. "Full moon, too." He waved them over. "Come on. Times a' wastin'. And you know the drill. No flying without the champagne." They joined him with the traditional toast.

As they walked to the balloon, Erin asked Corey, "You think you can do this again? Last time was a little iffy."

"I've got my sea legs now. Well, my balloon legs, I guess."

Greg's crew held the basket while each of them climbed inside.
"Ready, kids?" Greg's face flushed in excitement.

Corey saluted. "Aye aye, Captain."

The basket jerked as the balloon lifted off the ground. Corey gripped the sides but not as tightly as she had their first trip.

Erin placed her hand on top of Corey's. "Thank you for this."

They quickly rose atop the fir trees and into the most magnificent sunset Erin had ever seen. The sun was descending on the western horizon. Bright swaths of orange and red streaked across the sky as if painted there by a master artist. A mutual and comfortable silence fell between her and Corey.

Greg took them on a similar route over Grand Lake. He adjusted the flame so they dipped a little lower. In the middle of the lake, two fishermen in a boat lifted their hands in greeting. Corey and Erin waved back. Greg slowly raised them above the treetops and higher, yet even higher, until they again could see the Great Divide in the waning light.

Erin attended Mass once at a Boulder church. She had happened to look up just as the morning sun flashed through the stained glass. It had left her awestruck. It was as if God had spoken to her the instant the colors had burst into life inside the chapel. She felt His peace then... and she felt it now.

The full moon urged the sun along her journey to her resting place below the far horizon. Corey closed her eyes, and a slow smile spread across her lips. Erin turned Corey to face her.

An unspoken understanding passed between them, as hushed as the cool breeze sifting through their hair. She held Corey's face in her hands. Using her thumbs, she brushed aside the tears streaming down Corey's cheeks.

"I love you, Corey," she said softly.

Corey leaned in to kiss her, their tongues melding together as one. Erin's heart slipped into place. A place she'd hoped for but never thought possible. But she'd found it in Corey's love.

Corey trailed gentle kisses up to Erin's ear. "I love you, too, Erin." Erin trembled as the words whispered against her skin and nestled into her very soul.

* * *

"What are you thinking about?"

"What an unforgettable night this has been," Corey said with a sigh.

They were sitting on Corey's front porch chairs. Darkness had closed in fast once Greg had safely landed the balloon. In their time on the porch, Corey had been listening to the various sounds surrounding them—the chirping of the crickets, the occasional hoot of an owl, the hoarse croaking of the frogs rising up to them from the lake.

"And it's not even over." Erin stood and led her inside. No light was needed with the bright, full moon streaming through the partially closed blinds. Erin led Corey to the bed and sat beside her. "I want to go slow tonight."

Corey smiled. "I can do slow."

Erin was about to raise the hem of Corey's T-shirt, but Corey was faster and knelt down in front of her.

"Let me love you, Erin." She lifted Erin's shirt over her head and unclasped the front of her bra. "Remind me to send a thank-you card to whoever invented the front-clasp bra."

"Easy access *is* nice, isn't it?"

Corey pushed Erin back onto the mattress. She stroked her hands slowly from Erin's shoulders, lightly over her breasts until she reached her waist. She unbuttoned Erin's jeans and slid them down to the floor, along with her panties. Corey rested her cheek against Erin and relished the simple rise and fall of her stomach as she inhaled each breath. Erin brushed her fingers through Corey's hair. Corey raised her head to find Erin watching her intently.

"Take off your clothes." Erin said the words forcefully—it wasn't a request.

Corey stood up and quickly undressed, feeling Erin's gaze the entire time.

Erin shifted to lie back on the pillows. She offered her hand again. "Come to me."

Corey draped her body on top of Erin's but kept from pressing against her. She propped herself on her hands on either side of Erin and stared down at her.

"You wanted slow?"

Erin barely nodded.

"Then I'll start here." Corey leaned on one elbow and touched Erin's forehead with her other hand. "And work my kisses to here." She ran her thumb along Erin's mouth. "Then, I'll trail my mouth to here." She brushed the back of her hand against Erin's nipple which quickly became rock-hard. "Over to here." She tweaked the other nipple. "Then, I'll work my mouth over your stomach but not to where you crave it the most."

"Corey, honey."

"I'll start at your ankles and kiss my way up the inside of your thighs, then place my lips against the soft hair here." Corey skimmed her fingers through the triangle of light blonde hair nestled between Erin's legs.

Erin gasped. "*Corey.*"

"What?" Corey asked through a haze of lust.

"You don't have to write a term paper about it." Erin's mouth curled in amusement. "Later, maybe yes. Right now, no."

Corey bent over, kissed Erin's forehead, and worked her way down to meet Erin's lips. She ran her tongue along Erin's lower lip before dipping inside.

"Too much talking, huh?" she murmured.

"Mm hmm."

"All righty then." Corey deepened the kiss but didn't stay there long. She intended to deliver on her promises. After lavishing her attention on Erin's breasts, she sucked on the soft skin of her stomach.

"God, Corey."

Corey shifted to the end of the bed. Again, as she promised, she touched her lips to the inside of Erin's ankles and moved slowly up to the inside of her thighs, then placed a kiss on her mound. She raised her head.

"Watch me as I love you," Corey whispered.

The moon's mystical glow captured the intensity of Erin's blue eyes that, for a magic moment, never left hers.

Corey inhaled Erin's sweet scent and parted her soft, wet folds. She pressed her lips against her before encircling her clit. Erin moaned. She gripped Corey's hair and shifted her hips to the rhythm of Corey's strokes. When Corey felt the first pulsing of Erin's orgasm, she pressed two fingers deep inside.

"Oh, my God," Erin cried out.

Corey pulled her mouth away and marveled as the muscles in Erin's neck tensed. She continued to stroke until Erin's inner walls began to spasm around her fingers. She thrust deep inside one last time while Erin's body tensed. She waited until the spasms stopped and then slowly withdrew her fingers.

"Oh, God, Corey…" Erin's cheeks shone with tears.

"Hey, don't cry." Corey brushed them away.

"Come here, you." Erin took Corey's face in her hands and kissed her. "These are 'you blew my mind' tears."

"Oh." Corey stretched out beside her and pulled Erin into her arms. "In that case…"

Erin rested her head against Corey's chest and tapped her playfully on the stomach. "I do love you."

"I'm glad because I'm crazy about you, Erin Flannery," Corey said as she stroked Erin's shoulder. "Slow enough for you?"

"You even have to ask?" Erin mumbled before drifting off to sleep.

Once again, the smell of fresh coffee brewing woke Corey in the morning. She stretched and moaned as her muscles protested in response to last night's activities. She brushed her fingers along the space beside her. Erin wasn't there. But the sheet was still warm, so she knew Erin couldn't have been up long. The slight panic she'd felt the first time she awakened alone was now gone and replaced with a certainty Erin would always be there.

Corey put on her jeans and T-shirt from the day before and filled a cup of coffee. She pushed the door open and took a moment simply to enjoy the sight of the woman sitting on her porch. She approached from behind and kissed Erin's hair.

"Gorgeous morning, don't you think?" Corey said as she slid into the other chair. She took a sip of her coffee and turned to Erin when she didn't answer her. "Anything wrong?" Corey would find that hard to believe after the night they shared, but Erin's pensive expression worried her a little.

"Everything's fine, Corey, and last night was fantastic."

Corey waited for the "but…"

Erin chewed on her lower lip and stared down at her coffee. "You cried out in your sleep."

"I did?"

"You said Judy's name a few times."

Corey tensed in her chair. At first, she didn't remember the dream, but then that horrible night came rushing back to her.

Erin lifted a leg up underneath her and shifted to face Corey. "Tell me." She reached over and touched Corey's hand. "Please," she said softly.

To Corey's surprise, she shared every detail of her recurring nightmare—from Judy promising she'd try to come home early to the state troopers dripping rainwater on her hardwood floor, to blacking out and waking to Trooper Hendrickson's face hovering over her. They'd moved her to lie on the couch and placed a cool, wet washcloth on her forehead. She remembered sitting up, drenched in a cold sweat, clutching her chest, hoping then it was all a bad dream. She called her parents but was unable to say the words. Trooper Hendrickson took the phone from her and left for the foyer, quietly talking into the receiver.

Corey remembered rocking in her mother's arms as she sobbed. Her mom's whispered words of, "Let it out, Corey. I have you." Corey still felt the touch of her mother's fingers as she stroked her hair.

"The funeral was a foggy haze. I do remember standing at her graveside in the bitter cold. Snow was blowing, and the wind cut through my overcoat. But it was nothing like the ice-cold grief gripping my insides. I fell to my knees at her grave, pounded the snow-covered dirt, and yelled at her for leaving me."

At some point, Corey had started crying. Erin remained silent while she continued holding Corey's hand. When Corey was done, she was almost afraid to look at Erin. Afraid Erin would withdraw. But Erin got up and pulled her to her feet. She wiped her tears away and brushed her lips against Corey's.

"You're such a brave woman." She kissed Corey again, a soft, slow kiss that spoke of their passion. "I love you. I love everything about you… everything. And that includes the life you shared with Judy."

She clutched Erin to her chest in a tight hug.

"We're going to be okay," Erin said.

Corey smiled through her tears. "We already are."

Chapter 22

"Uh, Erin. Can we maybe slow down a little?"

Erin stopped in her tracks to allow Corey to take a break. They'd decided to hike the same Shadow Mountain Trail that Corey had taken several weeks ago. But Erin hadn't been with her on the way up then. She was used to rapid climbing in higher elevations and forgot that Corey wasn't.

"I guess you didn't go this fast when you hiked last time, huh?"

Corey leaned against the nearest fir tree, her breaths coming in short spurts. "No, I didn't, Sir Edmund Hillary."

"This is hardly Mount Everest."

"Maybe not for you," Corey mumbled. She took a deep swig of her water.

Erin rubbed Corey's back. "Do you want to put off going to the top?"

"Give me a few minutes, and I'll be raring to go."

Erin filled her lungs with the clean mountain air. She'd never get tired of this. She watched as Corey took another long drink of water. And she'd never get tired of this special woman.

Corey twisted the lid back on the bottle. "Ready."

"Why don't you lead the way and set the pace?"

Corey moved ahead of her. They kept quiet most of the way up. On occasion, Erin would point out a particular bird she knew or a chipmunk. They hadn't seen many hikers on the trail. Erin was glad. This was special, almost like they were the only people in the universe. Or at least in their universe.

They stopped at the stone base of the watchtower. Corey grimaced as she stared at the winding steps leading to the top.

"Another break?" Erin said.

"No, but this time, I'll let you take the lead. If you don't see me behind you, it means I took some time to admire the scenery."

"Right. Keep telling yourself that, and maybe you'll believe it."

"Get going and don't shoot down my excuses for lagging

161

behind."

They huffed up the steps. The muscles in Erin's legs protested with each effort. She glanced behind her and was surprised Corey was close by.

"Didn't... think... I... could... keep... up...?"

"Come on, Banner, one more flight."

They reached the top. Erin joined Corey in leaning over to catch her breath.

"You're just trying to make me feel better, aren't you?" Corey swiped at the sweat pouring off her forehead.

"No. I'm fine on the trail, but for some reason, the climb up these steps always gets to me."

Eventually, their breathing returned to normal. They approached the railing and took in the scene below them. Erin had been up to the observation deck too many times to remember, but it always struck her with a sense of awe. Three lakes lay before them. The largest, Lake Granby, was to the left of where they stood. Shadow Mountain Lake and Grand Lake lay below and to the right.

"I can't imagine growing up with this as your playground," Corey said with wonder in her voice.

Erin never had taken the gorgeous views for granted. She knew better. She'd visited other places in the States, especially while she was with Bonnie. But home was home. Nothing came close to beating it.

"I've never grown tired of it." Erin decided to play tour guide. "Grand Lake is the state's largest and deepest natural lake. They've measured one depth at 265 feet. It could be even deeper in parts, though."

"You're proud of this place, aren't you?"

"I am. Here's another interesting bit of information. The Ute tribe named the lake Spirit Lake because they believed it was the final resting place of departed souls." Erin became aware Corey had stilled beside her. The words rolled around her mind. She realized what she'd said and how it would remind Corey of Judy. "Corey, I didn't mean—"

Corey touched her arm. "Erin, please. What was it you told me the other night? You loved the life I shared with Judy?" Her smile was wistful. "Maybe that's why I was able to feel her with me the last time I stood in this spot. Maybe the Utes have it right." She leaned in and kissed Erin lightly on the cheek. "So, you said nothing wrong."

Erin hesitated before she broached something she'd been

thinking about. She wasn't sure if this was the time.

"You have your 'I'm in deep thought' expression going," Corey teased.

"I'm that transparent?"

"You don't know it, but you scrunch up your nose and bite your lip." Corey held Erin's hand that gripped the railing.

"I was wondering if... well, if..."

"You can talk to me about anything."

"I was wondering if you were planning on staying in Grand Lake." Erin rushed on with her words, afraid Corey might not want to talk about it. "I mean, I know you have the job at the lodge, but still, I wasn't sure if it was something you wanted to do permanently or if—"

"Hey." Corey gently grasped Erin's arm and forced Erin to face her. "I absolutely am planning to stay. It might have been a little questionable at first, but now? Now, I have every reason to stay, and I'm looking at the most important one."

Erin's shoulders slumped in relief. "I'm glad you feel the same way. We talked about my birthday and Christmas, but that doesn't mean the months to follow."

Corey lifted Erin's chin with her fingertips. "If you'll have me, how about all the years to come?"

At that moment, Erin's heart was so full of pristine joy, she was surprised it didn't leap out of her chest. "Yes."

Corey smiled. "Did I just propose?"

"As a matter of fact, I think you did." Erin grabbed Corey's T-shirt and tugged her closer. "You okay with that?"

"What do you think?" Corey met her lips and slowly and thoroughly kissed her, her body pressed tight against Erin's.

Erin didn't know how long they kissed, but someone clearing their throat behind them caused her to pull away from Corey. Over Corey's shoulder, a young couple was watching them. The woman had an amused expression on her face. Erin wasn't too sure what was going through the man's mind, but his mouth was gaped open.

"Didn't mean to interrupt," the woman said. "Did we, Mark?" He didn't respond. "Mark?" The woman turned to him and slapped his stomach with the back of her hand. "Quit drooling." She looked back at Corey and Erin and shrugged. "You know how guys are."

Erin and Corey edged away from the railing and walked toward the stairs.

"We'll leave the tower to you," Erin said as she passed them.

As they started down the steps, Erin heard the woman say,

"Jesus, Mark. Put your testosterone back in your pocket. That was embarrassing."

Erin and Corey made it to the next landing before they burst out laughing.

"What a memorable hike." Corey held her hand as they headed to the bottom.

"I know I'll never forget it."

Corey grinned at her. "Me, neither."

* * *

Corey was taking a Coke out of her refrigerator when her computer speakers indicated a Skype call coming through. She twisted off the cap and took a sip on her way to her desk. She settled in the chair and clicked the icon to answer the call. Her mom appeared on the screen.

"Hey, Mom. How are you?"

"I'm doing well." Vera moved closer to the webcam. "You look very refreshed. Are you resting more in between jobs?"

There was a good reason Corey was so refreshed, and her name was Erin Flannery. Corey hadn't told her parents yet how serious it had gotten between them. Was now a good time? Over a video call?

"I've been getting plenty of rest." Corey's mind suddenly filled with images of doing a whole lot more with Erin. She pushed them out. Mostly. "Um, Mom. Remember Erin, one of the co-owners of the lodge?"

Vera nodded. "I remember you telling me about her. If I recall, you weren't sure she liked you. But then you went to the fireworks celebration with her." She narrowed her eyes. "Are you blushing?"

For what had to be the thousandth time in her life, Corey wished she could will away a blush. It was physically impossible, but still...

"We've been seeing each other."

"Seeing each other? As in dating?"

"Yes. It's... it's pretty serious."

Vera waited a half a beat before speaking again. "Tell me about her."

Corey told her how amazing Erin was. Her mother interrupted with an occasional question as she went on to extol every one of her virtues. When she finished, she waited for her mom's pronouncement.

"You seem happy, honey."

"I am, Mom. I'm very happy. I love her."

"You have that glow about you. It's been missing for quite a while." Vera didn't need to say why. They both knew. "Let me get your father, and you can share your news with him. After you're finished, I need to talk to you about your house. I think we might have a buyer."

Vera stood up, and Corey's dad took her place in front of the webcam.

"What's this I hear about love?"

Corey should've known her dad would be close by. She went on to gush some more about Erin. Then she and her dad got into a deep discussion about construction. She had an idea and knew she could rely on his years of experience to help her in what she had in mind.

Eventually, her dad pushed himself away from the computer. "Why don't you shoot me your plans, and we can either talk about it on Skype or on the phone."

"Will do, Dad."

Her mom replaced her dad in front of the webcam. "You have an offer. You could counter, but with the market the way it is, I think the offer is fair. It's only two thousand below your asking price."

"That's fine, Mom. We'll go with what you think is best."

"You said you didn't have any need for the furniture there, right?"

"Right. My cabin's small, and it's furnished." Corey thought about when she and Erin might need more, but she'd discuss it with Erin first. She'd talk to Erin about her plans and make sure Erin felt the same way. After their trip to the observation deck the weekend before, Corey thought the feeling was very mutual. But she still wanted to ask.

"Your cousin's found a house nearby and is willing to buy your furniture. You can work out the cost between you."

"I'll give her a call."

"Technically, you don't need to be present for the closing. But you know me. I'm a stickler and always encourage the seller to be there. I'm not much for overnighting paperwork back and forth."

Corey hid a smile. Her mom was old-fashioned about her job, but it was something she loved about her.

"When does the buyer want to close?"

"Two weeks from Saturday."

The last Saturday in August. She'd learned Tess and Erin shut down the lodge the Friday before Labor Day. Other lodges in the area stayed open longer, some even into the winter, but Tess enjoyed having the winter season off. And from what Erin had shared, the lodge did enough business in the summer to more than make up for the idle months in between.

"Let me talk to Erin and Tess about it. They don't shut down the lodge until the next weekend. I may be able to swing it, but it would probably be a short trip."

"I hope you can stay more than one night. We miss you."

Corey heard the screen door to her cabin open and close with a bang. The sound of squeaking sneakers drew nearer and stopped behind her.

"Oh, I didn't know you were talking to someone," Erin said.

"Is that Erin?" Vera bobbed her head up and down and sideways as if trying to see around Corey.

Corey turned and motioned Erin over.

Erin, wide-eyed, mouthed, "Your mom?"

Corey tried to be discreet with her small nod.

Erin mouthed "no" and made a move to leave.

Corey stared at her hard to let her know leaving wasn't an option.

"Come closer where I can see you," Vera's voice insisted from the speakers.

Erin nervously straightened her hair and brushed her hands over her clothes. Corey pulled over a nearby chair for Erin to sit down beside her.

"My, you're beautiful." Her mom beamed at Erin.

"Thank you, Mrs. Banner."

"It's Vera. Now tell me all about yourself."

Corey was about to stand up when Erin dug her fingernails into Corey's thigh. Deep. Corey winced in pain.

"Corey, go get her a drink or something while we chat."

Again, Corey attempted to stand. When Erin dug in even deeper—enough that Corey was thankful she was wearing jeans—she reached over and pried Erin's hand off her thigh. She hurried quickly out of tripping range, thinking it'd be Erin's next course of action. She obeyed her mother's wish and went to the refrigerator to get Erin something to drink. She was about to reenter the room but hung back when she heard Erin laughing. Corey sighed in relief. She tiptoed in, trying to be as quiet as possible. She set the Coke beside Erin, but Erin didn't pay any attention. Corey left for the front porch to wait out their conversation.

About twenty minutes later, Erin joined her on the porch and plopped in the chair beside her.

"So? Was my mom as bad as yours?" Corey asked.

"Not quite. She's very nice. I can see where you get some of your finer qualities. But you look like your dad."

"You talked to my dad, too?"

"Yes, Corey, I met the parents. Between your meeting my mom and knowing Tess, I'd say we're definitely a couple. We were already, but this makes it official."

Corey let that sink in… it was a good feeling.

"She invited me to join you in Lansing in two weeks."

"You're kidding."

"What's that supposed to mean? Don't you want me to go?"

"No, no. I'm surprised, that's all. I didn't know how you'd feel actually 'meet meeting' them. Talking to them on Skype is one thing, but flying to Lansing is another. Don't get me wrong, it's great you had such a good talk. I mean, of course I want you to go and—"

"You can quit digging anytime, Corey."

"Huh?"

"The hole you're digging. I think it's deep enough." Erin winked at her.

Corey laughed. "I'm kind of clueless sometimes."

Erin knelt down in front of her. She spread Corey's legs apart and pressed in closer as she draped her arms around Corey's neck.

"When it came to following the clues I was giving you, I'm glad you had on your Sherlock Holmes hat."

Corey bent over and pressed her lips against Erin's neck. She nibbled her way up to her ear. "And what kind of clues am I giving now, Dr. Watson?"

Erin moaned. "I don't think Holmes and Watson had this kind of relationship."

Corey pulled away. "Problem?"

Erin yanked her forward again. "Ah, hell no."

* * *

Erin and Tess sat on one of the old swings dangling from the porch rafter. They were enjoying a quiet, late afternoon respite from their work. Emily was at the counter, and Erin had finished her paperwork an hour ago.

Tess took a sip of her iced tea. "No matter what, I never get tired of this view." She used her glass to gesture at the lake.

"I told Corey the same thing a couple of weeks ago when we were at the observation tower."

"How'd that go, by the way? You were a little quiet when you returned."

Even though she knew Tess liked Corey, she still sought her approval about their relationship. More than a little nervous, she blurted out, "She kind of proposed to me up there." She waited for Tess's response, but there was nothing. She ventured a peek to find her sporting a wide smile.

"And you said..."

"Yes. I said yes."

Tess set her glass down and reached over to give Erin a tight hug. "Oh, baby girl, this is wonderful. Remember me telling you months ago that if you opened yourself up to love, someone special might come along and fill the empty space in your heart?"

Erin remembered the conversation well and how she had a difficult time believing her aunt's words. "I do."

"I'm so glad Corey Banner came into our lives but, more importantly, into yours."

"I guess you approve?"

Tess slapped her lightly on the shoulder. "What do you think?"

Erin had been thinking about something and decided to ask her aunt's opinion on the matter.

"Remember the property we set aside south of the lodge and how you told me anytime I was ready, I could check into having a home built there?"

"I think I know where this is going, but yes, I remember."

"I've never been ready until now to see about building a home. But with Corey, I can think of nothing more special than having a cabin built from the ground up. One where we can make new memories. What do you think?"

Tess stared past Erin's shoulder. "I think you should ask Corey that question."

Erin turned around. Corey was standing there with a big grin on her face.

Erin got to her feet and went to her. "You weren't supposed to hear any of that."

Corey jerked her thumb toward the stairs. "Would you like me to leave? I mean, if you and Tess need more privacy—"

Erin didn't miss the twinkle in her eyes. She reached for Corey's hands. "I don't know if I'm moving too fast for you."

Corey laced their fingers together. "Would it make you feel better if I told you I've been talking to my dad about designing a cabin for us?"

Erin tried to comprehend what Corey was saying. It was almost too good to be true. "Seriously?"

"Seriously."

Erin pulled her down for a kiss, not even caring Tess sat nearby. Or that any lodger coming or going would see. Corey responded to the kiss, but Erin could tell she kept it from getting too intense. The swing creaked behind her.

"That's my cue to leave you two lovebirds to discuss whatever it is you need to while I take my iced tea back inside." Tess patted Corey on the back as she passed her. "Like I said before, I couldn't be happier."

"Thanks, Tess." Corey watched her enter the lodge and faced Erin again. "Want to show me the property?"

Erin spread her arms out. "This is it." She waited for Corey's reaction and was more than a little nervous.

Corey walked into the clearing and studied the land.

Erin tried to picture the place from Corey's perspective as if she were seeing it for the first time. They were partially surrounded by Douglas firs. Below them was a break in the trees offering a clear view of Grand Lake. The lodge was to their right, but the property was secluded enough that no one from the lodge would see it through the thickness of the trees.

"It's perfect."

In a surge of giddiness, Erin ran to Corey's open arms. Corey grabbed her by the waist and spun her in the air. Erin laughed as her feet left the ground.

"I'm so happy right now, I could shout it from the highest mountain in Colorado."

"You don't have to," Corey said softly. "I feel it right here with you in my arms."

Chapter 23

Corey tried not to be nervous as they approached the Lansing airport. Their two-hour afternoon flight to Minneapolis had gone smoothly, and the ninety-minute flight out of Minneapolis was turbulence-free. But it did nothing to quiet her queasy stomach.

She was taking her girlfriend home to meet her family. The enormity of the situation had hit her about midflight out of the Twin Cities. She'd noticed Erin had been flipping through the same airline magazine for what had to be the fifth time. Corey was so caught up in her own nervousness, she hadn't stopped to think about Erin.

"You all right?" Corey asked.

Erin shoved the magazine into the seat pocket in front of her. "Yes. Well, no. I think so."

Corey leaned over and said in a low voice, "They'll love you. Just like I do."

Erin furrowed her brow, clearly worried about the upcoming meeting. "They will?"

Seeing Erin's uneasiness alleviated Corey's anxiety. It forced her to quit thinking about herself.

"Of course they will. Why wouldn't they?"

Erin wouldn't meet her eyes. "I don't know…"

Corey thought she knew what was troubling Erin, but she wanted to hear her say it. "What's really bothering you?"

"They loved Judy."

There it is.

"And you were with her for six years, and I don't know." Erin's voice shook. "I'm not her."

Corey took Erin's hand. "Look at me, please."

Erin raised her head and met her gaze.

"No, you're not Judy. No one expects you to be, especially not me. Yes, Judy was special, but so are you. You're everything to me—you're kind, compassionate, funny, intelligent, beautiful, and—"

"If you say I have a nice personality, I'm going to smack you." Erin's mouth quirked into a small grin.

"Well, you *do*." Corey turned Erin's hand over and entwined their fingers. "But more than all those qualities, what you did for me was bring me out of the darkness and into the light again. Your love. You."

Erin blinked, and a single tear rolled down her cheek. "I want to lift this armrest, climb into your lap, and kiss you senseless."

Corey raised Erin's hand and pressed her lips against the soft skin. "Hold that thought."

"There's my sister," Corey said.

Erin craned her neck. An almost carbon copy of Corey stood beside a blue minivan and waved at them. The only noticeable difference was Betty had shoulder-length dark hair. Betty hurried around the front of the van and embraced Corey.

"I've missed you so much," Betty said as she held Corey for several seconds. She then looked at Erin. "You must be Erin." She didn't hesitate in giving Erin a hug as well. "Mom was right. You're beautiful."

"Thank you. Corey has told me so much about you and your sons."

"Who can't wait to see their Aunt Co."

"Co?" Erin said.

"They couldn't say my name when they first learned to talk. We shortened it for them."

Betty opened the back of the van, and they placed their bags inside. Corey and Erin slid into the backseat, while Betty settled in behind the steering wheel.

"Mom and Dad haven't stopped talking about your visit." Betty keyed the ignition. "Everybody's at their house. Except for Hank. He's at home with his friends watching the Tigers game." Erin caught Betty's reflection in the rearview mirror as she rolled her eyes.

Erin glanced at Corey who remained emotionless. Corey hadn't really talked about Betty's husband, and Erin got the distinct feeling Hank wasn't one of her favorite people.

Betty chatted about all the goings-on in their family. "Mom said the offer on your house is a good one."

"Yeah, it is. I'll be glad to sign off on it. I have to go over there tonight and double-check everything since the closing's in the morning."

"I wish you were staying longer than Sunday."

"Next week is the last week before the lodge closes," Corey said. "We need to get back and help Tess shut it down."

"Mom told me, but it doesn't change the fact I wish you weren't flying back so quickly. Are you both tired? I can never remember how jet lag works, if it's heading east or west that causes it."

"No, at least I'm not," Corey answered. "How are you doing, Erin?"

"I'm fine. I think the hour layover in Minneapolis helped when we changed planes. We could stretch our legs."

"Hey, I forgot to tell you. I called Penny before we left Grand Lake and invited her over tomorrow for dinner. Hope that's okay."

God. One more person to impress. Erin managed a smile. "It's fine. I look forward to meeting her."

The drive to their parents' house went fast. Almost too fast for Erin. She tried to stifle her anxiety as they got out of the minivan. Corey's parents, flanked by two young boys, stood on the stoop of the red-brick ranch house. Daniel had his arm around Vera. In person, Corey's resemblance to her father was even more prominent. Same thick, dark hair with only a few streaks of gray. Vera had her hair cut in a stylish bob brushed off her face.

"Hi, Mom and Dad." Corey set her bag down and gave them both a hug. She took Erin's hand and pulled her over. "I'd like you to meet Erin Flannery. Erin, these are my parents, Vera and Daniel."

Erin held her hand out, but Vera ignored it and hugged her, as did Daniel. Encased in the warmth of their embraces, Erin's anxiety dwindled down to nothing.

"Nice to see you in the flesh," Vera said.

Erin smiled. "Technology only goes so far."

"And these rascals," Corey said and ruffled the boys' hair, "are my nephews, Brady and Cole."

The taller of the two stepped forward and held out his hand. "Hello. Pleased to meet you. I'm Brady."

Erin stifled a laugh at the boy's formality but, at the same time, found it endearing. *Must run in the family.* She shook his hand while somehow maintaining a serious expression. "Pleased to meet you, too, Brady."

"The shyer one's Cole," Betty said.

Cole ducked behind his grandfather's leg.

"Hello, Cole."

Cole giggled and clutched Daniel's pants between his small hands.

"He'll warm up to you soon enough," Corey said as they headed for the front door.

"I have the spare room ready for you." Vera led them toward the hallway.

Erin looked around her and loved the coziness of the home. She noticed framed photos lining the mantel above the fireplace. One in particular caught her attention. It was a picture of Corey with her arm around a handsome, gray-haired woman. Erin didn't realize she'd slowed to a stop in front of the picture.

"We were camping in the Upper Peninsula. Penny took it."

"You look so... happy." She wasn't sure what she was feeling. It wasn't jealousy. It was more of a desire to know this part of Corey's life.

"We were." Corey put her arm around Erin's waist. "Just as I am now."

Erin relaxed her hip against Corey's and relished the feel of her solidness and of the truth behind Corey's words.

"Come on. Let's get our bags put away." Corey took her hand and led her down the hall.

"Mom, that was delicious."

It didn't escape Corey's attention that Vera had cooked her favorite meal—fried chicken with all the fixings.

Vera waved off her compliment. "Nothing special."

"It's my favorite, and you fixed it. That makes it special."

They'd shared a pleasant dinner with Betty and the boys. After they'd eaten, Betty and the kids left for home, while Erin, Corey, and her parents sat down for coffee. The conversation was light and full of laughter. It pleased Corey how easily her parents had welcomed Erin into the family.

"Dad, sometime before we fly back, I'd like to talk to you about those plans for the cabin."

"I thought this was a surprise."

Corey slipped her arm around Erin's shoulders. "It was supposed to be, but this one had the same idea and beat me to it."

"Good for you, Erin," Daniel said. "My daughter needs to be kept on her toes."

Corey checked her watch. "I'd better head over to the house before it gets any darker." She turned to Erin. "Would you like to join me?"

Erin seemed surprised. "I wasn't sure if it was something you wanted to do on your own."

Corey gave her a gentle smile. "Of course I want you with me."

Erin hung back as she followed Corey into each room of the three-bedroom ranch. Corey occasionally stood in place and closed her eyes, as if to relive some long ago, fond memory. Erin kept quiet, sensing this was Corey's time to heal even further.

After Corey's last pass of the house, they stood in the stillness of the living room. Corey ran her fingers along the wood grain of the fireplace mantel. She bowed her head for a moment and then straightened, took a deep breath, and let it out in one big puff.

"I'm ready to go."

Corey took Erin's hand and led her out the door. She locked up the house, and they got into her parents' Toyota. As they backed out of the drive and drove down the street, Erin broke the silence.

"How are you?"

Corey's expression was thoughtful. "It surprises me a little. I thought I'd be sad. But I feel like I've only ended a chapter of that part of my life, the life I shared with Judy." She took her attention off the road to briefly meet Erin's eyes. "Our story has only begun." She rested her arm on the console and held her hand open, palm up.

Erin placed her hand in Corey's. She laid back against the headrest and sighed with contentment. She thought of the months and years to come that she would share with this woman, and she was filled with joy. Corey was right. Their story together had only begun... and it had all the makings of a great book.

The following afternoon, Erin sat alone on a picnic bench in the backyard of Corey's parents' home. Corey had signed off on the house in the morning. This was the last get-together before they flew out in the morning. She'd felt at ease when she met Penny earlier. She saw how she and Corey could be best friends. Their camaraderie was instantly apparent with the way they cut up together.

Vera and Daniel were readying dinner, insisting Erin relax while Daniel barbequed and Vera prepared potato salad inside. Corey and Penny were playing tackle football with Brady and Cole. Erin laughed when Cole wrapped himself around one of Corey's legs and Brady around the other. Penny kept yelling at Corey to pass her the ball. Corey ignored her and struggled to keep her balance until she made it over the makeshift goal line. They all collapsed in a heap with Penny joining in on the fun. After Corey and Penny tickled the boys into hysterics, Corey handed the ball to Cole, and she and Penny followed him and Brady to the other end of the yard.

"She's good with them, isn't she?" Betty asked as she sat down across from Erin.

"She is."

"I can't tell you how happy I am to hear her laugh again."

Erin turned to face her and felt like she was looking into Corey's eyes.

"I know Corey's told you about Judy and about their relationship. But without seeing them together, I don't think you can fully appreciate the special love they shared."

Erin was beginning to get uncomfortable. Was Betty not happy for her sister? Or was she simply not happy with Corey's choice of a partner?

"We were afraid we were going to lose her two years ago. Judy's death demolished her. The times I'd call her and not get an answer scared me the most. You can imagine I pictured the worst-case scenario. I can't remember how many times I had to keep myself from jumping in the car and driving over to her house. But then I'd calm down enough to try calling again later. When she'd answer, I'd collapse with relief into the nearest chair." Betty brushed aside a tear. "I would've done anything to take away her pain. Day-by-day and week-by-week, she slowly crawled out of the abyss. But when she'd recovered enough to begin working with Dad, she was a shell of the sister I loved."

At the sound of Cole's squeal of laughter, they looked over at Corey. She was "tackling" Cole by picking him up into her arms. Penny ran interference against Brady by blocking his way each time he tried to get around her. Corey carried Cole toward the goal line and set him down right in front of it. He jumped over the line and held the ball up in the air in triumph. Corey yelled "touchdown!" and she and Penny joined the boys in a touchdown dance.

Betty pointed. "Do you know how many times I longed to see her like this again?" She reached for Erin's hand. "So, thank you, Erin. Thank you for bringing my sister back to me."

It took every ounce of Erin's restraint to hold back a sob. She blinked away her tears. "It's not a one-sided healing, Betty. I never thought I'd find love again. I'd given up when my ex walked out the door almost six years ago. I'd lost my faith and trust and thought it was hopeless to even dream of happiness. But Corey's given all that back to me. She's given me back my life."

"You both look way too serious." Corey walked over to the table while the boys and Penny continued playing football. "Everything okay?" She met Erin's eyes, her brow creased in concern.

"I think everything's absolutely perfect. Wouldn't you say so, Betty?"

Betty smiled. "Perfect is just the word I was searching for."

Later, after they'd had their fill of food, Penny left for a softball game. Before leaving, she'd made Erin promise to visit again soon. Erin leaned against Corey as they sat together on the picnic bench. She didn't know why she'd been worried. Corey's parents had welcomed her and set her instantly at ease. After her initial fear of Betty's rejection, she knew she'd not only received Betty's stamp of approval, she'd also gained a new friend. And Penny had definitely made her feel welcome.

"Erin, I hope you come back every time with Corey," Vera said.

"I'd love to."

"We probably won't be back until around Christmas, Mom."

"I understand, honey. Erin, I can't tell you how it makes Daniel and me feel to see light return to Corey's life. Thank you for that."

"When Corey left Lansing, she was searching for hope and peace," Daniel said. "I'd say she's found both in meeting and falling in love with you."

First Betty and now Corey's parents... Erin spoke around the tightness in her throat. "She's given me the same, Daniel, believe me."

Corey put her arm around Erin and kissed her forehead. "I'm glad you can see why I love her."

"After meeting her for myself, I can see what makes her so special," her dad said.

Vera stood and stacked their paper plates. Erin rose to help her.

"I've got this. Why don't you two either stay out here in the lounge chairs or go inside to the sofa and relax? You have an early flight tomorrow."

"Actually, I was planning on visiting the cemetery," Corey said. "I'd like to put some fresh flowers on Judy's grave."

Erin thought Corey might go the cemetery while they were in town, so it didn't surprise her. But she didn't want her going alone.

"Do you mind if I join you?"

"Only if you want to," Corey said softly.

"I do."

They drove to a nearby flower shop, and Corey picked up a spray of wildflowers. She told Erin they were Judy's favorite.

Corey was quiet on the drive, and Erin didn't break the silence. She knew Corey needed this, just as she'd needed the final walk-through at the house.

They pulled into the cemetery grounds and drove the circular drive to the back where only a few stones marked the graves. It was clear this was the newer part of the cemetery. Corey got out and lifted the flowers from the backseat. Erin remained inside, unsure if Corey wanted to go to the grave alone.

Corey leaned into the car. "Will you come with me?"

In answer, Erin opened her door and walked beside Corey as they approached the last row of graves. Corey stopped in front of a gray, marble marker with "Judy Darlene Wagner, April 17, 1973-October 31, 2010, Beloved Best Friend and Wife" etched deep into the stone. Erin noticed the words, "Beloved Daughter," were missing.

As if reading her thoughts, Corey said, "Her parents disowned her when she came out to them at eighteen."

Erin ached for someone she'd never met. "I wonder if they realize what a good woman they missed out on knowing and loving."

Corey wiped her face. "I never met them and didn't have any desire to. They hurt Judy. That was enough for me to never let them hurt her again." She bent over and yanked out some weeds that had taken root in front of the gravestone. She carefully laid the flowers on the grave and bowed her head just as she had at the house.

Erin did the same, knowing that Corey was praying.

"Amen," Corey whispered. As the word left her lips, a gentle breeze blew in and rustled through the wildflowers. She took a few steps away from the grave but stopped when Erin didn't follow her.

Erin stared at the wildflowers and then reread the words on the gravestone. She silently said her own prayer, thanking God for the love Judy and Corey shared. The love that had helped mold Corey into the woman she was today.

Erin reached for Corey's hand as they walked to the car.

On their drive to Corey's parents' house, Erin asked, "Are you okay?"

"Yes, and I'm ready to go home." Corey stopped at a red light and looked at Erin. "And my home is with you in Grand Lake."

"Good," Erin said with a catch in her voice as Corey's words settled lightly onto her heart like a soft downy feather. "Good."

Chapter 24

Corey patched the plaster where one of the lodgers had left a gaping hole. She'd already informed Tess, who would send the idiot a bill for the cost of supplies and labor as soon as Corey finished the work.

Although it was the last week, a few lodgers remained who would check out Friday morning. She and Erin had been busy since their return from Lansing. Erin promised everything would ease up after Friday. Bill Cooper was holding an "end of the season" dance the following Saturday night. Corey had to smile. Without any hesitation, she told Erin she'd go and couldn't wait to do some more two-stepping.

Corey hummed along to a tune on the radio. She spread the last coat of spackle over the hole until it was smooth. Next, she'd let the area dry again before sanding and Kilzing it later. Arms reached around her waist and a familiar body pressed against her from behind. Erin nuzzled her neck. "Hey, sexy."

Corey twisted around and was about to embrace Erin when she pressed her palm into Corey's chest.

"Whoa." Erin pointed at the front of Corey's long-sleeved Henley. "Your back is dry, but your front? It's a bit messy."

"You don't like messy?"

Erin stepped back, probably because of the wicked grin playing across Corey's face. "Don't you dare. I have to drive into Granby for some groceries, and I'd prefer not having to change before I go."

Corey set her spatula down on the lid of the spackle bucket. "Want some company?"

"I'd love to say yes, but Aunt Tess really needs you to finish this as quickly as possible. She's still hopping mad and wants to bill the guy. By certified mail, no less."

Corey glanced at the spot on the wall. "I don't blame her. The lodge is her baby. It was stupid for him not to tell her before he left. I think I know Tess well enough that she probably would've

179

charged him twenty dollars at the most for the inconvenience. I wouldn't be surprised if she doesn't send the guy a bill for two hundred if she takes into account my labor."

Three loud beeps sounded on the radio, interrupting the music. "The National Weather Service has issued a severe thunderstorm warning for Grand County, effective from now until two p.m. This includes the towns of Grand Lake, Granby, and Kremmling. Large hail, damaging wind, and torrential downpours are possible with this storm. The storm should move into the county in approximately one hour. Please stay tuned to this station for further updates."

A wave of fear coursed through Corey's veins. She gripped Erin's shoulders. "You can't go."

Erin winced in obvious pain.

Corey quickly released her. "I'm sorry. I didn't mean to hurt you. But you can't go."

"Honey, I think I know what's scaring you. I'll be fine. Granby is about a thirty-minute drive. I'll get there before the storm hits. I'll wait it out in Granby until it clears."

"Why don't you wait until after two?" Corey tried unsuccessfully to control the quivering in her voice.

"Because I promised Aunt Tess I'd buy some T-bone steaks for the cook-out tonight. She decided it'd be a nice treat for the remaining lodgers. I could go to Sam's in town, but I don't want to spend an outrageous price for smaller steaks when I could get a higher quality beef for less money in Granby. If I wait, I won't be back in time for the staff to start preparing the food. She already posted the time for the cook-out."

"But—"

Erin held Corey's hands. "Trust me when I say the weathercasters around here are notoriously wrong. I'm sure this is nothing more than our typical afternoon thundershower. If it'll make you feel better, I'll call you halfway there and again when I arrive in Granby."

Corey struggled to tamp down the terror that threatened to swallow her whole.

"Take some deep breaths," Erin said and breathed in herself, then let it out slowly. "Come on, Corey. Like me."

Corey joined her in trying to calm her nerves. Eventually, her pulse slowed down to its normal rate.

Erin leaned in and kissed her, running her fingers through Corey's hair. "Nothing will happen. I'll be back in about two hours." She gave Corey one more kiss before leaving for the door.

"I'll tell Aunt Tess how you're coming along on the repairs."

Corey watched as Erin disappeared from view. The loud banging of the screen door bounced off the walls of the small cabin. Corey tried her best to shake away the ominous finality of the sound.

With each passing minute and no appearance of the storm, Corey relaxed a little more. Erin had called not too long after she'd left and told her she'd not run into any bad weather. That was an hour ago. As she fastened the lid on the can of Kilz, distant thunder rumbled from the south. She remembered enough from the area maps she'd seen of Grand County that Granby was south of Grand Lake. The hair stood up on the nape of her neck.

She unclipped her cell phone from her belt and speed-dialed Erin's number. It immediately clicked over to voicemail. She tried to convince herself everything was okay. Reception was crazy in the mountains. She waited another five minutes and tried again, getting the same result.

Corey grabbed the container of spackle, sandpaper, and can of Kilz, and dropped them on the cart. She threw her tool belt on top and pushed the rickety cart into the storage shed. She entered the back of the lodge and hurried to find Tess. Maybe she'd heard something from Erin.

Out of breath, she slid to a halt at the front counter.

Tess held up her hands like a crossing guard. "Hey, where's the fire?"

"Erin… Have you heard from Erin?"

"I didn't expect to."

"I've tried reaching her but keep getting voicemail."

"That doesn't mean anything with the reception in this area."

The lodge phone jangled loudly. Corey almost jumped out of her skin.

"Rainbow Lodge," Tess answered.

Corey watched her face for any sign of bad news.

Tess paled and gripped the counter in front of her.

"What is it?" Corey practically shouted.

Tess silenced her with a cutting motion of her hand. "All right. I understand. They've taken her to St. Anthony's, but as far as you know, she's stable."

Corey's knees buckled. She held onto the counter for dear life.

"We'll get there as quickly as possible. Right. I understand we'll be driving through the storm." Tess's jaw tightened and her lips became a slash of white. "She's my niece. I will *not* wait until morning. We're leaving now." Tess hung up the phone. "Corey... Corey?"

Corey heard Tess's distant voice through the roaring in her ears. She tried to latch onto it like a life preserver.

"*Corey!*" Tess grabbed her hands she'd flattened on top of the counter. "Don't think the worst. They said she's stable. Come on. Let's go."

Corey fumbled in her front pocket and held out the keys. "I can't drive, Tess. I can't."

Tess took the keys from her. "I'll get us there. First, though, I need to call Kate."

Corey slouched in the passenger seat.

Tess repeatedly glanced over at her. "I don't need to worry about you, too, do I?"

Corey shook her head and tried to squash the overwhelming urge to throw up. The rain pounded on the windshield as the wipers tried to keep up with the onslaught of water sluicing over the glass.

"Another twenty minutes and we'll be there, honey." Tess didn't speak the remainder of the drive.

The rain had trickled down to a gentle shower by the time they arrived at St. Anthony's Medical Center in Granby. The rainbow that appeared overhead did nothing to raise Corey's spirits or ease her worried mind.

They approached the front desk of the emergency room. "I'm Tess Landers, Erin Flannery's aunt. This is her partner, Corey Banner. We'd like to see her, please."

The woman tapped on the keyboard. "She's in room ten. You go through the doors and turn right at the second hallway. Third room to your right." She reached under the desk and buzzed the door open.

Tess and Corey hurried down the hall. When they turned the corner, Corey slowed. It was as though she were slogging through quicksand with each step closer to room ten. Tess had gone ahead and stood in front of the doorway to the room. "You coming, Corey?"

Corey barely nodded. Tess entered the room. Corey stopped at the doorway and gripped the doorjamb when she saw Erin's condition. Her eyes were closed, her upper lip split and swollen. Bruises already formed on her cheeks, and layers of gauze encircled her forehead. Blood had seeped through and painted a splotch of red on the white material over her left eyebrow.

Corey broke out in a cold sweat. Buzzing sounded in her ears, and her peripheral vision had gone fuzzy to the point she thought she'd faint.

"Erin, honey? It's Aunt Tess." Tess took Erin's hand. "Corey's here, too." Tess looked over at her expectantly.

Corey couldn't do this. She bolted from the doorway and sprinted down the hall. She burst through the emergency room doors and fled to the outside. Even though the rain had picked up from its earlier light shower, Corey kept running until she reached a bench several feet away.

She clutched her stomach and bent over, sobbing and rocking back and forth. The rain drenched her hair and slid down her face. She was no longer in Granby, Colorado. She was on that couch in Lansing, shattered by the news of Judy's death. Corey couldn't break free from her memories despite the voice of reason screaming in her ear that Erin was very much alive and in a hospital room behind her.

She didn't know how much time had passed. Minutes? Hours? Someone sat down beside her. She opened her eyes. Tess met her gaze with a mixture of compassion and anger flickering across her face.

"I'm s-sorry, Tess. I really am."

Tess nodded once and then put her arm around Corey's waist. "She asked for you the second she regained consciousness."

Shame washed over her.

"Corey, I understand where your fear is coming from," Tess said. "But Erin's not Judy. She's still with us. And right now, she's hurting because you're not there."

Corey was about to speak, but Tess cut her off.

"You love her, and she loves you, and your love transcends all of what you're feeling right now, every bad memory and every nightmare scenario. Your love will see you through this, just as it will see you through all the bad times that lie ahead."

Tess gripped Corey's waist a little tighter as if to emphasize the importance of what she was saying.

"And yes, along with the joy, there'll be some sadness. You can't stop it from coming. But what you *can* do is swallow the fear lodged in your throat, get up off this bench, march back into that hospital room, and tell my niece you love her." Tess gave her a gentle smile. "This is where you say, 'yes, ma'am.'"

Corey wiped away the mixture of tears and rainwater from her cheeks. "Yes, ma'am."

"You go on in there to see her. I'm heading to the cafeteria to get some coffee. I need to call Kate back. I called her a little bit ago after I saw Erin and before I came out here looking for you. But I promised I'd call her once more. She was frantic with worry, as you can imagine."

They both stood. Corey grabbed Tess and pulled her to her chest. "Thank you."

"I'll tell you what I once told Erin months ago. You only need thank me if you heed my advice. Now get."

Corey slowed to a stop in front of room ten. She hesitated for a split second and then took the plunge and entered the room.

Erin shifted at the sound of Corey approaching the bed. Her beautiful eyes were full of hurt. Corey hated herself for putting that pain there.

"Hey, Erin." Corey moved beside the bed and held Erin's hand that lay on top of the covers.

"You weren't here when I woke up." Erin blinked away the moisture on her eyelashes and grimaced with the move.

"I know, and I'm sorry."

"Why weren't you?"

"I… I lost it standing in the doorway when I saw you like this. It's a lousy excuse."

"Corey, I understand my accident had to bring back bad memories for you. I do. But this is now. *I* am now. Right here in front of you. Now."

Corey bit her lower lip to the point she was sure she'd drawn blood. She didn't want to start crying again.

"You know what this reminds me of?" Erin asked. "Please look at me."

Corey raised her head.

"It reminds me of a scene from a lesbian romance novel where one of the main characters unrealistically runs off after a disagreement without talking to her lover. You know? Talking it over like normal couples do?" The corner of Erin's mouth lifted in a half smile. "Normal couples like you and me." Erin gave her hand a tug. "We work things out. We don't run away from a bad situation. That's not us."

"You're right." Corey bent over and with great care, kissed the top of her head. "I love you, Erin."

"I love you too, Corey. No more running. Promise me."

"I promise. It'll never happen again."

"Good. Now grab a towel from the bathroom and dry yourself off. Then find out when I can leave."

Corey heard the squeak of sneakers behind her.

"The doctor cleared you for discharge, Ms. Flannery." A nurse flipped through papers on a clipboard. "Your CAT scan was clear. You're to take it easy and have someone keep an eye on you for the next twenty-four hours." She addressed Corey. "I'd say that's you?"

"Yes. I'm her partner."

"Okay. Also, you're to make an appointment with your doctor in Grand Lake for a follow-up as soon as you can when you get home."

Tess entered the room and stood beside Corey. "We'll make sure she does."

"Let me rustle up a wheelchair, and you can be on your way."

Corey glanced at her name tag. "Thank you, Bea." Corey ducked into the bathroom, ran a towel over her head and body, and hurried back.

"I talked to two other nurses at the nurses' station," Tess was saying to Erin. "They told me you slid off of highway 34 right before you hit US 40 and landed in a ditch. I guess all that damage is from hitting your head against the steering wheel. I know you thought Bertha was a tank, but one thing she didn't have because of her age was airbags. It always scared me because I was afraid something like this might happen someday."

"You're talking about Bertha in the past tense. I take it she's totaled?" Erin asked.

"Unfortunately, yes."

"Damn."

"Don't worry, though. I thought I saw another Land Rover up for sale at Bill Cooper's ranch when I drove by the other day. Land Rovers are all that man drives. It's an older model but new enough to be equipped with airbags. We'll see how much he wants for it."

Erin attempted a smile. "Ow." She touched her lip and must have noticed their concern. "It's okay. You should've seen the other guy."

"The other guy?" Corey said.

"The ditch. I think I left a gash two-foot deep when I crashed."

Corey brushed Erin's hair away from her face. "I'm so thankful you're all right." She choked back her tears.

"Don't cry, honey," Erin said. "We have a long future ahead of us. Let's go home. After all, I need to heal up for Bill's last dance."

"Erin, I don't know—"

"Corey, we're going to the dance. It's my last chance to two-step with you until next summer."

Tess patted Corey on the back. "You can't argue with her. Stubborn, remember? Oh wait, I think I'm talking to the kettle."

Corey was confused. "Kettle?"

"You know? Kettle calling the pot black? You two are twins of stubbornness."

They shared in the much-needed laugh.

* * *

"Remember to dress warm, Corey." Moving slowly and deliberately, Erin tugged the University of Colorado sweatshirt over her head. Her bruises had faded to an ugly yellow, and her forehead was still sore. She'd had the stitches removed Monday. She ran her fingers over the raised area. The doctor said there would probably be a faint scar. But that was okay. It was a reminder of what she had almost lost and made her treasure her life with Corey even more.

Corey came out of the other room. "Is this all right?" She wore a Kelly-green Michigan State sweatshirt over a white polo. Her worn jeans hung on her loosely but were tight across the butt. They were one of Erin's favorite pair.

Erin straightened the collar of Corey's shirt. "It's perfect. Well, except for the school," she teased. "Ready to go two-stepping?"

Corey put her arms around Erin. "Do you remember the first time you asked me? I was scared shitless."

Erin pressed in closer. "And now?"

"Now, I'm ready to show 'em how it's done."

They'd been dancing for over an hour. Erin's feet were throbbing, and she was still a little sore from the accident, but she wasn't ready to call it a night. They took a break and approached the table full of buckets of iced beer.

Corey reached in and grabbed two bottles of Coors Light. She handed one to Erin. She twisted off the cap to her bottle and took three big gulps. "Damn. This dancing's hard work."

Erin elbowed her stomach. "You're not wimping out on me are you?"

"Aren't you tired? You know you're still recovering from your injuries." Corey's expression grew worried.

"I'm tired, yes. But I want to dance at least one more before we leave."

As the words left her mouth, Bill's band struck up the beginning notes of Anne Murray's "Can I Have This Dance?"

Erin set down her beer on the table and held out her hand. "And this is the perfect song to end the night."

Corey took her hand, and Erin led her onto the dirt dance floor. Other couples swayed to the music as Bill's daughter sang the words to the song. They held each other tight and shuffled along to the soft beat. Erin put her cheek on Corey's shoulder and sighed while she listened to Renee Cooper sing. The song was nearing the end. She raised her head and stared into Corey's dark brown eyes.

"So can I?" Erin said.

Corey questioned her with a raised eyebrow. "Can you what?"

She tilted her head toward the stage as Renee sang the chorus. Erin brushed Corey's hair off her forehead. "Have this dance for the rest of my life?"

Corey pressed her lips to Erin's ear. "Most definitely."

Erin grinned as she remembered their conversation on the observation tower. "Did I just propose?"

"As a matter of fact, I think you did," Corey said, repeating the same words Erin had spoken on Shadow Mountain.

Here in the arms of her love, Erin had found the missing piece of her heart. She breathed in the scent that was Corey and tucked this treasured memory away to revisit in the years to come. The last notes of the song swirled together and lingered above them like an unending melody to a dance.

A dance that would last a lifetime.

Author Chris Paynter   Photo Credit: Phyllis Manfredi

About the Author

Chris was born in a British hospital and happily lived a nomadic childhood as an Air Force brat, before settling in Indiana after her father's retirement. She graduated from Indiana University with a Bachelor's degree in journalism and a minor in history. After graduation, she worked as a general assignment reporter and a sports reporter. In her current position as an editorial specialist, she supports third-year law students in publishing a quarterly law journal. She continues to work on her novels, including *From Third to Home*, the final book in the *Playing for First* series, and her next stand-alone romance. Chris and her wife, Phyllis, live in Indianapolis with their beagle, Buddy the Wonder Dog.

Visit her website at www.ckpaynter.com. You can also find her on Facebook and Twitter.

Make sure to check out these other exciting
Blue Feather Books titles:

Clandestine	Cheyne Curry	978-1-935627-78-4
Pulse Points	Barbara Valletto	978-1-935627-79-1
Cresswell Falls	Kerry Belchambers	978-1-935627-95-1
Rebellion in Ulster	Angela Koenig	978-1-935627-76-0
Survived by Her Longtime Companion	Chris Paynter	978-1-935627-88-3
The Midas Conspiracy	Jennifer McCormick	978-1-935627-84-5
Lesser Prophets	Kelly Sinclair	978-0-9822858-8-6
Right Out of Nowhere	Laurie Salzler	978-1-935627-60-9
Appointment with a Smile	Kieran York	978-1-935627-86-9
Flight	Renee MacKenzie	978-1-935627-73-9
My Soldier Too	Bev Prescott	978-1-935627-81-4
Return of the Raven	Jamie Scarratt	978-1-935627-72-2
No Corpse Is an Island	Gato Timberlake	978-1-935627-74-6

www.bluefeatherbooks.com